Unmatched

Billie Jean Diersen

Unmatched is a work of fiction. Names, characters, places and incidents
described herein are either the product of the author's imagination or are used
fictitiously. Any resemblance to actual persons, living or dead, events or locales is
purely coincidental.

While this book mentions several Internet addresses that were active at the
time it was written, the author has no control over nor assumes any responsibility
for those sites or their content. Further, the author assumes no responsibility for
changes that occur to those addresses after publication.

For David, who lights my fire and makes all my dreams come true.

One

$\mathcal{I}$ held my breath as I watched my husband greet the blonde at the entrance to the bookstore. She was pretty, and tastefully dressed in skinny jeans and a pair of leather boots that matched her winter white sweater.

I'd spotted her a few moments earlier as she draped a tan jacket over her arm after emerging from a metallic sage Sebring and activating its alarm. I had wondered then if she was the one he was expecting, or if she was just another attractive thirty-something female looking to grab a latte and do some browsing before heading off to look stylish somewhere.

Walker seemed nervous as he held the door for her, and scanned the parking lot as if wondering if they'd been seen.

They had.

Her name was Tara, I knew. She worked in the airline industry but in what capacity I had no clue. She was thirty-four years old—four years his junior, and three years mine. This was as much as I could recall from the note I had found beside his keys on the desk that morning.

What a creep, you may be thinking. And how awful for his wife.

But Walker Browne is not an adulterous ass, nor is he a deceitful cad looking to boost his ego by toying with the affections of single women. Nor am I some jealous bitch hell-bent on catching her husband in a lie, or an embittered ex-wife stalking the man who did her wrong. Rather, I am a happily married journalist conducting research on Internet matching services with the aid of my eternally supportive spouse and his lovely, if unwitting, companion.

The idea originated, as is often the case, with a letter from one of my readers. By that I don't mean a fan or critic of the Sunday features I craft once a month for the *La Crosse Post-Courier;* oddly, no one but my colleagues and coworkers ever seem to comment on them. In truth, I'm referring to a devotee of the syndicated column wherein I dispense sage yet savvy advice to people looking to resolve interpersonal issues. Or so say my bio, my business cards, and my Wikipedia entry.

The letter had come from a thirty-six-year-old man with a question about online dating. Specifically, he wanted to know which of the Internet matching sites I would recommend, as he was tired of the bar scene and looking to meet a woman with a genuine interest in settling down and starting a family with a decent, hardworking guy. He claimed to be past the point where his self-esteem depended on his partner looking hot in a bikini, and while mutual physical attraction was important, he was more focused on meeting someone with brains, a solid character, and a good sense of humor who craved companionship and commitment.

I half suspected from his implied assurance of his own intelligence, sense of humor, and moral superiority that R.A., as he had signed himself, was truly hoping I would be the conduit for his love connection. Lots of readers send letters outlining the qualities they are seeking in a mate and/ or attesting to their own—often interesting—attributes. Many even invite me to print their addresses in the apparent hope it will generate personal responses from other readers. Mr. R.A., however, was unique in that, in addition to being full of himself, he had asked a question that would be of interest to me and his fellow readers. Thus, I decided to take him at face value and try to provide a considered answer.

Unfortunately, as someone who hasn't dated since the Internet was in its infancy and the term "cell" was used strictly in reference to the basic functional unit of life—as opposed to a mobile phone or the local branch of a global terrorist organization—I did not feel sufficiently qualified to respond. Although I had heard of several online matching services thanks to the ads they air on TV and radio, I knew relatively little about them. And while I'm frequently exposed to impromptu evaluations of the various means and methods of man-hunting by virtue of my profusion of single friends and coworkers, having already met my ideal match, I've paid next to no attention to the minutia. Obviously I would need to do some research.

Enter my team of trusted experts—aka Kristin, Natalie, Karla, and Rory—all of whom have tried online dating at one time or another.

The plan was to survey the gals and everyone they knew who had tried their luck at love on the Internet. I wanted to know which sites they had used, liked, disliked, and why; which had garnered the highest number of matches; and which had come up with the most viable potential partners. I would also ask them to share the best and worst experiences with people they had met online, their demographic and geographic details, plus anything else they thought might prove helpful to a rookie. With this in mind, I assembled a short questionnaire, e-mailed it to each member of the core team, and asked them to complete it and forward a blank copy to everyone they knew—male and female—who fit the survey criteria. From the responses I received, I would gain the data with which to offer Mr. R.A. an informed opinion.

While I waited for the results to—I dared to hope—*pour* in, I decided to do some surfing and see what resources were available to the romantically inclined. With search engines having advanced significantly since the days of *Jeeves*, I soon had a list of websites I could expect to find on the questionnaires when they came in, and from which I would identify the top three. The nominees ranged from the ubiquitous *match.com*, to the more ambitious *eharmony.com*; from the whimsical *cupid.com*, to the somewhat unsavory *letsbang.com*; and from *420dating.com*, which offers to match pot aficionados with other pot aficionados, to *fusion101.com*, which sounds like a service for physics students, but which—for reasons beyond my comprehension—actually caters to Christians.

After a while I began to feel like I did the time Walker conned me into going to a beer-tasting party, and I found myself staring at a tray of twelve short glasses filled with liquids that ranged in color from piss yellow to rusty cherry cola: I had no idea the market had become so specialized.

Embarrassed by my ignorance of a phenomenon as huge as online dating—especially one so closely related to my own vocation—I was glad for the excuse to fill the gaps in my education. Even if some of what I saw left me scarred or frightened for the future of humanity, it would be good to know the score, since according to one site's marketing, one in five relationships now starts online.

It occurred to me as I entered the contents of my list into a spreadsheet, that while identifying these sites had been easy, figuring out if and how they worked might prove a bit trickier. While some extol their virtues on the radio and TV (one, for example, claims to be responsible for more marriages than any other online dating site—although I harbor some doubt that *letsbang.com* was ever vying for the title) I had no objective information about their effectiveness nor the slightest clue as to how they work.

I realized then that if I were going to do this project justice, I would have to do more than make a list, conduct a survey, and crunch a bunch of numbers. I would have to visit the sites, get to know their cultures, and see what, if any, science was involved.

I decided to start with the larger, more popular, non-niche offerings. This would allow me to get a jump on researching those sites that were most likely to appear in the answers to my survey questions while enabling me to avoid whatever joys were to be found on *benaughty.com*—that is, unless and until it too turned up among the responses from one of the survey participants.

It was about this stage of the game that things started to get a little more complicated. This, to be perfectly frank, did not surprise me. As my fourth-grade teacher Mr. Matthews used to say, I have a knack for putting cement into things. Of course, what he would see as making things *harder*, I tend to view as making them *better*. "That depends," he would say," on whether you're making biscuits or building a skyscraper."

At any rate, having elected to review the top four sites appearing in the results of a Google search, I opened up a new browser window and—after checking my e-mail for the fifth time in two hours and finding not a single reply—typed *thematchcafe.com* into the address bar. I decided to start here because it was the only one of the four I had yet to see advertised on TV. This seemed as good a way to choose as any, I reasoned, since they otherwise all sounded alike to me.

What set *thematchcafe.com* apart, according to its home page, was its science-based system that could match members based on common values and other key components of compatibility.

Much as I wanted to be, I was neither surprised nor impressed by these claims. Rather, having heard advertisements for other sites making similar assertions, I was in fact doubtful and a bit dismayed.

Compatibility, in my experience, is underrated and highly misunderstood, so I had grounds to be skeptical. Too many people equate compatibility with similarity, as is implied by comments like, "We're both avid readers," "Sandy and I love Ron White," and "Jerry and I detest Indian cuisine."

While statements like these may provide clues as to whether two people will be able to find ways to pass the time together and/or identify restaurants they will both enjoy, they are hardly strong indicators of whether those people are suited to one another, much less whether they have what it takes to stay together over the long haul.

Which is why *thematchcafe.com* requires members to complete a mile-long questionnaire as part of its registration process. I knew this because (for the sake of research, of course) I had started to create a profile. In return for my effort, the site promised to send a report telling me how amiable, stable, and outgoing I am; how I process information; how I react to unexpected events; and how others may perceive and respond to me. I had to stop there, since for obvious reasons, *thematchcafe.com* doesn't accept members who aren't divorced, widowed, or otherwise single. Had I continued, I would have been asked to complete a second questionnaire wherein I would divulge to them how I like to spend my free time, what qualities I'm looking for in a mate, and how important those qualities are to me in general and in relation to one another.

This all sounded pretty cool—especially the part where they told me about my personality. That is not to suggest I don't already know what I'm like. I just wanted to see if they got it right and thus whether their questionnaire and software were up to scratch.

It was then that it hit me: How do the people who use online matching systems know they work? They may offer statistics like *"thematchcafe. com* is responsible for 4 percent of the marriages that take place each day in the United States and Canada," but what exactly does that mean? Were there 4 percent *fewer* marriages in North America before *thematchcafe. com* burst onto the scene? If so, is this necessarily a good thing? And does that 4 percent truly have a better chance of celebrating their fiftieth anniversary than the other 96 percent?

This inquiring mind wanted to know.

At first glance, it seemed the only way to determine whether the couples brought together by *thematchcafe.com* were more compatible—and thus more viable—than others would be to conduct a longitudinal study. This would involve recruiting a set of couples who met via *thematchcafe.com*, tracking their rates of separation, divorce, and perceived happiness, and comparing them to a control group.

Frankly, I did not have that kind of time.

Fortunately it didn't take me long to devise a simpler means of satisfying my personal and professional curiosity.

I would start by finding two people whom I knew were totally compatible, and have them register with *thematchcafe.com*. If the system worked, it would match the parties within days, if not hours, of the completion of their profiles. If that happened, I would accept the program's claims of superiority; if not, I would deem their science bogus and move on.

The next step was to find willing subjects. Unfortunately, as I learned upon closer inspection, *thematchcafe.com* required not only that members be single, but also not be cohabitating. This posed a serious threat to the plan since I didn't know any unmarried, non-cohabitating couples who were so utterly, completely, and obviously right for one another that I could trust the system to find them compatible enough to match them.

To be fair, I didn't know many married and/or cohabitating couples who fit that description either. In fact, among the four married women with whom I'm best acquainted in La Crosse, just one seems happy, and she testifies to that fact so frequently and fervently that I suspect she's full of shit. Even counting the married women I knew before we moved here three years ago, another whom I've known since I was a kid, and the two couples with whom Walker and I occasionally socialize, only two of the seven pairs are happy, and neither of the men involved were likely to want to take part in my research.

Having discounted everyone else, it became clear that the only way I was going to get the answers I sought was to become my own subject and enlist Walker's help. This would likely take some effort since, as a manufacturing systems engineer for the local brewery, he doesn't have a ton of spare time and, more importantly, would be less interested in the world of online dating than would an interpersonal advice columnist. On top of that was the fact that we were married, thus requiring us to lie on our profiles or get bounced at the door, as it were.

Working in my favor, however, were three things. One, Walker Browne is a techie and as such has an innate curiosity about almost anything that involves codes and algorithms. Two, Mr. Browne likes women. Not that I had planned for him to meet any of his matches at that stage of the game, but I knew that fact might come in handy at some point in our negotiations. Finally, the man loves to window-shop. He can spend hours looking at electronics, hunting gear, and golfing equipment he will never buy—unless it goes on sale—just for the thrill of seeing how it works, looks, or feels in his hands. This quality too would work to my advantage since *themantchcafe.com* allows members to view their matches without paying a fee.

I approached him with the idea that evening over dinner. I had been careful not to include any of his favorite foods on the menu for fear it would tip him off I had an agenda. I don't know how many more times I can rely on that tactic before he catches on and asks me what I want when he *doesn't* see his favorite foods on the table, but as of that moment reverse psychology was still working, so I opted to stay the course.

I didn't bother to bore him with the details about the letter from R.A. I felt it would suffice to talk about my interest in Internet matching sites and software, my plan to study the distinguishing features of one particular provider, and how I needed subjects to test my hypothesis.

"What is your hypothesis?" he asked with mild interest.

"I want to know if their science is valid."

"That isn't a hypothesis."

Oh, how I have suffered for having married a science major.

"Okay. My hypothesis is…" I racked my brain to locate the file containing the information from ninth-grade physical science. I had used hypotheses since then—most recently on a research design project in grad school—but while those memories are more recent, they were stored in older cells and therefore more likely to defy recall.

"Yes?" Walker interjected as he waited for the punch line. It wouldn't be intended as a punch line, but the odds were good my next words would make him laugh since I'm not as gifted as he is with scientific terms—which is why the only parts of a computer I use are the keyboard, monitor, and mouse.

"The science behind *themantchcafe.com*," I said finally, "is so advanced that it will match two completely compatible people immediately upon completion of their respective profiles."

"That hardly seems fair. You should give the system at least a day to fully process the scores and complete the functions that will allow the profiles to recognize one another."

"Okay. Well, I was going to give it a week or so anyway." In truth I had said *immediately* only because I wasn't sure how long it would take and I didn't want to scare him off by picking a time period he might perceive as a long-term commitment.

That'll teach me to analyze things to death.

Or not.

"That's an interesting idea," he mused. "Who are you planning to have as your subjects?"

"Funny you should ask me that, because I was thinking that would be you and me. No one else we know is compatible," I reasoned, "and it's not like I can run a longitudinal study on their clientele."

"Well, you could; but then you'd be waiting quite a while for the results."

"Exactly."

"Alright. So where do we start?"

That was way too easy.

Either the man was using my own tactics against me in hopes I'd psych myself right out of wanting his help, or he wanted something from me and was using my request as a bargaining chip.

"Okay," I said guardedly, betting on the latter. "What's your fee for this transaction?"

"That depends. What are you willing to pay?"

We both laughed. We had been here many times before but it never seemed to get old.

"Seriously, how am I to compensate you for your services?" I asked.

"And again, what are they worth to you? Are you, for example," he continued, stealing a crouton from my salad and exchanging it for a black olive, "willing to get me signed up and registered?"

"I would love to, but I can't."

"Why not? Wouldn't that help to ensure that the system deems our profiles compatible?"

"It might. But I want this to be a valid and reliable test of their program's capabilities. I don't want to skew the results."

In the end Mr. Browne agreed to complete his own profile, and I agreed to attend a dinner his company was holding for a group of visitors from Germany who were touring his facility the following week. Apparently there was a software deal in the works and he wanted me on hand, I could only assume, for entertainment value.

With that deal struck, I gave him the web address and a short set of instructions. One of particular importance was to list our former residence as his current address. We still owned the house after all—although the new owners had occupied it for the past two years per the contract for deed we'd been essentially forced into due to the sagging housing market—so it made sense for him to use a different address rather than risk having the system realize we live together and showing us both the door, so to speak. Another instruction of great importance related to marital status. Although

I hated to lie under any circumstances, we were going to have to fib on this one if our applications were to be accepted. I explained that to Walker, who joked he had no objection to saying he was divorced.

Other than those two items, I told him, he was free—nay, required—to answer all remaining questions truthfully and completely. Having only gotten so far into the questionnaire myself, I did not know what other mines might lie in our path, so I asked him to take his time and check in with me if he encountered anything that might pose a threat to the plan.

I finished my initial questionnaire the next day—using my maiden name, of course—and was going through my profile report when I got a text from Walker saying he had completed his own questionnaire. I texted him back with the invitation to sit down and review our reports together when his came back to see how accurate the system was in assessing our respective characters. If the reports were mostly accurate, I agreed to take them at face value and see what happened from there. If they were obviously way off base, I would scrap the whole project. Either way, I expected this aspect of the process to be pretty interesting.

Ultimately, there were no big surprises or major discrepancies in either report. Walker's seemed to suggest he was not compassionate, which I considered unnecessarily harsh and not entirely true; but as he had completed his own questionnaire, I attributed the difference between my perceptions and the program's conclusions to the fact that while I may witness his interactions with others, I'm not necessarily privy to what is in his mind. One noteworthy entry in my report, meanwhile, said I'm highly other-oriented; that I tend to want to help people solve their problems rather than assume they can solve them on their own; that those less empathetic than I may view my concern for others as excessive and intrusive; and that less autonomous individuals may become dependent on me to solve their problems. While I wasn't completely in agreement with this, I couldn't argue with it either. After all, what kind of an advice columnist would I be if I weren't interested in other people or their problems?

Instead, I focused my attention on the reports overall. I was amazed and impressed that a computer program could so accurately describe someone's personality and predict how people will respond to that person based solely on his answers to a questionnaire.

I was also relieved, as this meant we didn't have to start over with another provider. Time permitting, I could answer questionnaires all day, but I doubted Walker felt the same way.

There was little discussion of the project for a few days other than when we would find time to complete the final questionnaire. Apparently the system will create a set of matches for you based solely on what it learned from your initial questionnaire, and while I was curious as to who might be suited to an overly empathic counselor/journalist, we declined to view our lists until we had both completed the final questionnaire and we could be reasonably sure the system had what it needed to deem us compatible.

With this in mind, we allowed the system two full days to process our entries. Knowing how curious I was, Walker authorized me to check our matches without him, but since I had talked him into joining me in this odyssey, I decided to wait for him. I would need him there to console me, I teased, if the system ruled us incompatible and we were forced to file for divorce in order to bring the universe back into balance.

I may have been laughing when I said it, but I was a fountain of dejection when we sat down to view our matches forty-eight hours later. Not one of the thirty-odd names that appeared on Walker's list was mine, and none of the precisely five men with whom I'd been matched were named Walker.

"I don't get it," I marveled. "We've been together for almost fifteen years; we've always had great sex; we've never fought about money; and when we do fight about other things, we exhibit highly conciliatory behavior. How can *we* not be compatible?"

"I don't know," he replied without pointing out that conciliatory behavior comes a little more naturally to him than it does to me. "Maybe it needs more time. Let's give it a few days and let the software do its thing. I'm sure we'll be matched by the weekend."

To my chagrin, he was mistaken.

"There has to be a flaw in the system," I grumbled as I checked my matches that Sunday to find three more names but not one Walker in the bunch. He, meanwhile, was having a great time reading the names, ages, locations, and occupations of the forty-seven women now gracing his list. Of course, he would've been having just as much fun if he'd been reading names and model numbers of the various guns and accessories pictured in a *Cabela's* catalog, so I wasn't too put off by his enthusiasm vis-à-vis his potential girlfriends. I was, however, put off by how long the system was taking to tell me what I already knew.

"You did use your real name, didn't you?" I asked with annoyance. Since we weren't allowed to upload photos as a consequence of not being vested—that is, paying—members, I thought it prudent to inquire.

"Of course I did," he replied. "Why wouldn't I?"

I was about to answer in a less than conciliatory tone when it occurred to me that he had a point.

"I don't know," I offered instead. "We didn't talk about it, though, so I thought I'd ask."

Walker sat back from the desk as he logged out and closed the browser.

"Maybe you're right," he said after a moment. "Maybe there is a flaw in the system. Let's give this thing another two days and see what it comes up with. If we aren't satisfied by then, we can each go back and review our questionnaires to make sure we didn't inadvertently goof it up."

That sounded reasonable enough to me, although by then I had already ruled the program faulty. How it could have done such a great job analyzing our personalities and still not find either of us worthy of the other, I could not fathom, but I was determined to find the flaw.

With this in mind, I decided to go through my questionnaire with a view not only to finding errors in my responses, but also to collecting some data of my own. I planned to identify the type and scope of information they gathered in the two questionnaires, and consider it alongside what showed on my report. I would do the same with Walker's report after the deadline expired and he'd had a chance to review his profile and make any necessary corrections.

Meanwhile, in the interest of science, I proposed something a little more radical.

"What do you mean *I should meet some of my matches*?" he asked. "Have you lost your mind?"

I hadn't expected him to be wild about the idea, if only because it would require him to pay the two hundred dollar fee to become a full-fledged member. I planned to do the same, but with less than sixteen matches—compared to Walker's fifty—I was unlikely to be as busy as he would be—assuming he even went along with the plan.

It took some negotiating, but he agreed to go along with my scheme and imposed only two conditions. First, he refused to meet anyone from La Crosse. He was uncomfortable having his profile out there in the first place; he did not want to end up dating the sister or daughter of a colleague. Second, he refused to meet anyone anywhere *near* La Crosse. Instead, he would meet them in Waukesha, where we used to live; or Oshkosh, where we went to school; or somewhere in between. This meant meetings would take place on weekends, but that would also give us an excuse to visit our friends and families. I was all for that, and placed similar restrictions on my meetings, although by then I had already decided, compatible or not, I was holding out for Walker Browne.

Tara was the first of his matches I'd asked him to meet—okay, so perhaps begged would be more accurate—and I promised him there would be few others. I knew he wasn't all that keen on spending time with strangers, even if they were attractive female strangers. He was especially reluctant on this front since he didn't want to run into someone he knew who might get the wrong idea about him, or who might assume the woman with him was the wife he or she had never met, and inadvertently reveal he was married.

I was no more interested in him dating than he was, I had assured him; I just wanted him to meet a few of his matches and take some notes until the system figured out we belonged together—or at least until I'd gathered the information I needed to find the flaws preventing it from accepting we belonged together.

I realized upon concluding my review of the last few weeks that I was still sitting in my car in front of the bookstore. I had planned to leave the mall and, in fact, had asked Walker to text me when he needed me to pick him up. That plan sounded kind of silly now, since he and Tara might be wrapping things up any minute.

Still, as curious as I was to know how their meeting would end, I decided against lingering any longer. Better to go find something to do, I reasoned, than to sit and wait for this pot to boil.

Two

My girlfriend doesn't enjoy performing oral sex, but I think she just lacks confidence in her skill. How can I convince her to work on her technique so she enjoys it more?

I smiled patiently at the clerk who had posed this question—*sotto voce*, of course—and from whom I was accepting my credit card receipt upon completing our transaction at the local home improvement center about five days after Walker's meeting at the bookstore.

Such a query might have shocked your average shopper—and possibly earned the clerk a spot in the unemployment line. Fortunately for him, I'm accustomed to hearing questions of this sort from people who recognize me from my photo in the paper and thus I wasn't moved to complain. In fact, while I'm constantly amazed by the range of people who read my column, I'm no longer surprised when they approach, nor stunned by the nature of the questions they ask.

In such situations I generally draw a business card from my wallet and offer it to the inquirer, along with an invitation to send an e-mail. This is as much for his or her benefit as for mine. After all, it's hard enough to give a quality answer when you're not expecting the question; it's damn near impossible when you're standing at the checkout buying landscaping supplies with seven other patrons in line behind you wondering what's taking so damned long.

Under better circumstances I may take a moment to consider the question and offer an opinion or propose a course of action that would improve the situation or resolve it entirely. This is most likely to happen when I'm not dashing between errands or running late for a meeting, and when the matter is clearly not one of life and death.

Needless to say, Phil from Home Project Central got a business card.

In addition to encountering people looking for a personal consultation, I am occasionally approached by someone offering free appraisals of my performance. As often as not, these come from readers who think I could have done a better job with one letter or another and who, judging by how they phrase their remarks, seem to think I have the hide of a rhino.

Not that I object to either the impromptu queries or the unsolicited evaluations. As someone should have told a certain former Alaskan elected official: You can't thrust yourself into the public eye and then complain when people notice you; and you shouldn't say controversial things and then whine when people react. That said, it would be nice if some of these people showed me the same courtesy and sensitivity I show my readers.

That aside, I enjoy what I do. Even as it sometimes requires me to maintain my composure when utter strangers approach me with questions of a highly personal—and often sexual—nature, it's always nice to be recognized and to know you're trusted. I hadn't entered the field expecting that to happen, but it does great things for one's ego.

Another thing I hadn't expected when I first started helping people manage their interpersonal issues via the newspaper—as opposed to in a one-on-one or group setting, as I had before we left Waukesha—was how curious the readers would be about me. Are you married? they'll ask. If so, for how long? If not, why not? Are you happy? Do you get along with your in-laws? How about your parents? Your siblings? How are things with your boss? Your coworkers? Your neighbors? Are you gay or straight? Has your husband ever cheated on you? Have you ever cheated on him? Even if it had occurred to me that having a column would cause people to approach me on the street or in stores, never did I imagine how many would want to know about my personal life.

I could understand if they wanted to inquire about my qualifications for the job as one may before hiring, say, a doctor, a roofer, or a plumber. But for some reason, a good portion of the audience seems to think my sexual preference, my marital status, and even how well I get along with my brother are of greater significance than anything on my resume, and that knowing such things can tell them whether or not they can trust my judgment.

"Well, what do you expect?" asked Alethia Dornquast, as we, our friend Laurel, plus online dating survey recipients Kristin and Natalie—all of whom had worked at the *Post-Courier* at some point in the recent past— chatted in the bar of our favorite "girls' night" restaurant. "I mean, no offense, Roxanne, but I don't know why anyone would ask you for advice when they know next to nothing about you. It would be different if the paper would publish your *curriculum vitae* next to your byline; but without that, the public has absolutely no idea whether you're qualified to answer their questions or not."

She hadn't missed my point—that I found it strange so many readers are more interested in my personal experiences than they are my professional credentials. In fact, I suspect she had only bothered to open her mouth so she could say *curriculum vitae*—thereby demonstrating to all in attendance that she knew both how to pronounce it and how to use it in a sentence— and because doing so would make her the center of attention once again.

Prior to that she had been complaining to all of us how hard it is to find clothes in her size, and how she doesn't mind shopping for *jeans* in the children's section but that's not an option when you're looking for *career wear.*

Unfortunately one of our fellow patrons had had the unmitigated gall to interrupt Alethia's tale of woe to say how much she enjoys the column, and to ask if I had experienced sexual harassment in the workplace because I seemed to know what I was talking about in my response to the woman from Iowa whose boss refused to respect her boundaries.

It was on the heels of her visit that I had mentioned to the group how baffled I am by how many people want to attribute my "wisdom" to personal experience rather than education, training, or basic common sense, and by how curious some of them are about my personal life. I hadn't intended to steal the spotlight, but apparently Alethia felt I had, which is why she hadn't simply directed the conversation back to her wardrobe issues, but had also taken the swipe at me.

Alethia is an enduring problem of mine, and one I hope to solve without bloodshed since I suspect it would be difficult to maintain my career— not to mention my marriage—from a prison cell. She is not without good qualities; in fact, she's smart, kind to those she loves, and—in the right setting—can be highly entertaining. She is also pretty, has great taste in clothes, and is socially and environmentally conscious. Unfortunately, Alethia is also a narcissist who feels the need to draw attention to how smart, kind, entertaining, pretty, tasteful, and environmentally and socially conscious she is at irritatingly regular intervals. She also fancies herself an expert on a variety of matters far too numerous to mention, and is not content to simply say what she knows or thinks about a given topic and then let others do the same. Instead, she insists on interrupting others to reiterate her agreement or dissent, or to correct facts or terminology even when the party already speaking is well versed on the subject. Alethia also suffers from an abundance of pride in her husband, Greg, as evidenced by her seemingly incessant references to his brilliance and his contributions to our fine community as director of planning. I get that she's proud of the man, and I'm sure he's doing a wonderful job; but let's get real—it's not as if he's curing cancer.

These tendencies have become more apparent of late, and have had the impact of curbing the frequency with which I attend our gatherings. It has also had the impact of driving me insane—to use a technical term. I would love to hold an intervention where we all sit down with Alethia and explain where she's going wrong and how it's affecting the group, but no matter how gently we put it, no doubt her feelings would be hurt.

Why should I care? Obviously it's because I'm an intensely compassionate person who takes excessive interest in other people's lives, which incidentally can foster dependence among those who can't solve their own problems. If I were anyone else, I'd probably just tell the woman she's obnoxious and get it over with; but I doubt that would solve the problem since *Alethia the Wounded* would be no less irksome than *Alethia the All Knowing*.

In truth, Alethia wouldn't bother me nearly as much if her narcissism manifested itself purely as self-consciousness and self-interest. One can relate, after all, to someone who says she needs to diet and who is overweight; you tend to want to smack, however, a woman in size two slacks who routinely calls herself enormous in front of four friends who all wear at least a size ten, and whose only motive for saying it appears to be to induce them to remark on how trim she is. It's also easier to support someone who asks for leads and recommendations while looking for a job, than it is to congratulate a woman who lands a position with the county and then brags about all the strings her husband pulled to make it happen.

Kristin, who has the biggest heart of anyone I know but who has recently been the target of Alethia's worst remarks, has postulated that Alethia was one of the popular girls (aka the Plastics for those who've seen *Mean Girls*) at her high school back in her native St. Louis. I'm convinced, however, that she was actually an outcast—which makes sense given her poor social skills—and is making up for it by acting like a hotshot in her adopted community.

Thankfully, Alethia and I rarely cross paths outside of girls' nights, due to her status as a *Mover and a Shaker*, as she and Greg were dubbed in 2008 by *La Crosse* magazine. An urban monthly aimed at the thirty to forty set and run by the publishers of the *Post-Courier, La Crosse* covers the local arts and entertainment scene and features articles on noteworthy people, places, and events. It seems the two were recognized because of Greg's contribution to some downtown rehab project and Alethia's work on behalf of two area charities. That was before their daughter got in trouble at school and Alethia quit her part-time job in our marketing department to spend more time at home. The girl has since been remanded to a regional detention center—for reasons Alethia does not talk about in my presence—hence her return to work in 2010.

As neither a mover nor a shaker, I am not acquainted with anyone in our city or county government—other than Alethia and Greg—or with anyone who is affiliated with any civic or charitable organization. While this means I have to compete for jobs on the basis of my skills rather than my connections, that's a small price to pay for self-respect and for the privilege of not bumping into Ms. Dornquast every time I turn around. As hard to take as she can be when surrounded by her former coworkers, I hate to imagine what she's like with people she really wants to impress. Not that I have a clue as to who that would be. Given that we met three years ago and she drops names like my parents drop nickels in the slot machines at Ho-Chunk, I should probably have an idea; but since I generally tune her out when she's holding court, there's nothing in that file.

Ironically, it's only because of Kristin that Alethia and I are acquainted—a fact for which I've yet to thank her. It was she who invited me to my first girls' night after a farewell luncheon for Laurel two weeks after I joined the paper back in 2008. I had happened across the event while searching for the restroom, and was snagged by Kristin, who worked in HR and who needed a piece of documentation to complete my personnel file. After securing a promise to scan and submit the missing form when I got back home, Kristin invited me to stick around, and made it her mission to introduce me to the veterans and to keep me company. Based on what, exactly, I don't know, she apparently decided we should be friends, and later invited me to an off-hours gathering in honor of Laurel's new job at the end of the week. It was there that I met Alethia and Natalie, who had left her position in advertising sales a few months before I came on board.

Prior to that, I had worked only for and with myself writing the advice column, which was picked up for syndication about a year before we left Waukesha, and facilitating workshops on interpersonal communication. As a result, I hadn't actually had coworkers since about 2001.

We moved to La Crosse in 2007 when Walker was offered his current position at River City Brewing. With writing being suited to telecommuting and consulting being highly transferrable, Walker and I could find no compelling reason for him to turn down the offer. Even if it meant packing up our stuff and schlepping it all the way to the opposite side of the state, it promised to be a good move as it would be his first management job since finishing his graduate degree two years earlier. He had been a planner/scheduler for a rival brewery in Milwaukee then, and he was eager to move up, even if River City was a smaller facility.

After we got settled in our new place and there were no more walls to paint or furnishings to buy, I decided I wanted more to do with my day than read and respond to letters. My column was practically writing itself by then, and I had several weeks' worth of copy waiting in the wings. Not wanting to go back to facilitating workshops just yet, I approached the chief editor of the *Post-Courier*, Ken Lawrence, with some ideas I had for features, including one on relationships in the workplace that I'd already written and brought along as a sample. He was obviously not interested, but foolishly invited me to send him a copy of the other two when they were finished. I agreed, although I could tell he hoped I'd forget about it.

At some point between that conversation and the day I launched the e-mail with my two articles, Mr. Lawrence was apparently let go. Why he was removed remains a matter of debate among the former and current staff. Some say he was caught dipping his pen in the company ink. Others believe he'd gotten too liberal with the terms of his expense account. Still others think he had a falling out with a businesswoman who happened to be a friend of the publisher's wife. All of these things might be true, according to new Chief Editor Karla Collier, to whom my message was later routed, but none of them had anything to do with his departure.

"Kenny is a friend of mine," she told me at our first meeting after explaining how she came by my articles, "and the man was far from perfect; but he was let go for purely editorial reasons, so don't let anyone tell your otherwise."

I thought these were strange remarks since I had yet to meet anyone who would have told me otherwise. Still, I respected her loyalty, her discretion, and her directness, and decided I would endeavor to follow her advice.

She then went on to tell me how the publishers were looking to take the paper in a different direction, and they didn't think Mr. Lawrence was the person to make it happen. He didn't argue, apparently, and in fact recommended Karla for the job. He then called and told her to send over her resume, and provided her a glowing personal reference.

Although I got the feeling from Karla's body language there was slightly more to the story than I was hearing, I wasn't about to press for more details at that stage of the game.

From subsequent conversations, however, I determined that apart from giving her the heads-up that his position would soon be vacant, Karla would not have needed Mr. Lawrence's help in landing the job. Prior to coming to the *Post-Courier,* she had been an assistant editor of the *Twin Port Times,* a respected metropolitan daily serving Superior, Wisconsin, and Duluth, Minnesota. Before that the La Crosse native and UW-La Crosse grad had helmed the *Tri-County Chronicle*, a small weekly serving three rural counties in southeastern Minnesota. Like Walker, Karla had come to La Crosse to take a higher level job with a smaller company, but in her case, she was coming back home, not leaving it behind.

More creative, ambitious, and disciplined than her predecessor—as was obvious to me after just one meeting with each of them—Karla planned to grow the paper's circulation by adopting a new look and tone, and she thought I could assist her in that effort. Billing me as a guest editor, she offered me fifty column inches every third Sunday. The *Post-Courier* did not run my column at that point, but Karla planned to add it to their content the week before they ran my first Sunday feature. It seems to have been a good move all around since I'm still writing three years later and the paper hasn't folded.

With the spotlight firmly back on Alethia again, thanks to my decision to daydream rather than disagree with her, she was now speaking animatedly about some new project that's come before the planning commission, and how the Almighty Greg was going to save the economy by giving it his stamp of approval.

I considered interrupting her again, just for the fun of it, but resisted. I could think of better things to do with my time than pick on someone so desperate for attention—especially since she probably wouldn't notice I was trying to irritate her. Rather, I decided to wait for her to take a breath or a sip of her mai tai, and then announce to the group I had to get going.

"So what's the story with the questionnaire?" Natalie asked suddenly, simultaneously foiling my plot to escape and bumping Alethia out of first chair. "I know you said you're conducting a survey, but what's it for?"

"Questionnaire?" Laurel repeated. "What questionnaire?" Being one of my married friends, she hadn't received one, and thus had no idea what Natalie was talking about.

Worried she would feel left out, I quickly explained the purpose of the survey, to whom I had sent it and why, and how I intended to use the results.

As I expected, Alethia nodded the whole time as if she knew the entire story. Although she knew nothing more than Laurel did about the project, she wasn't about to appear even remotely curious about it. The woman may hate being out of the loop, but she hates *looking* like she's out of the loop even more.

"What I don't understand," she said as I was winding down, "is why you had to do a survey in the first place.

"I mean, with all due respect, Roxanne," she continued with precisely none, "if you're going to call yourself an advice columnist, shouldn't you already *know* how to handle the questions people will ask?"

I noticed Laurel brace herself. She knows what Alethia is like, and has apologized more than once on her behalf.

"She doesn't mean to hurt your feelings," she had said to the rest of us once after Alethia "invited" Kristin to housesit while she and Greg traveled to Bermuda and added, as a selling point, that it would be a vacation for Kristin as well since it would allow her and the boys to get out of their own little house for a week. "She just doesn't realize how she comes across."

"Well, perhaps someone should tell her," I had suggested at the time, but while they all seemed to agree, none of them volunteered to do so.

"I don't think that's fair," Natalie said in my defense before I could marshal a civilized reply. "Roxanne can't possibly know the subject of every letter she's going to get."

Natalie's great and, after Kristin, the second reason I come to these things. I like Laurel too, but she only attends about half of our gatherings, so I don't get to see her as much as the others. That's a real double-edged sword for me since if Laurel can't make it, Alethia generally cancels.

"That's true," Kristin added. "After all, I get all kinds of crazy calls down at the county personnel office, and I doubt you know now all you will ever need to about veterans' affairs."

Good point, I thought to myself. *But I wouldn't bet on Alethia ever admitting to it.*

It was largely due to Kristin's work in county HR that Alethia got the job in veterans' affairs in the first place, but she would never admit that either. Leave it to Shallow Al to think it's more impressive to have gotten a job because of her husband's influence rather than on the basis of her own skills and experience, or her former colleague's knowledge of them.

"Well, we're not exactly talking about a pastry chef being asked how to dismantle a bomb now, are we?" Alethia replied. "I'm just saying that since people write to Roxanne for advice about relationships, and since one in five relationships starts online, perhaps she should know something about online dating."

I watched Laurel brace herself again and I wondered if she truly was afraid I would respond with violence, or if she just thought Alethia deserved to get smacked.

I had no intention of smacking her, of course, although I confess to having fantasized about it in the recent past. In reality, however, I don't believe in violence except when it's necessary to protect oneself or others from harm. Thus, there would be no smacking, slapping, scratching, clawing, or hair pulling from my side of the table, even if Alethia herself seemed out for blood.

In truth, while I was offended by her tone, I really couldn't dispute what she had said. She wasn't wrong, after all. She had only voiced aloud what I had chastised myself for just weeks ago. Okay, so maybe she had said it with less than helpful intentions and with her trademark lack of tact; and maybe she'd ripped off her stats from the same TV commercial I'd seen to make herself sound like an authority. That didn't mean I had to fight fire with fire, or sink to her level.

"You're right," I admitted instead, although it almost killed me. "I should know something about online dating, which is exactly why I decided to conduct the survey. It may sound like a complicated process, but since we can't trust the providers themselves to give complete, accurate, and unbiased information—and since as a married woman, I am barred from joining at least the most reputable among them—it seemed the best way to educate myself on online dating services was to consult the people who have already used them."

I don't know why I was trying so hard to keep thing civil. I honestly didn't care what Alethia thought of me or, for that matter, if I ever saw her again. I guess I just didn't want to make the others uncomfortable, even if she was incapable of showing them that kind of consideration.

"I trust this puts to rest your concerns on behalf of my readers," I concluded after a brief pause. "Now if you'll please excuse me, I need to use the ladies room."

Only Kristin remained at the table when I got back. Alethia had apparently decided to leave after my mini monologue, she said, and had insisted on paying Natalie and Laurel's share of the tab since they both had birthdays coming up and we didn't yet have a plan in place to celebrate them.

This made me laugh. Alethia rarely paid one cent more than her share of anything when we went out, but could always be counted on to make a big deal about it whenever she did. Kristin and I had joked about that on our way into the building that night, and she laughed with me again after explaining how Alethia had talked Natalie and Laurel into leaving when she did by saying she had gifts for each of them in her car.

"Why didn't she just bring them in with her?" I asked, shaking my head. "Was she afraid you and I would feel left out?"

"More likely she was afraid we'd try to take credit for them the way she does whenever someone else brings one of us a gift."

We laughed again, and each had another drink in honor of the refreshing lack of tension before calling it a night.

Walker was already home when I got back to the house that evening, and since the night was still fairly young, we took the opportunity to have a glass of wine, chat about the day, and discuss the status of our research on *thematchcafe.com*. He had just finished the notes I'd asked him to take on his date with Tara, so we decided to start there. Afterward, we would go over the printout of his current matches and decide which of the lovely ladies he would contact next.

The purpose of these missions, as he liked to call them, was to get a sense of his dates' personality and other traits in hopes of isolating the characteristics the system thought made them compatible with a gadget head/manufacturing guru/hunter-gatherer/WEB Griffin fan, and subsequently identifying why the system hadn't matched him with yours truly. Since he could view their profiles but not their personality inventories or their responses to the questionnaires, it seemed the only way to do this was to learn as much as we could about his potential matches ourselves, and try to determine how the system had deemed them suitable for Walker Browne.

To that end I had devised a three-part survey for him to complete after each date. He knew that was part of the deal when I first pitched the project to him last month, and had even offered to help me put it together. I relieved him of his duties in this regard, however, when he suggested I have him ask and personally confirm each woman's measurements, and I realized he wasn't taking it seriously.

The first part of the survey was a Roxanne Browne original. It contained spaces for him to record general details such as age, education, and occupation, plus areas to enter observable traits like appearance, voice, and mannerisms. It also contained areas where he could record the type of information a woman might disclose in the course of conversation—such as likes and dislikes, goals, and family history—and things she would reveal about herself in the process, such as her level of self-confidence, intelligence, values, and sense of humor.

The second portion of the survey sought information from which I would create a personality inventory. Loosely based on the reports Walker and I had received from *thematchcafe.com* after completing our initial questionnaires, this portion of the survey aimed to assess a subject in terms of her interpersonal behavior and demeanor. Obviously this was not an ideal tool since it would provide few clues as to how the subjects saw themselves or how they interacted with people who knew them well, but it was the best way I could come up with to identify what each of Walker's matches had or did not have in common with one another and, more importantly, how similar or different they were from me.

The final section of the survey was essentially a mock-up of the questionnaire that members of *thematchcafe.com* take after receiving their personality inventory, which asked about hobbies, interests, and what one absolutely must have and would not accept in a partner. Walker would complete this portion—to the best of his ability, that is—from the information he had gathered over the course of the date or the preceding online chat. In my opinion personality and demeanor, which the second portion of the tool was designed to assess, were more reliable indicators of compatibility than, say, the title of the last book one had read or whether or not one likes sushi; but since *thematchcafe.com* considered that sort of information when creating matches, I thought it prudent not to discount it.

Once the survey was completed, I asked Walker to read it with a view to retaining as much of what I wanted him to learn about his dates as possible. I didn't expect him to memorize the form, and I specifically asked him not to appear to his subjects as if he were conducting an interview, but aside from these guidelines, I left it to him to decide how to get the information in question.

And so, like the gem that he is, Walker had reviewed the material, gone out with Tara, and completed his first packet of notes, which he handed to me as we sat down with our wine. On top of the stack was a printout containing the names, ages, and occupations of the women he had most recently been matched with through *thematchcafe.com*.

"So who's it going to be?" he asked as I scanned the sixty-odd sets of demographic and other information.

"Don't ask me. I'm not choosing the women you're stepping out with."

Walker laughed. "Why not?"

"Because I don't want to skew the data, silly."

"Besides," I added as I handed back the sheet, "you wouldn't be asking me whom to meet if we weren't married, so it doesn't make sense for you to ask me just because you're pretending to be single."

"Actually, I wouldn't have to *ask* you whom to meet if we weren't married, given how eager you were to set me up back in college."

"Maybe. But that was an entirely different situation."

"How so?"

"Well, for one thing, we're supposed to be divorced now, which means you would have left me—since I would never dream of leaving you—which means things between us would not be amicable, which in turn means we would not be having this conversation."

"Second," I continued as Walker shook his head, "the goal is different. Today I'm conducting research. Back then I was just making excuses to talk to you."

"Why?"

"Because I liked you."

"And you thought the best way to convey that was to have me date your friends?"

"Most of them were just acquaintances, really; and it's not as if I expected things to work out between you and any of them."

"Is that so?"

I nodded. "Did you think it was just a coincidence that everyone I set you up with was either boring, stupid, or crazy?"

"Yes—not to mention an indication of your taste in friends, if I'm honest."

"Well, you were wrong on both counts. I was just keeping myself in your orbit until you woke up and realized you wanted to date me."

Walker laughed again. "Why didn't you just ask me out?"

"Because I figured if you were interested, you would have asked *me*."

The plan had almost backfired, I recalled with a laugh, as Walker had apparently concluded I was off the market. This information came to me by way of my classmate, Shannon. As she told it, Walker had suggested the two of them get together with me and my boyfriend over spring break since neither they nor I had plans to go to Florida.

Lucky for me I realized the flaw in my plan, and when it was obvious things were not going anywhere between him and Shannon, jumped at the chance to invite Walker to a movie.

"So you were deliberately setting me up with people you thought were wrong for me," he recapped now, "so you could eventually have me to yourself?"

"Basically."

Walker shook his head again. "I had no idea you could be so devious."

"I know. That's because I look about as threatening as a Care Bear."

"So," I continued, nodding to his printout. "Who's the next lucky contestant?"

"You're really going to make me choose, huh?"

"Yep."

"Okay. Then I guess I'll go with Jamey."

"Jamey?" I repeated, having expected him to go a different direction. "Why?"

"Because she's from Eau Claire."

"And?"

Walker shrugged. "And Eau Claire girls are easy."

"Excuse me?"

I shook my head as Walker started to laugh.

"Okay, okay. You're hilarious," I assured him. "Now seriously—why Eau Claire?"

"Because it's about four hours from there to Waukesha, which means we and Jamey are less likely to have any friends or relatives in common."

"I hadn't thought of that."

"Neither had I until Tara asked where I'd gone to high school and I had to decide if it would be safer to lie or tell the truth. Turns out she's a transplant from Northern Indiana, so there was no cause for alarm, but I realized then that to minimize the risk, I should probably steer clear of women from either Waukesha or Milwaukee."

"Good thinking."

That decided, Walker and I took our glasses to the kitchen sink, and then headed upstairs, where he inquired about my visit with the gals, and I told him of my run-in with Alethia.

"Shall I break her kneecaps?" he offered, "or put anthrax in her air ducts?"

He was kidding, of course. He had made similar proposals with respect to my last employer before I decided to quit, and about everyone from whom I've since gotten hate mail. As tempting as the offer was, as usual, I declined.

"I don't have to put up with her that often," I reasoned, "and I'm not usually the one in her line of fire."

In fact, it's usually Kristin who suffers for Alethia's excessive self-esteem and who takes the bulk of her crap. This has always made a sort of sad sense to me, since Kristin is a single parent with a difficult ex, and Alethia loves to gloat. She doesn't go about it directly, of course, but with pretentious displays of compassion, and patronizing references to Kristin's pluck.

Natalie is also single and has an outright ass for an ex-husband, but these details are offset by the fact that she has money and connections that put Alethia's to shame. Divorced since leaving the *Post-Courier*, she drives a little blue convertible she won in her settlement—along with the deed to a brand-new two-bedroom condo overlooking the river. She has also since joined the board of directors of the United Fund for the Arts and Humanities and the Wisconsin Humanities Council. Unable to feel superior to Natalie on economic or social grounds, Alethia compensates by making wholly unsolicited offers to update her hair and makeup, and volunteering to serve as her personal fashion consultant when she goes shopping for clothes or home furnishings. There is absolutely nothing wrong with Natalie's look or her choice of home décor, mind you. It's just that Alethia believes her taste is superior to Natalie's, and wants everyone to know it.

Not that Natalie ever seems to notice. Easygoing and secure in herself, she declines Alethia's offers like generous gifts she's unable to accept, and never appears to perceive the implied insult.

In the entire three years I've known these women, Laurel is the only one I've never seen Alethia put down—directly or otherwise—which may explain why Laurel finds it so easy to defend her. It probably doesn't hurt that Alethia worships the ground Laurel walks on, as evidenced by regular assurances of her beauty and frequent offers of back rubs, manicures, and foot massages. If someone was that eager to get her hands on my body, I would have to wonder if she had something other than friendship in mind, but Laurel seems totally unfazed by all the ass-kissing, and insists Alethia is only being nice.

Although Kristin and I joke that Alethia's flattery and superfluous attention are indicative of latent sexual attraction, a more likely explanation is that Laurel is the only one of us that Alethia considers her equal. A former Miss La Crosse County, Laurel was third runner-up for the title of Miss Wisconsin while a senior at Viterbo University in 1994. In addition to being gorgeous and highly intelligent, she is a gifted athlete with an incredible singing voice and an enviable career. An accounting major, Laurel started as a clerk in the billing department at the *Post-Courier* right out of college, and stayed on after she got married in order to put her husband, Marty, through dental school. She continued there, taking time off to have their kids, and had worked her way up to the coveted role of circulation director by the time Marty finished his training in 2005. She quit three years later when Marty decided to strike out on his own and asked her to run the business side of his practice. Since then, she has helped make his office one of the three most profitable in the area.

Despite all her success, Laurel is less sure of herself than almost anyone I have ever known. She is also one of the sweetest and most generous people on earth and, not surprisingly, the one to whom Natalie and Kristin turn when they need support or a kick in the pants. Her nurturing manner puts them at ease and allows her to say what they need to hear even when it's not what they *want* to hear. Thus, it is my fervent hope that one day Laurel will take advantage of her unique position with Alethia and convince her to stop being such a pain in the ass.

"Why don't you tell her yourself?" Walker had asked the last time I shared this fantasy with him. "After all, you're the relationship expert in the group."

The man had a point. Unfortunately, I am also the *newest* member of the group and as such, am in no position to police the others.

"At least she didn't regale us tonight with tales of how Greg wooed her," I concluded, "or how ecstatic they still are despite being married for seventeen years."

"Seventeen years?" he marveled. "How old was she when they got married? Twelve?"

"Thirteen, actually, or they would have needed parental consent."

"Are you serious?"

"No I'm not serious—but thank you for playing along."

"Thanks also for mentioning how young she looks," I continued as I prepared to brush my teeth, "since she neglected to point that out herself for a change."

"Think nothing of it," Walker teased back. "I'm just happy I could help."

"Meanwhile," he added after setting the alarm and turning back the covers. "If Mr. and Mrs. Perfect have been together for seventeen years, why didn't you rope *them* into being the subjects of this little project of yours?"

I shrugged. "Mostly because I've only met Greg twice and thus I don't know how compatible they are, but also because the invitation would go straight to her head, and I am not willing to inflate that ego any more than it is."

Three

As per our plan, Walker contacted Jamey the next day via *themcatchcafe.com* and, after a brief chat, invited her to meet him the following Saturday. They decided to meet in the Wisconsin Dells, which would make the trip about a two-hour drive for each of them if we still lived in Waukesha, but would take us just ninety minutes since we were only coming from La Crosse. I felt somewhat guilty knowing Jamey was driving one hundred thirty miles vice Walker's ninety; but as he so eloquently pointed out as we packed up the car that morning, she likely would mind driving the extra distance far less than she would the fact that she was meeting a married man whose only interest in her was to gather data for a study on modern courtship.

Unable to argue with that logic, I decided it made more sense to focus on the positives of the plan than to feel guilty on Jamey's behalf. I would make it up to her, I resolved, by buying some fine chocolates for Walker to give her as a token of my secret appreciation, and by having him cover all the costs associated with their date.

One of the aforementioned positives to the plan was that it would allow me to visit with my parents, whom I hadn't seen since Christmas three months before and who were unavailable when we were in Waukesha for Walker's last date the previous Saturday. Bunny and Mack, as they are known to everyone but complete strangers—by whom they are referred to instead as Bernadette and Royce Mackie—live in Oshkosh, and under normal circumstances would have been more than happy to drive down and meet us in Madison or Milwaukee. As it happened, however, they already had plans to visit my older brother, R.J.—or, as he's known to almost no one but our grandmother, Royce Jennings Mackie, III—in Chicago that weekend and would not be passing through Milwaukee again until long after we needed to leave on Sunday.

Not wanting to miss them again, I had picked up the phone only moments after Walker had finalized his plans with Jamey, and—without elaborating, of course—invited them to meet us for dinner in the Dells. I didn't exactly have to twist their arms since it's only a ninety-minute drive for them too, and—more importantly—their favorite casino is right down the street from the restaurant, and less than a mile from our hotel.

Another positive aspect of the plan was that it forced me to sit still for more than twenty minutes, which I normally can't do at home. This made it possible for me to review the notes and other materials I had collected for an upcoming Sunday feature, and to put together an outline of what I wanted to cover. This, in turn, gave Walker the chance to enjoy the scenery along the interstate in relative quiet before having to face the visual cacophony that is the Wisconsin Dells.

When people from greater Wisconsin and her neighboring states think about the Dells, they generally think of recreation, and lots and lots of refreshing water. When Walker Browne thinks of the Dells, he thinks of overstimulation—and lots and lots of irritating tourists.

This is not unreasonable since according to available statistics, the Dells attracts more than five million people each year to its numerous water parks, resorts, campgrounds, RV parks, indoor and outdoor amusement parks, theme parks, museums, hotels, motels, and restaurants. That's one million more than the number of people who visit the Grand Canyon in a given year, and about twice as many as visited the National Zoo in Washington, DC in 2010.

Statistics like these make the Dells highly attractive to investors, but they make it completely unappealing to a man whose idea of relaxation is floating down a lazy river in an inner tube with a cooler full of beer in tow, or sitting on a rock with a shotgun and a paperback waiting for a deer to wander into view. Which is why Walker stopped accompanying his family on their annual pilgrimage to the Dells well before he had reached the age of majority. It is also what prompted me to ask why he had chosen to meet Jamey there in the first place when so many other viable locations existed.

"Because the Dells are the halfway point between Eau Claire and Waukesha," he had replied as if it were a silly question, "which made it the most equitable place in terms of driving time."

"Okay, but you could have asked her to meet you in Tomah and just let her think you're gallant."

"True. But that may have suggested a level of interest that I think would be inappropriate and unfair to convey under the circumstances."

"Besides," Walker added with a teasing wink as I recognized his words as a parody of some of my own, "given the pain you've suffered over the fact that she's driving thirty-six miles further than we are, I hate to imagine how distressed you'd be if she had to drive eighty-two miles and we only had to drive forty."

Okay, so the Dells it would be.

Fortunately, we were going in the off-season when the outdoor attractions would be shut down, and there would be fewer people competing for access to the indoor ones. This didn't make the place much more alluring to Walker since he objects as much to the attractions as he does the tourists— which makes sense, since you wouldn't have one without the other. Still, he was somewhat appeased by the knowledge he wouldn't have to park in Outer Mongolia, and by the fact that he wouldn't have to fight to the death for a turn on the go-karts.

While he was out, I filled the in-room Jacuzzi, switched on the TV, and managed to waste ten bucks on what may have been the greatest cinematic disappointment of my entire life.

The film was a new release about two teenagers who track down the man who donated the sperm their mothers had used to conceive them. It had been a huge hit in the theatres last year and earned several Golden Globe and Oscar nominations, but if I tried all day and in more than one language, I could not explain why.

Perhaps I wasn't looking hard enough, but I could find absolutely nothing in the relationship between these two women to explain why they were together, much less why they bothered to work it out after one of them had a fling with the sperm donor. In fact, aside from giving one of them a slightly less feminine look and painting the other as an earthily sexy nurturer, there was nothing to explain why they were partners. It was almost as if those involved in the production thought the fact that the women were lesbians, and that one of them was a bit butch, was enough to explain why they were in a relationship.

Maybe I'm alone in that I watch movies with more interest in the relationships between the characters than the average person does. But if I were a physician and a film tried to pass off an actor in full makeup and a healthy glow as a patient in kidney or heart failure, the makers should expect me to notice, and for it to influence my opinion of the movie.

Even if I do pay more attention to the relationships between movie characters than most people, I am definitely not alone in picking up on things that are relevant to my work or hobbies. Just as my dad objects when an actor who's playing a marine is shown wearing his hair down around his ears or in a uniform with the wrong insignia, so do lots of moviegoers react to inaccuracies or inconsistencies that are relevant to their own lives and experiences.

I shared some of these thoughts—in condensed form, of course—with Walker after he returned from his date with Jamey, then asked him to share his first impressions.

Apparently things went well for them at "the area's largest indoor fun center," where they had lunch, played a few games, rode the go-karts and bumper cars, and sat down to enjoy some ice cream before parting company.

"Sounds like the perfect first date," I mused when he had finished the briefing on their date.

"I wouldn't go that far."

"Why not? Didn't she let you kiss her?"

Walker cringed.

"I wouldn't have been able to kiss her even if I'd thought that was part of the deal," he confessed. "She reminded me way too much of Lisa."

That would be our friend Lisa Paulsen.

Let the record show that his aversion to kissing Lisa—or even someone who reminds him of her—is not a comment on her looks. In fact, Lisa is an attractive woman with striking gray eyes, a great figure, and a wardrobe to die for. In addition, she is educated and creative, and has a taut sense of humor, which is how I knew Walker's reaction was also not a comment on her intellect.

The problem is that behind those striking eyes is a crazy woman. By that I don't mean someone who paces in front of convenience stores talking to invisible companions or one who should be confined to a peaceful pastel setting and encouraged to arrange flowers or make pottery all day. Nor do I refer to the freewheeling spontaneous types who stay up too late on work nights, drop five hundred bucks on a pair of shoes when the impulse strikes, or suddenly decide to jet off to the Bahamas or Vegas just before lunch on Friday mornings once a month.

What I mean is the highly functioning, deceptively coherent, slow-burning crazy of the kind that middle-class nightmare thrillers like *Basic Instinct* and *Fatal Attraction* were made. Like many villains of these bourgeois fear fests, Lisa is somewhat out of touch with reality when it comes to romantic relationships. What sets her apart, however, is that she has never had one. Well that, and the fact that she is probably not homicidal.

In case I've given the impression I'm kidding or guilty of hyperbole, I should add that I have had some genuine concern for Lisa's mental stability for about as long as I've known her, which has basically been my entire adult life.

We met in graduate school at UW–Madison in 1996 when we were assigned to the same group to do a project on propaganda and public opinion. Since our home had the space and was centrally located between those of the group members, I would host our meetings and the others would bring snacks. I noticed right away Lisa would always share what she would bring but would never so much as try what anyone else had brought. I found this strange but assumed, as I think any reasonable person would, that it was due to either food allergies or some other medical issue. At one point, however, I tested this theory by putting out some of the same items she had brought to previous meetings and was surprised to see her bypass them just as she had everything anyone else had ever contributed. This was my first clue that Lisa was, shall we say, different.

Aside from this quirk, we seemed to have a lot in common, which is why we continued to hang out after the term was over and we no longer had any courses together. She didn't have a lot to say outside the realm of school and work, but what she did say was generally interesting and often amusing, and gave me no reason to think she was odd in any way except with respect to other people's food, which by then I suspected was evidence of a latent eating disorder. By that point she had also started sampling whatever happened to be on offer at our place but continued to say she was still full from lunch to justify not having more than a few bites. Since she also spoke frequently of the gym—where she went every evening and sometimes in the morning to make up for whatever gastronomic sins she may have committed the previous day—I figured she was dealing with at least some mild body image issues, if not developing or recovering from anorexia nervosa.

Since we hadn't known each other long and were not well acquainted, I kept my thoughts in this regard to myself and hoped I was wrong. Had she not appeared so hale, I might have voiced my concern; but as she was a seemingly healthy size nine, I decided to keep my nose out of her business—at least until I knew her better and could do so without feeling like what my grandma would call a *buttinsky*.

Given how little she spoke of personal matters, I didn't expect that to happen any time soon. I've always been more open and effusive than most of the people I know—with the exception of Alethia, who finds herself endlessly fascinating, and my friend Caroline, who isn't exactly quiet when she's at ease but who tends to babble when she's feeling nervous or self conscious, which is about 80 percent of the time—so I wasn't annoyed or otherwise put off by Lisa's reticence. I was, however, concerned for her well-being and as time went on, increasingly curious about her background.

As I endeavored to get Lisa to open up for the sake of either allaying my fears or enabling me to express them, I became keenly aware of just how hard it is for me to keep my own mouth shut. It didn't help that she asked a lot of questions and seemed happy to let me ramble—about school, my friends, my family, and whatever personal or cultural issues happened to be on my mind at the moment. This made me wonder if she was deliberately keeping me talking so she could avoid speaking herself, or if she let others to do the talking out of habit. Still, sensing from her contact seeking behavior that she liked having me around, I did my best to make her feel comfortable talking to me, and tried not to monopolize the conversation.

Among the first topics of a personal nature that Lisa did mention to me was her parents, who were technically foster parents but with whom she kept in touch since she had lived with them from about her eleventh birthday until she aged out of the system when she turned eighteen. The Kadlecs were evidently good people who treated Lisa and their other foster daughter, Karen, as if they were their own children. According to Lisa, they would have adopted both her and Karen, but could not afford to do without the monthly stipend they received from the state in exchange for their services as foster parents. Now that Lisa was grown and living on her own, Leonard and Trudy had taken in another girl, as they had when

Karen moved out, but continued to invite her to dinner for major holidays, and never failed to acknowledge her birthday.

Lisa also told me about her one known sibling—an older sister named Lara—who had run away from home when Lisa was ten, and whose departure had led to her mother's depression, alcoholism, and eventual institutionalization, which in turn had necessitated Lisa's going into foster care. Evidently her father had left well before Lara ran away and thus was not available to help her mom cope with her disappearance or care for Lisa. I had a feeling that her mother's depression had preceded—if not precipitated—the departure of both Lisa's dad and sister. For while the loss of both her husband and her child may have exacerbated her mom's problems and given everyone a convenient explanation for what had happened, the family had unraveled far too readily after Lisa's dad took off for things to have been all that peachy before he flew the coop.

Whatever had caused the first fracture in Lisa's family life, I wasn't particularly shocked by her disclosures. By then I had figured her story was going to be either a tragedy or a snooze, and had prepared myself for both.

My mom had helped to prepare me in this regard well before I'd even met Lisa. She had spent time in foster care, although for a much shorter period of time, and had lived with one relative or another and both sets of grandparents on and off from the age of five until she was fifteen. Unlike Lisa's mom, my grandmother was widowed and her kids were never formally taken away from her, but she did struggle with depression as she fought to support Bunny and her siblings with just a high school diploma and limited job skills. Bunny talked about her experiences a lot while I was a kid, and effectively beat into my brain the importance of getting a college degree, building a strong work history, and having an arsenal of life insurance in case things don't go according to plan.

Thanks to her stories—which I didn't exactly appreciate at the time but for which I am now richer and grateful—and her constant harping on me to be independent, I reached adulthood fully prepared to support myself and to not appear shocked whenever I encounter someone whose life wasn't quite the velvet cushion mine was. In fact, it is likely because of how easy I've had it that I'm drawn to people whose upbringing and experiences were different from mine. After all, a velvet cushion may be safe and comfortable, but it's rarely exciting or even noteworthy.

That said, I haven't handled all of Lisa's disclosures with the ease I did those about her family. Her next revelation a few weeks later, for example, left me speechless for perhaps the first time in my adult life, and is the reason Walker reacted the way he did upon encountering her doppelganger.

In that conversation, Lisa admitted to stalking Tim Richards, a reporter from a Madison TV station. Apparently she had overheard one of her coworkers telling another about having met him at a party the previous weekend, and had e-mailed him from work with a story idea to get his contact information. A couple weeks later, having succeeded in getting his cell number, she contacted him again under a false name, and pretended to have met him at the same party where he had met her coworker—whom she deliberately did not mention. The guy obviously believed he'd met "Angie" and was either too nice to say he didn't remember, or was hoping she was hot and/or easy, because they wound up chatting for hours that night and at regular intervals thereafter. Eventually she also became friends with Tim's brother, Troy, who was also his roommate, and who asked her to send him a picture so he'd have a face to go with the name. Unwilling to send a photo of herself, Lisa instead set up a ghost e-mail account and sent him one of an old friend. Smitten, Troy made repeated appeals to "Angie" to go out with him, but she always managed to have a conflict.

This arrangement was working beautifully and likely would have continued to do so were it not for Lisa's need to impress a former classmate. Having run into Mia at the mall one afternoon, Lisa apparently felt moved to tell her that she and Tim Richards were friends, and that she'd been invited to a party at his house. This much was true, of course; in fact, Troy had planned it for the express purpose of meeting "Angie," although she, for obvious reasons, was not planning to attend. When Mia expressed doubts about the veracity of Lisa's claims—which apparently she had cause to do, so there's clearly a history there—Lisa decided to prove it by forwarding some photos Troy had sent her, as well as the invitation to the party. Realizing then that Lisa was telling the truth—at least her version of it—Mia begged Lisa to let her accompany her to the party. When Lisa refused, Mia announced she would go by herself since she had both the brothers' address and phone numbers. This forced Lisa to admit she hadn't met either man, and that she'd been talking to them under a false identity. Although Lisa begged her not to, Mia went to the party anyway but promised to keep up the ruse. After a few drinks, however, she told Tim the truth about Lisa. He later called to confront her, then told her off and told her never to contact him or Troy again.

I learned of all this on the morning of the party when Lisa called and frantically asked for my help. She told me the whole story and—

fearing Mia might deliberately or accidentally reveal her secret—asked if she should call Troy and tell him the truth before Mia did. I told her it depended on what her objective was. If all she wanted was to come clean and put the whole matter behind her, that would be the way to go. If, however, she viewed confession as a path to preserving their friendship or the possibility of a romantic relationship, she was barking up the wrong tree since that train likely had left the station—to mix at least two metaphors—the minute she started lying. She argued that the brothers might be more forgiving than I am, and that confessing might be the only way to maintain her relationship with them. I doubted any guy would be inclined to forgive what she had done, and said as much. In the end, though, she chose to wait and hope that Mia would keep her word but was, ultimately, disappointed.

I am deeply embarrassed to admit now that I was so focused on helping Lisa find a solution that day that I didn't fully process the real problem until that evening when I was telling Walker about it as we were getting ready for bed, and I saw the look of horror on his face.

"You do realize your friend is insane, don't you?" he asked when I paused.

"I do now."

Knowing what I did by then about her background, I was not surprised to learn that Lisa had trouble forming healthy attachments. Although my mom had never "stalked" anyone the way Lisa had Tim Richards, she does tend to keep track of the people she has known over the years—even those with whom she no longer keeps in touch—and to put more effort into nurturing friendships and helping people with their problems than anyone I know. Perhaps this is just a facet of her highly social nature, but one could argue that part of it comes from having experienced so much turmoil and loss as a kid. Likewise, while Lisa may have been predisposed to crazy behavior by heredity, my training and expertise tell me that people who create alternate identities and conduct relationships under false pretenses—when not motivated by financial gain or fraud, that is—are more likely than members of the general population to lack emotional security and to have experienced a significant loss.

Having not been harmed personally by Lisa's actions, and believing that everyone is entitled to one lapse in judgment, I decided not to hold the Tim Richards incident against her and to never mention it again. Although I wondered what exactly had moved her to choose him—and created a mental file of the events in case they became relevant in the future—I continued to spend time with her as I did my other friends, since she was otherwise a perfectly normal human being.

Over the next several years, our interactions became more limited due in roughly equal shares to physical distance, our respective commitments, and Lisa's devotion to her various obsessions.

One such obsession came to my attention just after we finished grad school, when Lisa moved to Seattle. Evidently her personal trainer had told her he was moving there to manage some great new facility, and invited her to look him up if she ever got out that way. I knew she was moving to Seattle to pursue a new job opportunity, but did not know about the personal trainer until she called one day to complain he had given her the cold shoulder when she showed up at his new place of employment. Obviously the poor guy hadn't expected her to take his invitation literally, and now he didn't know what to do. Things only got more awkward, she said, when she told him she had just moved to the area, and she couldn't understand why.

I explained as gently as I could that he probably hadn't expected to see her, and didn't know how to react. I added that he might have taken from the nature and magnitude of her actions that she had romantic intentions, and didn't know how to tell her his feelings were not reciprocal. This seemed to upset her, for she then challenged me to explain why he'd invited her to look him up if he hadn't wanted to see her. I speculated he was just being polite, since people often say things like that when they move away, but don't necessarily expect acquaintances to turn up unannounced—much less move in next door.

I did not speculate as to whether he may have gotten a restraining order or a permit to carry a firearm as Walker suggested when I told him about it later, but I did carefully explain that people generally don't go to such great lengths to be near individuals with whom they have a business relationship—like dentists, dog groomers, or personal trainers—unless they also know them socially. Although she claimed then to have moved to Seattle for other reasons, she came back to Wisconsin six months later, which told me I had been correct to surmise otherwise.

A similar situation occurred a year ago when she became obsessed with a guy who lived in the apartment down the hall from hers. After speaking to him once as he passed by her doorway with a basket of clothes, she started keeping track of when he did his laundry, and made efforts to do hers around the same time. Periodically she would call to update me on their interactions, ask my impressions, and bemoan the fact that he hadn't asked her out. Based on her history, I feared she was misinterpreting his behavior, but suggested—in the faint hope I was wrong—that she invite him to lunch on the grounds that he might be shy and need some encouragement. She refused, but continued to obsess over him until gas prices went up and she was forced to move to a place closer to work.

These days she's fixated on a guy at her gym. They've spoken a few times and she recently tweaked her routine to increase the odds that they'll run into one another. That much is perfectly normal in my book, but in truth I'm afraid it's only a matter of time before she's rifling through his locker or hacking the gym's membership files in search of his personal information. She's already acquired a towel and pair of socks he dropped one morning on his way to the showers. Convinced he had left them for her to find so she'd have an excuse to approach him later—as opposed to, say, because he was in a hurry—she washed the items and put them in her gym bag with a view to returning them the next time she saw him. Unfortunately, he hasn't been back to the gym since then, which has her upset and worried he's avoiding her. I said that's unlikely since she hasn't given him reason to avoid her; but since experience tells me there may be more to the story than I've been told—and since he most definitely would be avoiding her if he knew just the bits I know—I also suggested she turn the items over to the front desk and forget about the guy.

That's the challenge of being friends with someone like Lisa. As much as I'd like to accept what she tells me as the truth, because of all the lies she's confessed to telling others, I have to take everything she says with a grain of salt. Moreover, because there is so often a gap between reality and Lisa's interpretation of events, I can't necessarily trust what she says even when she has no apparent reason to lie.

To be fair, I honestly don't think she intends to lie, or even to mislead. I just think she sees how things are and how she wants them to be, and the line between them sometimes gets a little, shall we say, blurry.

In any case, I never find out about any of Lisa's "relationships" when they first start, which makes me suspect that, at least on some level, she knows her behavior is bizarre and wants to keep it a secret. Like the bird who loses it when the hunter approaches her hiding spot in the movie *Bambi*, however, the suspense gets to her, and she just can't help but give herself away.

Why she chooses to involve me in these adventures is anybody's guess. Although I haven't come right out and told her she's crazy, I have told her that I'm concerned and I think she should get help. Specifically, I've said she should find someone who can help her explore the reasons she is more comfortable with what are essentially imaginary relationships, with a view to being able to someday have a real one.

I knew that hearing the truth would be hard for her and might cause her to terminate our friendship, but felt it would be worse for her in the long run if I failed to speak my mind. To my surprise, although we don't see as much of each other in person these days, she has yet to kick me to the curb.

No doubt part of the reason I'm still in the picture is that she doesn't have anyone else in whom she can confide. Aside from her foster family, not one single person has been in her life as long as I have. From what I understand, she does have relatives and childhood friends who live not far from her in Brookfield and with whom she could connect, but for some reason—fear of rejection or painful memories—she wants nothing to do with them.

Another reason she keeps me around is that I accept her for who she is. Although I have told her she needs help and have encouraged her to do things she doesn't want to do, she knows I am not going to mock her or dump her for feeling or acting like she does. She also knows that, while I'm going to call things as I see them, I'll do so as delicately as possible.

With all of this in mind, it likely comes as no surprise that Lisa—unlike all my other single friends—was not among the list of trusted experts who received my online dating survey. Had she been sane, she would have had some dating experience and thus some valuable wisdom to share. Likewise, had she been sane, she would have received a survey and had other friends to whom she could disseminate it for me. Unfortunately, her attachment issues prevent her from forming meaningful relationships, thereby inhibiting her ability to receive the affection and other rewards we need as human beings, and preventing her from acquiring the experiences that could help her improve her social skills and thus build better relationships in the future.

From the sound of things, Lisa's look-alike did not have this problem. In fact, according to Walker, Jamey had many friends about whom she talked a lot—in mostly positive ways—and was a frequent performer at her local karaoke bar.

So it wasn't Jamey's outward appearance, per se, that made her less desirable in Walker's eyes; it was her resemblance to someone who, as his carpenter father would have put it, is "half a bubble off."

"I just kept imagining how Lisa might behave after a date with someone she'd met online," Walker confessed after sharing with me Jamey's specific physical similarities to Lisa, "and while I know it's unfair to compare

Jamey to someone she doesn't even know exists, I could hardly look at her without thinking 'stalker.'"

Fearing that trauma—if not the passage of time—would dilute his memories, I persuaded Walker to let me drive on the way home tomorrow so he could work on his notes.

Meanwhile, we switched the channel over to *The Outlaw Josey Wales,* which I'd seen advertised before opting to unwittingly waste my money on pay-per-view. Westerns aren't exactly my cup of tea, but I figured Walker deserved a reward for spending the afternoon with Jamey, and thus did not object to his watching it while we waited for my parents to get to town.

It occurred to me as we waited for Bunny and Mack to call and report that they were about ten minutes out that Walker may not have been alone in having plans to stay in the Dells after his date today. What if Jamey had decided to take advantage of the off-season rates and spend the night in town without its usual horde of tourists? What if she had brought someone along and the two of them were planning to have dinner at the same restaurant where we planned to eat? What if she saw the four of us and decided to come and say hi to Walker? How would he explain his presence, and more importantly, how would he explain me?

"I wouldn't worry about it," he said when I couldn't hold back my concerns any longer. "She didn't say anything about having a friend ride along, or hanging out in the Dells for the weekend."

"That's great. On the other hand, I'm pretty sure you didn't mention you'd brought your wife, or that you were having dinner with your in-laws."

"That's true. But then, I had a reason to leave that part out and unless she's married too and also had a spouse stashed in a hotel—in which case you have even less to worry about—she probably would have mentioned it."

"What makes you so sure?"

"As I said, the girl was talkative."

"Besides," he added after planting a peck on my cheek, "even if she does plan to stay here tonight, there are plenty of restaurants in town, so odds are we won't run into her."

That sounded an awful lot like what my dad would call famous last words, but there wasn't any more time to argue since the opening lines of "Mack the Knife" were playing on my phone, thereby signaling to me that he and Bunny were making their final approach.

Four

Dinner with my parents is always interesting. Bunny and Mack have been married since they were both nineteen years old, so they've had a lot of adventures together, which they cheerfully recount aloud, in part or in full, with little to no prompting and in such a way that gives one the impression they wouldn't even need an audience. There are times, in fact, when it seems as if even in the presence of other people, they see and hear only each other. This never bothered me as a kid, since it allowed me to retreat to the pit of my mind and to ponder whatever was going on there without appearing rude or disrespectful toward anyone, but it does sort of explain why I didn't start talking until I was old enough to make friends of my own and spend time away from the house. Up to then, and for even a short while thereafter, my parents and their friends thought I was unusually quiet and thought I might need treatment for selective mutism. In truth, however, with them and my equally gregarious brother to compete with, I just couldn't get any airtime.

As an adult now, I find my parents quite amusing, and often wonder what I missed by tuning them out and leaving the scene as a kid. My mom's friend, Birdie (whose given name is Meadowlark—which explains the source of her nickname but not necessarily why she prefers it) used to say "Spending time with Bunny and Mack is like being on the set with Lucille Ball and Desi Arnaz, or on the soundstage alongside Burns and Allen." Being too young to have seen or heard either of these characters, I naturally had to spend some time at Google and YouTube to fully grasp her assessment the first time I heard it, but ultimately concluded she was right.

As with Lucy and Desi and George and Gracie, there are certain themes woven into Bunny and Mack's dialog. These include the condition of their backyard, which is perpetually in a state of flux, owing concurrently to Bunny's seemingly pathological need to alter her surroundings and Mack's affinity for sleeping in on weekends; and their latest road trip, which generally includes reviews of the various restaurants they visited along the way.

Another frequent theme in any conversation with my parents is the paucity of navigational and conductive skills among Wisconsin drivers. As natives of the Badger State, one might expect them to laud the abilities of their fellow Cheddarheads and to condemn those of motor vehicle operators elsewhere, but my folks pride themselves on their objectivity and are more than willing to go against the grain. Then again, since they've lived in and/or driven through forty of the fifty states as a result of Mack's military service and managed to find the drivers in each progressively more appalling than the rest, Wisconsin was bound to have the worst simply by virtue of being the state in which they currently live.

Among the topics discussed on this particular occasion were the earthquake and tsunami in Japan, the Jasmine Revolution, UN airstrikes in Libya, and the equally earth-shattering news that my brother had acquired a new girlfriend. R.J. had been playing the field for about a year up to then after having split—amicably and peacefully, of course; the Mackies aren't prone to drama, and acrimony just isn't our style—from Emily, his partner of twelve years. Though for a while they were enemy cohabitants who could hardly bear the sight of each other, once they decided to go their separate ways, they were able to sit down and craft a fair and mutually unsatisfactory division of assets. They still see one another periodically, owing to all the friends they have in common, and apparently go out for dinner or drinks about once a month, but that is subject to change if things become serious between him and his new gal—especially if she's the jealous type, as was the case with Emily's predecessor.

Julie—or *R.J.'s Ferrari*, as Mack called her—was beautiful, exciting, and expensive. As one might guess, it wasn't just the initial investment that made things tricky; it was the upkeep. The only daughter of a defense contracting executive, Julie was supported by her parents in a style that allowed her to pursue her primary passions, which were apparently to shop and to be seen in trendy restaurants and nightclubs. This was back when

R.J. was working toward his real estate license and had neither the time nor the means to indulge her as often as she expected him to. Having no goals of her own—other than to never wear the same outfit twice—nor any reason to work, she could not fathom why R.J. needed to put so much time into his career, and routinely accused him of cheating on her. As if that weren't enough to prove her unworthy of my brother's affections, she would throw a fit if he spent even one minute longer at work than was necessary, and would drive through his school parking lot to make sure he was in class and not out with someone else. What someone like R.J. was doing with a woman like Julie is anyone's guess. At any rate, he put up with her for about five months until the day he received both the results of his real estate exam and an ultimatum. Given the choice between excluding his friends from the ensuing celebration or never seeing her again, he wisely opted for the latter and told the spoiled brat to get lost.

According to Bunny, there didn't seem to be much danger of that sort of thing happening with his new flame. Although she'd only met Serena twice, she got the sense that she did not lack a work ethic, manners, or confidence. An accomplished chef, she was apparently brighter and prettier than Emily, and thus had no reason to feel threatened by her or anyone in R.J.'s past. Of course, Bunny knew as well as I did that jealousy has nothing to do with reason, but I decided not to argue that point and instead chose to solicit more pertinent details about Serena.

As I did so, Mack and Walker went to their happy place where they talk about their trucks, hunting, and guns. Mack had recently found a great deal on a Master Sportsman Leafy Cut Camo Suit at Fleet Farm. I confess I had no idea what this was at the time, but Walker was most impressed. In fact, so excited was he at the prospect of owning what I later learned was basically a set of nylon cammies to which someone—and my money would be on a bored wife or a scorned ex-girlfriend—had taken a knife or pair of scissors, he decided to drive out to the nearest Fleet Farm first thing in the morning and if they were out of stock, continue on to Oshkosh and wherever else he had to go to get one. That would potentially add two to five hours to our drive home since the closest store was about sixty miles east of the Dells, while the closest three after that—including Oshkosh—were all at least another sixty miles north, south, or east of there.

The circuitous route didn't exactly appeal to me at the time, so as Bunny chatted about her latest projects and voiced her disapproval of all the union-busting efforts that were cropping up since the Republicans swept the 2010 gubernatorial elections, I set my mind to figuring out how to get

Walker his new costume without traveling all the way to Lakes Superior and Michigan. Not that I begrudge him more hunting gear or the chance to spend his own hard-earned money, especially since he'd been kind enough to both start dating again and visit the Wisconsin Dells; I just figured there existed a more efficient way to acquire a Master Sportsman Leafy Cut Camo Suit than touring all of southeastern Wisconsin. Realizing I could use the power of the Internet to avoid wasting both time and fuel, I rejoined the Bunny and Mack show that was still in progress.

By then Mack and Walker had moved on to the time-honored tradition of slaughtering large feathered bipeds with arrow-tipped projectiles. Hunting—like fishing, basketball, and golf—is largely lost on me. Despite having grown up with a man who hunted every spring and fall unless he was sick or deployed overseas, I had no interest in such things, and apart from knowing the difference between a long gun and a handgun, I could not tell one firearm from another. Bunny is the same way, and to this day teases Mack whenever he's eying a new rifle by gushing about how *brown* it is; how it's made of wood *and* metal; and how it takes real *bullets* and has a *trigger*.

The whole routine is beyond hilarious, and makes even my dad laugh, but I imagine we feel the same way about their guns as the guys do whenever we pick up a new pair of black pumps: They all look about the same and serve the same purpose, so why would you need another pair?

Happily, it's all in good fun. My parents respect each other's needs and interests, and to my knowledge, have never argued about money or how to spend it. That's not to say they don't argue; they do their share of that. It's just that you're more likely to hear them fighting about the location of a particular store or restaurant, how far away it is, and how best to get there, than you are to hear them arguing over bills or the cost of hunting gear or a surplus of ladies' footwear.

"So how are things at the paper?" Bunny asked upon completing her assessment of Serena. "Still getting your share of column space, I see."

She and Mack have subscribed to the *Post-Courier* since almost the second I was hired and although I'm almost forty, make a point to read and share with their friends nearly everything in print that bears my name. Mack isn't quite as enamored with the advice column as the features. A practical man who joined the marines with a view to serving for four years but ultimately stayed for twenty more, Mack thinks most people who write to me make their lives harder than they have to be, and says I shouldn't waste time and column space on folks who are obviously too stupid to live. Needless to say, I did not inherit my so-called excessive empathy from Mack.

Bunny, on the other hand, enjoys the advice column every bit as much as the features. A fan of *Dear Abby* up until the copyright was taken over by Abby's 'hopelessly ungifted' daughter Jeanne, Bunny could read advice columns all day—especially those dedicated to niche topics such as health, etiquette, and car care—and has written a letter or two in support of or in condemnation of the wisdom, or lack thereof, imparted by my contemporaries and forebears in the field.

It was with this in mind that I gave her a brief summary and a few highlights on my current feature, and quickly moved on to the letter from R.A. and the research I'd been doing as a result. Until then I hadn't told her or Mack why Walker and I had been on the road two Saturdays in a row. I had only said we needed to be back East for work reasons, which they accepted without question, and had invited them to meet up at some point along the way.

As I expected, Bunny was intrigued. Whereas another mother may have been concerned and warned me against letting my husband spend time with man-hungry single women, mine was more interested in what his matches were like, and what I had learned.

"Not much at this point," I admitted. "Walker's only been on two dates so far, and he hasn't even completed his notes on the second one yet."

"Well, what is he waiting for? Doesn't he know how much I hate to be kept in suspense?"

"Who doesn't?"

"Exactly."

"So have him do it now," Bunny only half joked. "I mean, certainly that's more important than Mack's new wheels."

By that she meant the new pickup they had bought just after Christmas. Between the military discount and all the end-of-year incentives, the dealer had made Mack an offer he couldn't refuse, and he was now giving a somewhat-envious Walker a typically dramatic play-by-play.

"I doubt either of them would agree," I observed amusedly. "Besides, even if he had finished the notes, I wouldn't have anything to report."

"Why not?"

"Primarily because I wouldn't have read them."

"*Why not?*"

"Because there's nothing to learn from just two sets of notes. I need a lot more data before I can devise any theories," I explained—

unnecessarily, really, since as a sometime social scientist herself, Bunny knows as well as I do that for the results to be valid, a study generally has to involve more than two subjects, "and even more in order to test those theories and formulate a reasonable conclusion."

"Maybe so. But that doesn't mean you can't review the data as it comes in. After all, aren't you curious as to what these women are like?"

"Of course. But I also want my theories to come from the data, not the other way around."

"Oh come on, Roxanne."

"I'm serious, Mom. Walker is doing me a huge favor by helping me with this. The last thing I want to do is skew the data and nullify the whole project."

"I understand that. I just don't think peeking at his notes will do the project any harm."

"It may not, but you and I have watched enough *Law & Order* to know what happens when people come up with theories before they've collected all the evidence. Suddenly they're looking for facts and figures to support a certain line of thinking, and missing or discounting details that would point them toward the truth."

I could see from her expression that Bunny thought the risk of such a thing happening in this case was both minimal and totally worth taking if it appeased her inner voyeur. I also knew from experience that patience was not her strong suit, and that she rarely lost a battle regardless of the strength or weakness of her argument.

"I'll tell you what," I offered by way of compromise. "I could use a research assistant anyway. So how about I scan and e-mail you the packets as Walker completes them, and you can review them and enter the data onto the spreadsheet for me. That way the data gets entered, you get to satisfy your curiosity, and I don't have to worry about my results being colored by bias."

Bunny shrugged.

"Why not?" she said, as if she didn't care one way or another and was doing me a favor rather than salivating at the thought. "I could use the distraction since there isn't much yard work to do this spring."

"Perfect. Then I'll send you the first two packets when Walker finishes the one from his date with Jamey, and I'll send the others as they are ready."

"Sounds good. So how many women do you want him to meet before you think you'll have enough data?"

"I'm not sure. At least ten. Maybe twenty-five."

"*Twenty-five*? What is that? Like 90 percent of his matches?"

"More like thirty."

"*Thirty*?" Bunny repeated. "Are you seriously telling me that Walker Browne has been matched with seventy-five women?"

"Seventy-eight, actually—as of yesterday morning, anyway. Could be up to *eighty*-eight by now."

"It seems *thematchcafe.com* employs the morphine drip method of information delivery," I explained when Bunny appeared puzzled, "and adds new names to your list of matches almost every day. I can't say whether this is due to the fact that new people are constantly joining and thus being found compatible, or if it's a tactical feature that's been built into the software for the purpose of keeping people coming back to the site. All I know for sure is that within two days of joining, Walker had over thirty matches, and by the end of the week, he had over forty. By the second week he had over fifty matches, and as of yesterday, he had almost eighty."

"Wow. And is that nationwide?"

"Nope. That's just in Wisconsin."

"So what you're saying is that there are nearly one hundred women in the state of Wisconsin who are looking for a marriageable man, and whom the system decided would be compatible with Walker Browne?"

"Yes."

"That is unreal."

It bears mention here that Bunny's disbelief was less a comment on Walker's desirability than a sign of just how out of touch she is when it comes to the singles scene. Although many of her friends are divorced, none of them are officially in the market for a new mate, so she has no concept of just how many people are looking for love.

"So what about you?" she asked, suddenly returning to voyeur mode.

"I think I'm up to around forty now."

"*Forty*? Is that all?"

I nodded. "Apparently there are fewer men looking for eligible thirty-something writers than there are women looking for thirty-something engineers."

"I can't believe that. What on earth did you put on your profile—that you have rabies?"

"Apparently—or at least its social equivalent."

"Seriously, Roxanne. This doesn't make sense. You should have at least as many matches as Walker does."

"Well, thank you for the vote of confidence, Mother, but it's not necessary. I honestly don't care how many matches I have since I'm not looking."

"I get that, but don't you find it strange that you have so few matches compared to Walker?"

"Not really."

"Aren't you at least curious to know why?"

"Not really."

"Well, I am."

"Really, Mom? I am shocked beyond words."

"Ha, ha. So did you really list writer as your occupation? Or was that a joke too?"

"Nope. My profile says I'm a writer."

"Ah. I bet that's the problem. When you get home, you should change that to 'self-employed.'"

I didn't bother to tell her I didn't have to go home to change anything. I could log into my account from almost any computer or smartphone on earth, but that wasn't the point.

"Thanks for the tip, Mom, but I think I'll just leave things as they are, since as I may have mentioned, I'm not really looking to meet anyone.

"Besides," I added somewhat defensively, "Walker and I are trying to keep things as close to the truth as possible. After all, if the system works like its developers say it does, it should match us on the basis of who we really are."

"Agreed. But you really are self-employed, so that wouldn't be a lie. And given how many men are threatened by intellectual women, I think you'd have more matches on your list if they didn't know you were a writer."

"I can't imagine they'd be any less threatened by someone who was self-employed. But again, it doesn't matter how many matches I have, since I'm not. Actually. Looking.

"Besides," I continued, "I don't think the bias against intellectual women is as strong among men of my generation as it is with the men of yours. And in truth, I wouldn't want a man who was put off by an intellectual woman and neither would you. So I would have listed writer in my profile even if I was looking to meet someone—if only to weed out all the sexist jerks."

"Good point."

I knew that would get her. My mom may be intensely competitive, insanely curious, and almost criminally voyeuristic, but she is above all a feminist.

"So how are you choosing whom he meets?" she asked, having exhausted the previous topic.

"I'm not. We decided this needs to be about as natural a process as possible, so I'm having Walker do his own choosing."

"And how is he choosing?"

"Mostly by location and logistics."

"My God, how boring. But I suppose I should have expected that. The man is an engineer."

"Which is exactly why he's helping me. If he were anything like Natalie's husband, or any man on your side of the family, there is no way I would have asked him to do this."

"That's fair. And at least he's not picking women because they do or do not look like you," Bunny mused, "or because they resemble his mother or Angelina Jolie."

"Exactly. Plus, the process needs to be random or we might wind up seeing a pattern in what is just a coincidence."

Bunny shook her head. "No offense, Roxanne. But sometimes you're as big a techie as Walker is."

"Why, thank you, Mother. I'll take that as a compliment."

"I wouldn't have it any other way, Sweet Pea."

"Still," Bunny continued with a smile. "I think you could have a little more fun with this project. I mean, I know you're more comfortable with the clinical and analytical aspect of things; but you shouldn't overlook or discount the value of the emotional and sensual."

"Perhaps. But as much as we want to believe that choosing a mate or a sex partner is an emotional and sensual process, in truth it's as much—if not more—about biology and chemistry. People may think they're attracted to this person or that person because of his or her size, shape, looks, personality, or manner, but it's because their brains have determined from these and other features that his or her genes would combine favorably with their own and thus they should mate. So while people may think they're being brought together by emotions, they are in fact being driven by genetics and evolution, and thus biology and chemistry."

"I know. But we speak of biological and chemical phenomena in emotional and sensory terms for a reason, Roxanne. After all, would you have gone out with someone whose opening line was, 'Your eyes, nose, hair, and body type suggest to my brain that our genes would combine favorably to advance the human race'?

"Don't answer that," Bunny instructed as I started to ponder her query. "For all I know that's how you and Walker wound up dating."

It was in fact I who first mentioned that Walker and I would likely produce highly attractive and intelligent children, not the other way around. That remark was made during a conversation about genetics and heredity several months after we'd met, however, and thus was neither a proposition nor an opening line. Saying so wouldn't have helped my case much, however, so I decided to keep these details to myself, and simply acknowledged Bunny's joke with a giggle.

"So what about the Internet research?" she continued with an affectionate grin. "How's that going?"

"Fine. I haven't gotten all the surveys back yet, but I hope to get the rest this week."

"I see. And have you found anything of interest in the ones you've received, or are you waiting to find out until you've collected all of that evidence too?"

"Of course—although you would be interested to know that I did happen across some rather disturbing information while downloading one to my holding folder yesterday."

"Oh?"

I nodded. "Evidently one of Kristin's coworkers is a member of *ashleymadison.com*."

"What's that?"

"It's a social networking site that connects married men with eligible younger women, and openly markets itself the 'most recognized and reputable extramarital affair company.'"

"That's disgusting."

"Tell me about it."

"So what's this guy doing with one of your surveys if he's married?"

"Oh, he's not married. At least, not anymore."

Bunny laughed. "Go figure."

"Anyway, the disturbing part for me isn't so much that he was looking to cheat. That's his business as far as I'm concerned. My problem is that Kristin has a crush on him."

"Oh my."

"Exactly."

"So are you going to tell her?"

"I'd like to."

"But?"

"But if I tell her, it's going to change the way she feels about the guy."

"As it should."

"I don't just mean it will make her not want to date him. I mean, it will cause her to lose all respect for the guy, and change the way she treats him."

"As it should."

"Perhaps. But the respondents were told the surveys would be completely confidential, so I don't feel quite right about telling her."

"Roxanne, I know you. You'll feel even worse about *not* telling her."

"Only if they wind up together."

"Which they definitely *won't* if you tell her."

"I know," I sighed. "So, for now at least, I'm just going to have to play it by ear. If it starts to look like something's going to happen between them, I'll have no choice but to speak up. But if, as is my fervent hope, nothing transpires between them, I won't have to say a word and I can just forget the whole thing."

"That seems like a rational approach."

"I'm glad you think so, since it's the only one I've been able to come up with."

"The real trick," I added without confidence, "will be keeping close enough tabs on the situation so I can act before they wind up in a state of bedded bliss."

Bunny laughed. "That's funny," she said with pride. "I'm pleased to know you haven't lost your way with words."

It must be said that spending time with Bunny isn't just entertaining; it's also pretty good for my soul. Her curiosity and interest in others make her a great listener, and she's generous with compliments, which are always sincere.

That would hardly be remarkable since I'm her daughter; but in truth she's like that with everyone, not just her family. She'll compliment complete strangers on their clothing or hairstyle, and randomly approach seniors to see if they need help with their shopping or getting to their cars. She's also drawn to accented foreigners like Charlie Sheen is to hookers, and can be relied upon to flatter them with greetings or phrases in their mother tongues to put them at ease. On top of that she remembers everyone's name and birthday, and approaches everyone she encounters in the course of her day as if they're doing her a favor just being in the same place she is.

That is not to say that Bunny is always placid and pleasant. She has a glare that can cut steel and the tongue and wit to match, all of which I've seen her use on those who made the mistake of returning her goodwill with rudeness, irritation, or disdain, or who treated anyone else badly in her presence.

Her support for me and R.J. knows no limits and extends to even the minutest of things. My earliest memory of this is from sixth grade when I complained that R.J. and his friends were making noise and infringing upon my ability to read a book. So moved was she by my choice of words and her desire to show it that she clasped her hands beneath her chin and with a smile said, "I'm just so glad to have a daughter who knows the word *infringe*." Events like that became so common that it was almost embarrassing. Yet, I soaked it up like a sponge, and endeavored to learn big words and to demonstrate my facility with them at every opportunity.

She made sure not to let it all go to my head, of course, by playing devil's advocate and reining me in whenever she found my commentary sanctimonious or my attitude verging on conceit. To that end, she regularly reminded me of the advantages I had that other people didn't have—not the least of which were a houseful of books and two parents who loved and supported me—and that I would have turned out differently without either one or the other. As a result of these and other reminders, I came to learn that people should be understood and not judged and that caring advice can accomplish more than criticism.

From there we moved on to the subject of midlife crises, something with which Bunny has developed a mild obsession of late. Although she hasn't experienced one herself, two of her closest friends have, and both were in their early forties at the time. Both had jettisoned their husbands— one justifiably, I'm told—to pursue relationships and activities they had abandoned in favor of marriage and motherhood. These events had come to the fore, it seemed, after her and Mack's friend Keith went off the deep end and left his wife for an old flame with whom he'd reconnected via the Internet.

"I would certainly hate for something like that to happen to you and Walker," she was saying now. "Or like what happened to your counterpart Ms. Halifax."

By that she was referring to fellow advice columnist Alison Halifax, whose fame, following, and fortune I've yet to achieve. Syndicated since 1997, she's carried in over two hundred papers, and has published three books, including two compilations of letters and one scholarly tome on kids and divorce. She also hosts a weekly online chat, and has appeared on numerous daytime and evening talk shows.

Essentially all we have in common—besides the fact that we both dispense advice—is that her dad's company makes military weapons and my dad has fired some of them.

Apart from those stated above, the most glaring dissimilarity between me and Ms. Halifax is that she recently left her husband—comedian and "shock show" host Race Baker—for her high school sweetheart with whom she'd reconnected through a reunion themed website and who incidentally happened to have three kids who were likely going to teach her a few new things about kids and divorce. It was a scandal that generated more than a little buzz in the digital media and earned Ms. Halifax the scorn of a sizable portion of her readership who felt she had failed to practice what she so often preached about honesty, loyalty, and respect.

"You've got nothing to worry about, Mom," I replied. "After all, I'm only thirty-seven and in case you've forgotten, I married my first love."

Bunny smiled.

"I know that," she said almost sadly as if harkening back to the high school dances I never attended, and all the prom dresses and satin pumps she never got to shop for because I didn't date until after I'd gone to college. "I guess that's kind of what worries me."

"*Worries you?*"

"Well, maybe not 'worries me' *per se*. I guess what I mean is that not everyone who leaves their spouse does so to chase down a memory or the ghost of their youth. Some do so because they want to experience things they feel they missed or because they think they settled too soon."

I searched Bunny's face to see if she might be speaking from personal experience, but could find no evidence to support that conclusion. As usual, she and Mack were holding hands on top of the table and taking turns sipping from the same glass of wine. Having also noted that they'd exchanged more than a few affectionate winks as they carried on their respective conversations with me and Walker, I decided she wasn't projecting, but instead working through another bout of what we all lovingly call her Worst-Case Scenario Syndrome.

"Trust me," I said with a smile as I patted her knee. "I have never felt that way. Nor do I ever expect to.

"But I promise," I added to both reassure her and inject some necessary levity into the situation. "If I ever feel myself on the brink of a midlife crisis, a major depressive episode, or an unusually severe craving for chocolate, you will be the first to know."

Bunny laughed. "Smart-ass."

"Better than a dumb-ass."

"I guess."

That settled, Bunny and I paused to observe and await the conclusion of Walker and Mack's conversation.

With this in mind, I nudged Mr. Browne's foot under the table, thereby activating the Polite Interruption System, which we deployed whenever we were behind schedule, looking to change the subject or end an exchange altogether.

Having sensed my message, if not the reason for it, Walker performed the requisite stretch and asked me if I needed another glass of wine.

"No thanks," I replied per the Polite Exit version of our script. "But I do need the restroom."

Bunny reached for her handbag. "I think I'll join you."

"And then you and I should get going," she informed Mack, who nodded and indicated to the server to bring the bill.

We left him and Walker to tie up loose ends, which involved a brief discussion of Mack and Bunny's annual Independence Day barbecue and bonfire.

"So what else is new?" Bunny asked as we made our way toward the restrooms near the front door. "Besides your research projects, I mean."

Knowing that Bunny is keenly interested in people—and especially in people from the old days—I took the opportunity to share some juicy news about a girl R.J. had dated back when we were stationed in California.

Marie Antonnette Luchanski is notable both for her name—which itself is notable not only in that her parents chose to call her after the ill-fated queen of France, but also because they did so without agonizing over the spelling—and for the fact that she was the one girl who broke my brother's heart.

Marie and R.J. started dating as sophomores in high school, and broke up at their junior prom following a course of events we all fondly refer to as the Great Monterey Date Exchange. As Bunny tells it—and she is the only one who *can* tell it since Mack was out of town and I wasn't really tuned in to my brother's activities at that point in time—that was the night R.J. went to the prom with a short curvy blond in a pink dress and left with a tall skinny brunette in a blue one. The brunette in question was Marie's best friend, Jess, an apparently awkward girl whose beau of three weeks had started dating her for the express and undeniably perverted purpose of publicly dumping and humiliating her. After making good on that plan, which he'd hatched with his pals on the football team, he approached Marie at the entrance to the gym, where the two of them proceeded to make out as if the world were coming to an end. Ever the cool-headed gentleman, R.J. decided to make the best of a bad situation by inviting Jess to get some punch and have their photos taken, and by offering her a ride home when Bunny came to fetch him at twelve.

Not having been in the car when Bunny dropped R.J. and Marie off at the restaurant where they were to meet up with Jess and her date, I wasn't the least bit confused or concerned when the girl who got in the car with him at midnight did not look familiar. From Bunny's reaction and the ensuing conversation, however, I soon learned that the girl in question was not Marie, but Marie's now former best friend.

Recently I had learned that Marie had just pleaded guilty to her second DUI. In addition to losing her license and serving ninety days, she was placed on probation, ordered to complete a substance abuse treatment program, and to perform three hundred hours of community service.

This news came from Caroline Conway—nee McNamara—who was my first real best friend. We met in middle school when Mack got orders to the Defense Language Institute in Monterey, California. Although we were classmates for only a year and had been friends for barely two before Mack got orders to go back to the East Coast, we managed to stay in touch thanks to the dedication of the postal service and the genius of Alexander Graham Bell. After we graduated from our respective high schools, Caroline went to secretarial school and got a job working for the city, followed by another at the courthouse in Salinas where she moved when she married her husband, Thom.

"R.J. had no idea what a favor that girl was doing him when she dumped him," I said after conveying to Bunny the news about Marie. "With her daddy issues and addiction to drama, she would have brought him nothing but trouble."

"How do you know it's the same Marie?" she asked as I joined her at the hand dryer. "There must be plenty of women with that name in Monterey County."

I laughed.

There may be plenty of Maries, I mused privately, and there may even be a couple Marie *Antoinettes*, but I doubted there were any Marie *Antonnettes*—much less with the last name of Luchanski.

"No doubt," I admitted to avoid a potentially lengthy debate on the frequency of names and the average person's ability to misspell them, "but Caroline had a raging crush on R.J. for most of her life, and was keenly aware of his social interactions right up to the day we moved away. To bottom line it: Whether the woman was going by her given name or using an alias, Caroline would have recognized Marie Luchanski anywhere."

"Wow. I never knew she had the hots for R.J."

"You weren't supposed to. Caroline swore me to secrecy."

"Still, I'm a mother. You'd think I would have noticed."

I couldn't disagree with that. Whether it's because she's a mother or not, I can't say, but Bunny is far more likely to notice things that aren't there, than to miss the things that *are*.

"Perhaps," I said instead. "But that's probably for the best. She'd probably die if she knew I was telling you now."

Bunny smiled.

"So how is Caroline these days?" she inquired as I signaled for Mack and Walker to join us. "Last I recall she'd married some insurance executive."

"Oh, you know Caroline," I euphemized in the interest of time. "Never a dull moment."

That's not to say that Caroline's life was exciting. Tumultuous would be a better word for it, and disastrous probably the best, since every three weeks or so, Caroline can be found dangling at the end of her rope thanks to Thomas, who is a nice enough guy but, due to a weakness for poker, makes it a challenge to make ends meet, much less save for the future.

But as I didn't have the energy to bring Bunny up to speed on all the drama plaguing Caroline these days, I decided to let the matter drop. If she was interested in hearing more, she would ask me again when we weren't standing in the lobby of a restaurant preparing to part company. At that point, I would be perfectly happy to share all the gory and glorious details that—along with slot machines, family gossip, and shrubbery—make my mom's life worth living.

Five

It may not seem like it given my commentary at times, but I don't set out to analyze the people I know, or treat them like clients or curiosities. At the same time, however, it's hard to ignore the behavioral and attitudinal clues, which taken together, explain why some people enjoy relatively happy and productive lives while others dwell in misery or discontent, and why some are adept at avoiding negative or toxic situations while others keep making the same mistakes and running into the same kinds of problems over and over again.

That said, it's even harder to resist the urge to study the less contented members of my circle, and to observe how they handle themselves in various situations. This helps me understand how they make the choices they do, and predict how they'll behave under certain conditions. It also enables me to draw conclusions about other people with similar qualities and tendencies, and to imagine what they will do under like circumstances.

In this way I guess I'm like Bunny, whom I often tease or joke about being a social voyeur, but who—like the guy who satisfies his lust for cutting flesh by becoming a surgeon instead of a serial killer, or the woman with an flair for fallacy who spends her days writing romance novels instead of inventing Internet aliases and pretending to have a life—is just using her unique gifts for good rather than evil. In her case Bunny has tamed what might otherwise be characterized as an unhealthy fascination with the experiences of others by, among other things, mentoring at-risk youth, counseling abused women, and—more recently—peering frequently into the lives of her adult offspring. Freud called this—that is, the ability to channel potentially harmful impulses into socially acceptable behavior—sublimation; I call it a positive alternative to ostracism and incarceration. By any name, it is a tendency I obviously share, as evidenced by my choice of career and my affinity for dissecting the actions and motivations of my friends.

Among those I've been studying in La Crosse is Laurel, whose pursuit of contentment has been hampered by astonishingly low self-esteem. Despite all she has to recommend her, she frequently puts herself down; compares herself negatively to her sisters, friends and colleagues; and allows Marty to make unflattering remarks—about the fit of her clothes, and the size, shape, and firmness of her bottom—without objection or consequence. She also lets him dictate how the family spends their money, weekends, and vacations, and will not suggest alternate courses of action even when she and the kids have other ideas because—and I quote: "Marty doesn't care what anyone else wants or thinks, so why start a battle I know I can't win?"

It is clear from her tone and manner that Laurel's purpose in describing her deficiencies and recounting Marty's offenses is not to draw attention to herself or to solicit compliments, support, or reassurance—as undoubtedly would be the case if we were talking about Alethia—but to get her friends' take on things to see if they align with her own. In fact, Laurel is the polar opposite of Alethia in that she tends to shun the spotlight, and will defer to anyone on virtually any topic with the exception of business management, on which she is the obvious and undisputed expert.

It is also clear that Laurel's low self-esteem can be attributed to how she was raised. From what I've gathered during our private chats, it was considered inappropriate, if not unseemly, for her to be proud of herself or to even acknowledge her own positive attributes and achievements. Maybe this was how her parents approached the rearing of girls or children in general; or maybe they didn't want her siblings to feel inadequate or inferior by comparison. In any case, at some point in her youth Laurel learned to deflect compliments and to downplay her abilities and accomplishments. Along with this came a significant amount of criticism, which was probably meant to motivate her to work harder, but which simultaneously primed her to expect and accept unwarranted negative assessments and treatment as an adult.

Were it not for the moderating effect of these tendencies and experiences, Laurel would have acquired the confidence that people of her intelligence, talent, and character deserve. This may not have endeared her to women whose own lack of self-esteem moves them to envy or spite, or to men who are intimidated—vice fascinated or charmed—by self-assured women; but it may have elevated her expectations with respect to interpersonal relationships, and enabled her to better manage Marty or avoid him altogether.

Conversely, Laurel's lack of self-esteem has lowered her standards vis-à-vis relationships and rendered her entirely too accepting of arrogant jerks and others to whom a more confident person wouldn't give the time of day. This is no doubt why she is so tolerant of Marty's insensitivity and despotic approach to the administration of their household. It's also why she is so forgiving of Alethia's rudeness and chronic self-absorption. In truth, if Laurel didn't have such a dim view of herself, she would have set them straight or dumped them both a long time ago.

Unfortunately, the direct approach is rarely the one taken by even accomplished women with abysmal self-esteem, as I've learned from observing my friend Janine. Like Laurel, Janine is an attractive, caring, and intelligent woman who has worked her ass off so her spouse could pursue his dreams of personal success, and so their children can have the kind of experiences he wants them to have—whether the kids want them or not.

From the moment we met—in the concessions stand at the local community fitness center where we both worked over the summer between our junior and senior years in high school—I could see Janine lacked a backbone and had a poor self-image. She wouldn't put herself down or negatively compare herself to others like Laurel does, but she would let Dean—whom she'd been dating for two years by then and whom she married less than a year after we graduated from high school—get away with remarks and behavior that were rude and insulting, and which suggested a level of arrogance and need to control that would have sent a more self-assured and discerning woman running in the opposite direction.

Janine gamely tolerated Dean's crap for what seemed like an eternity, just as I feared she would since the moment I first laid eyes on him when he came by to collect her after work one night. The guy didn't even bother *pretending* to be a decent human being like creatures of his kind usually do when their girlfriends or wives are among friends or anyone else who might be called to testify against them in the future. Rather, he stormed up to the counter and without so much as a hello demanded to know why she hadn't been waiting in the parking lot as instructed. He went on to inform her that, since she couldn't follow directions, they would not be seeing the movie she had chosen, and that if she didn't like it she could just find herself another ride home.

I remember standing there watching—as Janine obediently nodded, asked me to clock her out, and hurried after him to his Monte Carlo—and wondering what century we were in, and why the hell she hadn't told him to take a hike. It would have been different if he'd simply expressed a desire to see another film, and if they couldn't agree to see a different one that night but the original next time, offered to drive her home before going to see it with one of his friends. But to bark at her like a dog in front of other people and threaten to leave her behind if she didn't like his plan—before she'd even said a word for or against it—was unnecessary, and far more than any self-respecting woman would ever accept.

It reminded me of the many scenarios I'd overheard my mother describe whenever she talked about domestic abuse in my presence. *Why would she put up with that?* I marveled. *Why doesn't she tell him to fuck off?*

"Maybe she just really loves him," one of our coworkers suggested after I absently verbalized my shock and disgust aloud.

She, like far too many young women even today, thought Dean's behavior was perfectly acceptable. She thought Janine was lucky just to have a boyfriend, and saw no reason why she shouldn't let Dean set the conditions of the relationship. I, on the other hand, had seen and heard enough about this kind of thing to know his actions that night were just a taste of things to come, and that Janine should get rid of the jerk *posthaste*.

"That's not the point," I argued back. "No one deserves to be treated that way, and she's crazy to let him get away with it. She may love the guy, but by tolerating that kind of shit now, she's basically telling him he can treat her like trash and she will not object."

Eighteen years, three kids, and countless insults and unpardonable offenses later, Janine finally decided she did object—which she conveyed in a predictably passive and pusillanimous manner. Emboldened by an unexpected promotion at work and the attentions of a guy in her new office, she lost the sixty pounds she'd gained in her subconscious campaign to drive the famously shallow Dean away, and instead of declaring independence, embarked on an affair with her daughters' allergist. Eventually his wife caught on and Janine was forced to tell Dean of her transgressions before the doc's future ex-wife made good on her threat to do it for her.

From the moment Janine told me about her then week-old affair with Doctor Ron—as she insisted on calling him before, during, and since their little fling—I knew she was hoping to get caught and praying that the discovery of her infidelity would motivate Dean to either pack his bags or change his ways. Unfortunately, instead of taking off or atoning for his sins, he chose to stick around and punish Janine for hers. Over the next couple years, he exacted his revenge by turning their kids, their parents, and all but her closest friends against her; and by spreading the word that she was a raging alcoholic slut who had given him hepatitis C, and with whom he had no choice but to stay because his landscaping business had failed—thanks, naturally, to the stress caused by Janine's selfishness and immorality—and he couldn't afford his own health insurance.

As her closest friend and confidant, I knew she was innocent of all but one of his charges, and that she had been motivated to it as much by Dean's cruelty and indifference as by Dr. Ron's smoldering glances. Having wasted untold quantities of breath over the years urging her to assert herself with him and her parents, I also knew she wouldn't fight back, and that she would never be free of Dean unless *he* decided to leave *her*. This, of course, was never going to happen as long as she was making money and Dean could say and do what he wanted, and so Operation Smear Janine continued unfettered.

Having grown up in a home where asserting herself was prohibited, futile, and occasionally dangerous—and fraught with guilt over wanting more love, attention, and respect than Dean and her parents thought she deserved—Janine was incapable of defending herself. Thus, Dean was able to control the spin, eliminate all but her staunchest allies, and come off more sympathetic than Elizabeth Edwards, Sandra Bullock, and Maria Shriver combined. Finally, with nothing left to lose, Janine threw in the proverbial towel and flew the coop.

So while no one knew that Dean had refused to comfort and console her after she miscarried their second pregnancy, her entire family heard—and amazingly believed—that Janine managed to get drunk on an almost nightly basis for more than a decade without missing a single day of work. And while none of them knew that long before she sought comfort in the arms of Dr. Ron, she had been crying herself to sleep for years because Dean refused to touch her after she gave birth to their third daughter—because he wouldn't 'risk' a fourth girl by going for a boy and he couldn't 'trust' her to use birth control—they had no trouble swallowing his claim that she'd bedded every willing man within a ten-mile radius of her office. And while no one but her cousin Molly and I knew she couldn't buy so much as a pack of gum without permission—even after Dean's business folded and she became the sole breadwinner—not one member of their circle doubted it when he said she'd emptied their bank accounts and refused to give him money to support the three girls she left him to raise by himself.

All of which makes you wonder: Are these folks the stupidest people on earth? Or are they just unfathomably sick in the head? After all, who else but a dolt, lunatic, or sexist jackass doesn't realize that a man whose once notoriously virtuous and obedient wife has an affair and subsequently leaves him will say literally anything to cast her as a harlot and himself as a saint?

That is not to say Janine deserves none of the blame for how things turned out. Certainly she could have taken the direct approach toward getting what she needed from Dean by speaking her mind and refusing to back down when he resisted. Failing that, she could have suggested—and, if necessary, insisted—that they seek counseling to resolve their issues. Likewise, upon realizing that things weren't going to improve, she could have told Dean she wanted a divorce instead of taking comfort in the arms of another man. Once she was busted, she could have owned up to her feelings and explained her actions instead of running for cover and allowing Dean to launch a wholesale attack on her character. That she kept her mouth shut all that time is less a testament to her strength and patience than evidence of her paralyzing fear of confrontation, disapproval, and reprisal.

There are several other examples of how badly Janine played her cards over the years, but her biggest mistake was not taking the girls when she left. Having lived with Dean as long as she did and knowing what a manipulative shit he was, she should have known better than to trust him to play fair and not accuse her of abandonment after convincing her it would be better for the kids if they weren't uprooted from their home at the same time their parents were separating. Unfortunately, she was so happy with how well he took the news she wanted a divorce that she failed to question his uncharacteristic civility and consequently was stunned when he told the court she'd walked out on him and the children, and successfully petitioned for sole legal and physical custody.

So while Janine may finally be less one jerk, because she lacks the skill and the will to assert herself, she is also minus three kids, her reputation, and a fair share of the assets. And while she no longer lives under the same roof with a tyrant, because she can't—or won't—fight back, he still manages to control her by constantly screwing around with their visitation schedule and periodically threatening to haul her back to court.

Sadly, she's unwilling to do the hard work required to avoid an equally tragic sequel. Instead of taking a break from men and trying to understand what went wrong with Dean, she's running around and latching onto guys who seem nothing like him on the surface but are his exact clones on the inside, or getting used by dirt bags who sense her hunger and desperation, and drop her like a hot rock after they've had their fun. Meanwhile, she's effectively cut her closest friends—as in those of us who've seen her through every crisis up to and including the divorce—out of the picture, and instead spends her free time with her latest boyfriend or partying with other newly divorced and unhappily married women who share her inexorable need for male attention. All of which ensures that Janine will get from future relationships exactly what she got from Dean: disrespect, despair, and loneliness.

Like Laurel, Janine has her parents to thank for who and where she is today. For it was they from whom she learned that love and respect are conditional benefits to be conferred upon girls for doing what they're told, and who taught her to never stand up for herself or expect her ideas or opinions to be taken seriously. It probably didn't help that the first guy to ask her out turned out to be an ass who shared her parents' philosophy and would go on to treat her worse than they did. Still, having witnessed firsthand how they speak to her and how they behave if she so much as *thinks* about going against their wishes—it's clear who taught Janine to fear disapproval and to put everyone else's needs above her own. Likewise, it is clear who stunted her confidence, and turned her into a magnet for a creep like Dean.

Having watched all this play out over the better part of two decades, I know better than to expect Laurel to take swift or decisive action toward improving her situation. Rather, I imagine she'll accept the status quo until something or someone forces her hand. She may say she's doing it for financial reasons, or for the children—which is ludicrous since kids are no better off living in a war zone, or with a man who fancies himself their mother's lord and master, than they are having parents who are divorced. In truth, however, it is her low self-esteem that will keep Laurel from rocking the boat or moving on to better things.

That said, Laurel has a few things going for her that Janine does not and which will make her life better regardless of whether she jumps ship or stays the course. One such advantage is that she doesn't need validation from Marty or any man. She may tolerate the cruel and insensitive remarks he makes at frustratingly regular intervals and let him call the shots at home, but she is not inclined to alter her appearance to win his favor, and often rebels by bending or flouting the rules when he's out of town. This stands in sharp contrast to Janine, who spent years fine-tuning her hair and wardrobe to suit Dean, and would never have dreamed of defying him even behind his back. Likewise, whereas she doggedly pursued Dean's approval, and took responsibility for the cooling of both his heart and libido, Laurel is happy for the excuse not to shave her legs, and admits to wondering—hopefully—if Marty is "getting it" elsewhere. And whereas Janine zealously avoided spending even one night away from Dean and to this day is loathe to sleep alone, Laurel isn't the least bit perturbed by all the trade shows and conferences Marty attends, and looks forward to having their bed to herself a few times a month. Moreover, when he's away, she doesn't hit the town looking for someone to fill the void or linger after her kids' soccer games to chat up the coaches and unaccompanied fathers; instead she rallies her pals around her kitchen counter or lures us to a favorite eatery for some good food and lively conversation. Finally, she doesn't greet every man in her circle with a hug and a "Hey baby." Unlike Janine, who I'm sure is only trying to sound friendly and confident—as opposed to seductive or salacious—Laurel keeps her hands to herself and gets validation not from being desirable to men, but from being loved and appreciated by her family, friends, clients, and colleagues.

With these observations in mind, it is reasonable to assume Laurel won't resort to passive aggression, or allow her future to be ruled by a need for male attention. Even if she doesn't wake up one day and swiftly file for divorce, neither will she start sleeping in the guest room or stop wearing her wedding ring hoping Marty will feel bad and clean up his act. Nor will she waste her time trolling the bars, contemplating tramp stamps, or parading around in her daughter's low-rise jeans. She'll be too busy celebrating with the friends who stood by her, and if it's not too late, making up to her kids for all the things they couldn't do under Marty's regime. If they're still around, she may also take a stab at reconnecting with her parents whom she only sees about twice a year, owing to Marty's belief in their innate inferiority—and who, despite having done little to foster her self-esteem when she was a kid, would never take Marty's side or let him manipulate them because they have more respect for Laurel than Janine's folks ever had in her.

And therein lies the second difference between the two. Although both women had parents who undermined their confidence, Janine's failed her further by constantly reminding her of her limitations, warning her off of challenges, and voicing amazement at—as opposed to applauding or taking pride in—her successes. To add injury to insult, they have always sided with anyone who has ever said a word against her, and would intentionally shame her or withhold affection if she ever dared to go her own way. Without this added "bonus," Laurel won't have to worry that the two people who should be squarely and steadfastly in her corner will take Marty's side or become his accomplices in the assassination of her character.

Nor will she have to worry that her parents won't support her efforts at building a new life. This is because while they did not lavish her with praise or allow her to take pride in herself, they refused to let her rest on her, well, laurels, and did not encourage her to settle in any sense of the word. In fact, they always believed she could do better in both her career and her choice of mate, and openly wondered if Marty was worthy of someone of her abilities and potential.

This is not the case for Janine's folks, who routinely reminded her of her shortcomings and how they would limit her romantic prospects. Although they initially condemned her relationship with Dean—not because he wasn't good enough, of course, but because they were afraid of the influence he would have on their ability to control her—once they saw the writing on the wall, they switched gears, and in a bizarre variation on the Oedipal theme—wherein a boy accepts that he'll never have his mom to himself and decides instead to buddy up to his father—they allied themselves with Dean and from that point on, encouraged Janine to obey the man, and to do whatever else it took to keep the peace. Recently they've surprised me by lending her the money to cover her attorney's fees, but given their penchant for blackmail and extortion, I suspect they've only done so with a view of using it as leverage in the future.

The third and probably most important difference between Janine and Laurel is that Laurel acknowledges what went wrong in her relationship with Marty, and plans to take steps to ensure she doesn't wind up with someone just like him—or worse. That's not to say she intends to seek counseling or some sort of training to improve her confidence so she can make a better choice next time around. Rather, if she and Marty split up, she plans to forego dating altogether and focus on her kids and career. Laurel admits this sounds a bit lonely but says it's her only option since she's always been attracted to men who think they're smarter than she is and who need to be in charge. That's not likely to change just because she takes a class or spends a few hours on an analyst's couch, she adds, so she's better off going it alone.

Although I find it sad and a bit disheartening that someone with as much going for her as Laurel has would throw in the towel after a few rough rounds, I can't say it's entirely unwise. Especially given what I've encountered in my line of work, I can't say with any degree of certainty that she could, even with intensive therapy, change the patterns and processes that draw her to men like Marty. Some habits truly are impossible to break.

Despite its drawbacks, Laurel's approach is still superior to Janine's, which typically involves drinking and going home with the most persistent guy in the bar, and crossing her fingers that he won't dump her or be an even bigger ass than Dean. That may sound like an oversimplification of her tactics, but as the one whose phone rings when things go awry, I can affirm that it's not an exaggeration. More importantly, while it may keep her busy in the short term, it will do nothing for her self-esteem in the long run, and may lead to pregnancy, disease, assault, or even homicide. Laurel's plan carries none of these risks and will serve her better if she and Marty part company.

That's not to say her attitude won't change. Freedom tends to look different up close than it does from afar, and as with a cancer diagnosis or a lottery jackpot, you can't know what you'll do with it until it becomes a reality. So Laurel may say she'd rather retire than get back in the ring, but that perspective may be the product of frustration and as such, may shift once the source of her frustration has been quashed or removed.

This, of course, assumes Laurel is being honest with herself in the first place. Although she may think she has a firm grasp of her true feelings, I've been around long enough to know that people will convince themselves of all kinds of things to gird their hearts and minds against disappointment and embarrassment, and that many who say they'd rather be alone do so to avoid sounding desperate or because they don't want to squander their energy looking for someone they're afraid they'll never find.

With this in mind, I generally urge anyone—male or female, friend or fan—who has recently ended a long-term relationship to stay out of the dating pool for a while. Instead of meeting new people, I advise them to get to know themselves, and to figure out what they want out of life and in a life partner. Additionally, they need to learn to distinguish decent people from the duds; to replace destructive communication patterns with healthy ones; and to develop the skills and habits to get what they need. That way they won't end up with a Marty, a Dean, or the human equivalent to a high-performance Italian sports car. More importantly, they won't waste the best years of their lives waiting for their partner to leave or die so they can finally live and be happy.

Ideally that wouldn't happen to anyone—either the first time around or the second. Ideally, everyone would marry the right person for the right reasons, having been totally honest about their intentions and their expectations, and armed with the skills to cooperate and negotiate. That so many people go into it with none of these is not only perplexing, it's downright disturbing.

Just as disturbing is how many parents raise their daughters to be passive and insecure. Given how detrimental these characteristics can be to a girl's immediate and overall quality of life, one would expect parents to promote confidence and independence instead. Although (as Bunny is fond of arguing) some folks are too busy putting food on the table and keeping a roof overhead to focus on their children's emotional development, I doubt meeting basic needs was a struggle in either Laurel or Janine's case. After all, both come from two-parent households that could afford a home in the suburbs, college for their kids, and two family vacations a year. In fact, the only differences between their childhoods and mine—apart from the fact that I was encouraged to be myself and to speak my mind while they were silenced and shamed—are that I had moved about nine times before tenth grade while they each lived in the same house until they got married; and they were raised in Catholic homes while I had a secular upbringing. Given how many confident and contented Catholic girls and military brats there are on earth, one can reasonably conclude that having parents who favor guidance and praise over criticism and commands, and promote assertiveness and autonomy over blind obedience and dependence, has a greater impact on one's emotional well-being than do religion, economics, or a nomadic lifestyle.

Even if one accepts the idea that single parents and poor families have a harder time fostering confidence in their children, it doesn't necessarily follow that married couples and families with higher incomes will have it any easier or are any more successful. In fact, as Laurel and Janine's examples illustrate, insecure and timid women can be found among even middle-class families, just like their more confident and assertive counterparts.

The relationship between these qualities and girls' behavior and choices during adolescence and adulthood cannot be overstated. Having a positive self-image and an assertive nature enables girls to pursue interests, activities, and friendships that allow them to acquire skills and develop a sense of belonging and accomplishment. Having a positive self-image and an assertive nature also influences girls' expectations as to how they will be treated and perceived by other people, and how they will respond when those expectations are not met. It also reduces the likelihood that girls will be drawn to or tolerant of rude, narcissistic, or insecure men—who are, with few exceptions, the kind who need to control, abuse, or otherwise mistreat women. More importantly, it renders them less attractive to abusive and/or sexist men, who are threatened or otherwise put off by confident women—thereby sparing them the hassle of avoiding or ditching them later.

And the advantages of self-esteem and assertiveness to girls don't end there. In the highly unlikely yet not entirely unheard-of event that she winds up living with a man who has cunningly concealed his insecure, controlling, or abusive nature throughout their entire courtship, a strong, confident woman will be better equipped and thus more willing, to act in her own best interests. Likewise, the assertive woman whose theretofore pleasant, reasonable, and rational spouse starts to exhibit jealousy, bitterness, or other signs of instability in response to, say, disappointment or perceived injustice, will be better prepared to deal with him than would someone who lacks confidence and self-esteem.

Obviously it would be better for all concerned if there were no rude, insecure, controlling, or violent men on the planet in the first place. Unfortunately, achieving that fantasy means changing the way some people raise their boys, which has little chance of catching on among those who need it most. And that alone wouldn't solve the problem, since there are still many generations of grown men among us who treat women like dogs, slaves, and punching bags, and who believe they are within their rights to do so. The only way to get rid of that lot would be to exterminate them—either en masse or one by one—which is likely to be met with more than a smidge of resistance.

Fortunately, many parents do succeed in raising decent boys who have no need to hurt or dominate anyone. Walker and his brother, Carson, are living proof of this. Although they grew up in a home that was fairly traditional in terms of gender roles—Mrs. Browne cooked, cleaned, and did the shopping; Mr. Browne managed the money, the yard, and the cars—neither acts as if he feels superior to women, or resents or feels threatened by them. In fact, based on their actions among friends, colleagues, and family members, it's clear they respect men and women equally and would never use coercion, intimidation, or violence against anyone who didn't pose a bodily threat to themselves or someone else. At the same time, neither has trouble acknowledging his mistakes and both exhibit conciliatory behavior in the face of conflict. Like all true gentlemen, Walker and Carson are secure in themselves and, as such, have no need to attack, criticize, or control others to compensate for their perceived faults or weaknesses.

Not that I would have settled for anything less. Unlike many of my contemporaries, I've never been patient, bored, or needy enough to tolerate the company of rude, sexist, or otherwise offensive people, no matter how smart, good-looking, talented, fun, or interesting the source of that behavior may be.

No doubt this goes a long way toward explaining why I didn't start dating until my second year of college. Although I attended functions with male friends and went out with groups that included members of the opposite sex, I didn't go out with anyone on my own until an exchange student I met at a neighborhood picnic asked me to accompany him to the Paine Art Center. I'm not sure that even qualifies as a date, given that I only went as a favor to his host family and didn't realize the guy had romantic intentions until I noticed him closing his eyes and sniffing my hair as we moved about the gallery.

Also contributing to my late arrival to the dating scene was the fact that the bar had been set pretty high by my dad. Mack would've been a hard act for anyone to follow, and I doubted there were many guys of my generation who could measure up. Moreover, thanks to my friends and Bunny's associates, I knew the perils of settling for less than what you want in a partner, and was convinced that the precise combination of strength, sensitivity, and smarts I desired was unlikely to be found among men who had never left Wisconsin and hadn't been through Marine Corps Boot Camp. This no doubt carried over into my interactions with the guys I encountered and made it clear to all but the clueless and the cocksure among them that I was, for whatever reason, off the market.

I'm sure some in my orbit assumed from my persistent solo status that I was batting for the other team; but while I was in no rush to get serious with a guy, neither was I attracted to girls. The bottom line is that I didn't expect anyone to trip my trigger, and thus saw no point in dating when I could be reading, writing, or drawing instead.

If anyone settled in our marriage, it was Walker, who probably could have dated anyone he'd wanted if he'd had just a trace of caveman DNA and been willing to work it, as the saying goes. Intrigued by his wry sense of humor, his relaxed, easy-going temperament, and his charming science-geek-meets-outdoorsman demeanor, I pursued him—obliquely, of course, at least until I realized that subtlety is not the province of mellow, gentlemanly engineers and had to get more obvious about it—and happily discovered he was amenable to spending time with someone who was creative, outspoken, and more than a little curious. It probably helped that I'm not the sort who draws hearts and flowers on her notebooks or imagines life as a fairy tale, and who had sufficient self-esteem that I didn't need to be worshipped, flattered, or pampered.

As a result, we were able to forge a fair and equitable relationship that had many in our orbit scratching their heads. Although we didn't understand their bewilderment, just in case they'd seen something we'd missed on our way to the altar (or more accurately, City Hall—something for which Walker's mother has not fully forgiven us) we decided to proceed with the proviso that if it didn't work out, we'd part company with no hard feelings.

The first time I mentioned this—at lunch with Bunny and her younger sister, Charlotte, a week before the wedding—the latter nearly lost her mind.

"Marriage is hard enough," she fretted, pursing her naturally plump lips for emphasis, "without people going into it expecting to fail."

I remember suppressing a laugh.

Aunt Charlotte isn't as progressively minded as Bunny is, but she is definitely as outspoken. In her case, however, the candor is less a matter of conscious assertiveness than a lack of a verbal filter. To bottom-line it, as both the youngest and the official "pretty one" of the bunch, she could get away with just about anything and therefore never had to learn tact or self control.

It bears mention here that Aunt Charlotte isn't prettier than my mom. In fact, she'd be a dead ringer for Bunny if you put her in an auburn wig and slipped a pair of hazel contact lenses into her denim-blue eyes. Charlotte only got designated the "pretty one" because she's the baby and a blonde, and because Bunny had already been designated the "smart one."

That's not to say that Charlotte is any less intelligent than Bunny. It's just that because she was beautiful and, again, the baby, she was never required to think for herself, or encouraged to develop her mind.

"It's not funny," she had added reproachfully, mistaking my look of chagrin for amusement. "With one in every three marriages failing within seven years, I wouldn't think you'd treat it like such a joke."

Much is made about statistics like these—and I admit it sounds bad. But people tend to hear *one in three marriages* and assume it means one in three *first* marriages. Few of them realize that this figure includes not only people who are getting married for the first time, but also those who keep trying and failing at marriage—or as I call them, repeat offenders. By this I mean folks like Elizabeth Taylor, who wed way too many times in her lifetime because she didn't believe in sex outside of marriage, and Bunny and Charlotte's younger brother, Mel, who's been married four times and engaged twice more because he has a Sir Galahad complex and keeps rescuing damsels in distress—from cruel husbands, et cetera—only to lose them again when they realize he's a possessive maniac, and they head for the hills to avoid being smothered by his devotion.

Often accompanying these facts—by which I mean the rate of divorce, not the mating and dating habits of Uncle Mel—are ideas about where to lay the blame, and lots of hand-wringing over the fact that someone should be doing something about it. People are too self-centered, the concerned will lament, and unwilling to work together or compromise. They think society should revere marriage and protect it at all costs—that if it weren't for the breakdown of the family, America's kids wouldn't be so messed up.

Some of that may be true and warrant attention, but it's also true and worthy of note that not everyone who lands in divorce court gets there as a result of selfishness or sloth. And while I'm all about communication and negotiation, it can be difficult—if not impossible—to reason with the kind of man who thinks he's infallible and refuses to listen to anyone, or who believes his *Y* chromosome entitles him to berate, intimidate, or abuse those he deems inferior. Yes, women can be just as obnoxious—R.J.'s Ferrari is proof of that—and they should not be tolerated. My point is that—at least when the problems don't boil down to negotiable issues like priorities, roles, and responsibilities, but instead to intractable arrogance and insensitivity and/or emotional or physical abuse—it is unrealistic and wholly irrational to expect the aggrieved party to stick around waiting for things to get better.

Ironically enough, it is usually those in the most deeply dysfunctional relationships who don't know when to give up the ship. Unlike people who leave relationships for frivolous or superficial reasons, those with serious, insuperable grievances and thus justification to walk away, are the least likely to do so. Rather, they'll stay in a relationship long after it has gone sour, and well past the point at which it's remotely salvageable.

Then again, in my experience, the signal to abandon ship comes well before it starts to sink and oftentimes before it even sets sail. After all, decent men don't wake up one day and suddenly start slapping their wives around; nor do faithful husbands become cheating bastards overnight. Likewise, ambitious women don't turn into drugged-out slugs in the blink of an eye, nor do kind and generous souls become selfish, venomous nags in the time it takes to drink a cup of coffee. Rather, there are signs that someone doesn't respect you, has a temper, is unhappy or can't be trusted, just as there are signs pointing to the exit ramps on the freeway. People may deny they exist or try to rationalize them away; but the evidence that a person lacks empathy, or has other serious issues that prevent him or her from building and maintaining equitable and meaningful relationships generally appears before any vows are exchanged, and almost always before there are kids or financial issues to prevent a swift and smooth departure.

In Janine's case, the first clue that Dean was such a creature surfaced on their first date, although it escaped her notice as a harbinger of doom until we were well into our second bottle of wine a few weeks after she left him. As she told it, at some point that evening they had stopped off at a convenience store for a snack and, after they'd set their respective items on the counter, Dean picked up the candy bar she had placed next to her soda and, without a word, put it back on the shelf. Given that they'd already agreed to go Dutch that night, Janine knew he hadn't done this because he thought she expected him to pay for her items and didn't have the cash to cover it. And given the pack of mini donuts next to his Coke, it was also clear that he had no moral or political objection to the consumption of refined sugar. Rather, as he was kind enough to confirm in front of two of his friends the following weekend after Janine suggested that they split a piece of cheesecake, the problem was that she needed to lose a few pounds and therefore had absolutely no business eating sweets.

Now I'll concede that preventing your date from buying candy or ordering dessert isn't exactly a hanging offense, nor does it qualify as violence or abuse. It does, however, suggest that someone is a world-class jerk with whom one probably shouldn't go out again. For even if coming between you and your sugar isn't enough to make you want to cut a man loose, then surely the manner in which he does it should be. Meanwhile, if you're the kind of person for whom none of Dean's actions would be a deal breaker, then you probably should stop dating and send me your address because you are in dire need of an intervention.

It may sound harsh to suggest ditching someone based on one or two acts of thoughtlessness or insensitivity, but it's the best move all around. It not only keeps that person's problems from becoming your problems, but it also keeps those problems from escalating, thereby saving both parties a lot of grief. Besides, ditching someone because he's rude is far more honorable than ditching him because he's short or has bad hair, and ditching someone before you've had sex with him is infinitely easier than ditching him after you're married or after you've had his baby.

That's not to say relationships can never be preserved or that no one ever deserves a second chance. In fact, were I in Janine's shoes, I might have gone out with Dean again following the candy bar incident—after seeking and securing a suitable explanation and apology, that is. Then again, since controlling bastards aren't generally drawn to women like me, it's unlikely that Dean would have asked me out once, much less twice, so the point is moot.

Still, there are situations where patience and understanding are called for and thus a second chance is warranted. Misunderstandings and mishaps, for example, frequently occur in the early stages of a relationship when the parties are nervous and trying to put their best foot forward; and giving someone the benefit of the doubt is perfectly reasonable when it is obvious that the root of the problem was anxiety or confusion as opposed to arrogance or contempt. The same applies to long-term relationships whose parties may have started to take one another for granted or are so comfortable that they don't always stop to think about what they're saying to one another. Under such circumstances, I generally advise people to give their partners the opportunity to apologize and to make amends before ruling the behavior unforgivable and calling it quits.

In my experience, even relationships where one of the parties has committed adultery can often be saved. When a wayward spouse has made a full and voluntary confession, for example, and provided the infidelity was unpremeditated and unprecedented, a second chance is definitely in order. Under such conditions—and provided the unfaithful party vows to aggressively avoid temptation in the future, works diligently to fulfill his or her promise to make amends, and agrees to submit to periodic monitoring until such time as the partner feels comfortable—trust can be restored and the marriage can be saved.

Policies and tactics like these, however, should be employed only by those who are equipped to deal with conflict directly, rationally, and without shame. Women like Janine, who are afraid to confront a guy for outright rudeness and can't distinguish pushy from direct, don't have what it takes to create and sustain an equitable relationship, and should limit themselves to first dates until they do. This may seem a bit coldhearted, but one can't rely on hope to deliver a good mate or on faith to ensure he'll stay that way. After all, even the kindest person in the world can have a bad day, and if you can't muster the nerve to confront rude or obnoxious behavior in someone you've just started dating, you don't have a prayer of dealing with that—or worse—once you're in love or taken the vows.

Then again, women with low self-esteem aren't famous for acting in their own best interests. So while those with strong self-esteem are okay with being on their own—and in fact usually prefer it to putting up with someone who isn't right for them—those without it are so desperate to fill the void, they'd rather date the wrong man than invest the time and energy developing the qualities and habits required to attract the right one. Likewise, instead of standing up to a jerk they should have avoided altogether, they'll marry him, and almost certainly live to regret it.

Which is why I am just as likely—if not more so—to chastise people for hanging on too long than I am to accuse them of giving up too quickly. It's easy to stay unhappy and go through the motions waiting for something to happen to change the course of your life. It's hard to admit that you've made a mistake; that the person you married isn't the man or woman of your dreams but Adolf Hitler or the Bitch of Belsen; and that you could've avoided him or her if you hadn't been so desperate to be loved or get laid. People—but women especially—need to remember that they have choices, and that if they expect respect and are willing to be the bad guy once in a while, they can avoid marrying and having children with the wrong person, and never have to choose between the devil they know and the devil they don't.

Such were my thoughts as we started our journey back to La Crosse the next morning, with Walker in the passenger seat working on the notes from his date with Jamey. Having succeeded in finding a Master Sportsman Leafy Cut Camo Suit in his size online as we were packing up, there had been no debate over whether to drive all over Badgerland looking for one. Thanks to his easygoing nature and the excitement over the impending arrival of new gear, he was more than happy to let me drive—especially since it meant he wouldn't have to make time to do the notes after work one day next week.

He'd already chosen his next date, and arranged a meeting for the following Saturday. Her name was Erica, and she was a thirty-six-year-old grant writer from Steven's Point. Noting that, like me, her occupation required her to collect data and write persuasively, I wondered what other skills and interests I might have in common with Walker's many matches. In the interest of time and science, however, I decided to contain my curiosity. There would be plenty of time to ask questions later, I reasoned; for now it was best to let the man work in peace.

Six

D ue to several factors—both natural and manmade—I was unable to fulfill my promise to e-mail Walker's notes to Bunny the following week.

The first of these was the traffic we hit on our way home, which was backed up for several miles thanks to an overturned semi that had blocked both westbound lanes of I-90 about halfway between Mauston and Tomah. Although I considered the inconvenience a relatively small price to pay for having lured a woman out to the Dells to meet a man with no intention of seeing her again, Walker was a bit less sanguine.

"I paid for luring her out there by spending the day surrounded by tourists," he observed. "For dealing with this traffic, I think I now deserve some other form of compensation."

"Would you settle for a set of Master Sportsman Leafy Cut Camo Undies to go with your camo suit?" I offered. "I doubt they sell them anywhere, but if you'll let me run by Walmart for some kitchen shears, pantyhose, and brown and green markers, I can probably fashion you a pair."

Although he declined this offer, the mention of the camo suit seemed to appease him enough to keep him from griping as we inched our way down the freeway toward the stretch of shoulder where traffic had been diverted to get around the semi, and back onto the two lane black top toward home.

The second factor contributing to my delay in satisfying Bunny's curiosity about Walker's activities was my scanner, which on Monday morning decided it would rather be a paperweight and, thus prevented me from converting the hard copies of Walker's notes into electronic files. The blasted piece of plastic, glass, and whatever else scanners are made of had proven itself temperamental in the past so I knew it was only a matter of time before it bit the dust; I'd just hoped it wouldn't crap out on me before I could make time to find a new one that suited my admittedly limited but specific needs.

Good things may come to those who wait, I could imagine Bunny saying as I disconnected and reconnected the unit several times—and eventually banged on it with different objects and from various angles—in a questionable effort to revive it *but bad things happen to those who procrastinate*.

In any case, the death of my scanner—while tragic—was hardly an emergency since the only person who expected to receive anything from me in the immediate future was the bearer of the aforementioned wisdom. With that in mind, I shoved the scanner in the closet—mostly to get it out of my sight but also to see if a couple days in the hole might teach the recalcitrant beast a lesson—and decided to do some comparison shopping at midweek.

When I finally brought home a replacement—with far less enthusiasm than Walker displayed upon carrying his camo suit through the door, I would add—I still had to connect it, install the drivers and software, and complete the set up so it could function as I wanted. This would have been a piece of cake had it not been for the layering/compatibility issues that sparked a contest of wills between the scanner and the printer, which prevented either from doing its job while the other was connected—and which suggested that, like Harry Potter and his nemesis, Voldemort, one could not exist as long as the other lived.

"You could have avoided all that if you had opted for a printer-scanner-copier," I reminded myself as I uninstalled and reinstalled both components in a different order. "True—but where's the fun in that?"

In truth, I'd gone with the basic scanner-copier out of loyalty to my printer, which I've had since college and has served me better than any I've encountered since, and out of a preference for how it handles the paper when you order up a job. Nowadays, most of them fire sheets off the roller with the force of a rocket—as evidenced by the last three units to occupy Walker's 'command center' in the den, and send them flying off the desk and onto the floor.

Eventually, I got the system reconfigured and—due to an irritating inherited inability to rearrange anything without cleaning—my entire office dusted, detangled, and decluttered. By then, of course, it was time to make dinner, which alone would not have been a complicated affair but would be difficult to accomplish while unstapling packets of paper and laying them one at a time on a platen to be captured and stored electronically. Having determined that even Bunny wouldn't put feeding her curiosity over feeding her husband, I decided the packets could wait another day and vowed to get to them first thing Thursday morning.

Unfortunately, Mother Nature had other ideas for that day, as evidenced by the rain, thunder, and golf ball-sized hail that preempted our alarm clock by about twenty minutes. Not content to frighten the bejeezus out of those of us with skylights over our beds and anyone who had the misfortune of owning a vehicle but not a garage to store it in—she decided to throw in some lightening, flash flooding, and straight-line winds that took down several trees and knocked out power to our quadrant of the city soon after Walker left for work. Having determined via a call to the electric company that the outage was under investigation and repair was expected within two hours, I used the occasion as an excuse to do nothing productive and sat down to catch up on my reading. Four hours, three magazines, and one boring room-temperature lunch later, I picked up my cell phone again and dialed the power company, whose automated outage management system indicated that the repair window had been extended to midnight.

Apparently that estimate, too, was inaccurate, as we learned when Dr. Greg Forbes—whose report I'd been watching on The Weather Channel when we lost power that morning—suddenly reappeared on the set in the living room at 8:52 p.m. By then of course, Walker and I had already eaten dinner out—at the closest restaurant to our neighborhood that had power—and set up the generator with a view to keeping our phones charged and the fridge cold. With the generator running in the garage and the extension cord having to pass through the doorway from there to the kitchen, we had no choice but to leave both the exterior and interior garage doors ajar. By then I'd also arranged for us to sleep in the living room since it was the only way I could think of to deter any gang of thugs who hoped to take advantage of our vulnerable situation and conduct their next rash of home invasions in our neighborhood.

A true believer in Murphy's Law, I was not the least bit surprised when the power came back on just minutes after we'd finished preparing to hunker down for the night. In fact, although I didn't say so—since, like sharing the wish you make before blowing out your birthday candles, voicing your intention only hampers the magic—I had only insisted on preparing to spend the night without power to induce our portion of the grid to come back online before it was time to go to sleep. If instead we had chosen to sit in the dark listening to the meat thawing in the freezer or waiting for our phones to discharge, we wouldn't have had electricity for days—guaranteed.

And so, although it meant I had a lot of stuff to put away the next day, Walker and I were able to sleep in our own bed, and to wake up to the gentle beep of our digital alarm clock, as opposed to the bone-rattling, brain-shattering clang of the old fashioned wind-up model Walker uses when he goes hunting. Other options existed, of course, besides the deceptively dubbed Baby Ben. Specifically, I refer to our cell phones, which enable users to be awakened by one of several pre-installed tones, and our regular alarm clock, which could have been brought down with the bedding from the guest room and plugged into the generator. But as circumstances and Walker's almost pathological aversion to being late for work—even in the face of emergencies and other unforeseen events—would have forced him to set the wind-up anyway—thereby proving I'm not the only member of our household given to superstitions and irrational fears—it didn't make sense to bother with them.

I had just finished remaking the guest room bed and returning the clock, the extension cord, the flashlights, and spare batteries to their rightful places—having already eaten breakfast, drunk my coffee, and kissed Walker good-bye—when my phone rang. Recognizing the area code but not the number, I decided to let it go to voicemail and to find out what—if anything—I'd missed after a long hot shower.

Having just utilized Murphy's Law to my own benefit the night before, I probably should've expected the call I ignored to be an important one. While answering it may not have turned the caller into a telemarketer or kept the day from spinning completely out of control, doing so—or at least listening to the voicemail message right away—would have enabled me to know what was happening an hour earlier, and given me more time to prepare for what came afterward.

The call had come from Renee, a former client of mine, who said she desperately needed to talk, and asked me to call her back as soon as possible.

Having heard words like these from Renee several times since we met six years ago in Waukesha, I did not view them as cause for alarm. That's not to say Renee is histrionic or prone to exaggeration. In fact, every last one of her personal challenges is serious enough to warrant life changing action. Unfortunately, Renee refuses to take life changing action, which makes it hard for me to take her problems—and her commitment to solving them—seriously. In fact, more than once, I have cited Renee's case—anonymously, of course—as evidence that failing to learn from the past guarantees it will be repeated, and staying with someone for the sake of being with someone is a supremely bad idea.

Like Janine and Laurel, Renee has issues with self-esteem that have impaired her ability to build healthy, satisfying relationships. In her case, however, the problem is severe enough to qualify as a full-blown inferiority complex, which has given her an arrestingly high tolerance for assholes, batterers, and emotional sadists. Said complex developed courtesy of her mom, who used to—among other sick and twisted things—force Renee's head into the toilet and flush, and tell her she hated her and wished she'd never been born.

Among those who have both benefited from and contributed to Renee's condition are the four men with whom she has had serious relationships since high school. The first of these was Jeff, who called her names and smacked her around for a couple of years, but never broke any bones. Next came Lonnie, who liked tequila and would throw her down the stairs whenever he had too much—which was often—and who contributed a broken clavicle, a fractured wrist, and a couple concussions to her medical history. Grant was better in that he preferred to throw things *at* her instead of hitting her or pushing her down the stairs, but worse in that if she ducked, he would continue to hurl things—cans, candles, chairs—until something connected with her head or a limb and she needed stitches or an icepack.

Three years after being dumped by Grant, Renee met Vance, who batters her emotionally rather than physically. This makes him no better than his predecessors in my book, but renders him vastly superior in hers. Consider that along with the fact she thinks he's brilliant—which, compared to her exes, I suppose he is—and you can probably imagine just how much pain and humiliation she'll tolerate from him.

Another difference between Vance and Renee's former beaus is that he lacks a conscience. So while his predecessors knew enough to be sorry for what they'd done to her and to be on their best behavior until the bell rang for the next round, Vance never apologizes or tries to make amends. In fact, his conceit is such that he never even admits to being rude or hurtful, and often denies having said anything at all. And since emotional abuse leaves no marks, there is never any evidence of what he's done, nor any injury she can prove. Thus, when she complains about how he treats her, Vance can say it's all in her head and never has to admit to doing anything wrong. On those rare occasions when he doesn't outright dismiss her complaints, he'll say it's her own fault, and if she wasn't such a nag/bitch/moron, he could treat her better. Moreover, when she tries to bolster her case by telling him how others perceive their relationship, he'll argue that all her friends are either biased against him because of all the lies she's told them, or they're a bunch of jealous losers who don't want her to be happy.

Like his physically abusive counterparts, Vance's hostility and cruelty stem from a wicked cocktail of narcissism, sadism, and profound insecurity. This explains why when Renee does something he doesn't like—which is often since his compulsive need to berate her demands that the rules be constantly in flux—he can't just say so and move on like a reasonable person would. Rather, he has to rant and rave about how stupid/ugly/annoying she is, and compare her to his sister, his secretary, or any other woman to whom he knows she feels inferior. He's also fond of humiliating her by blowing up at family gatherings and accusing her of deliberately "ruining everything" by pissing him off and then "acting" sad or scared when he tries to set her straight. He may change his tune later that day—if, say, he wants sex or needs a favor—but will call her a vindictive bitch or accuse her of emotional blackmail if she fails to respond to his contrition with the speed and enthusiasm he expects.

Even if I knew none of this—and Renee had no history of dating abusive men—based on Vance's controlling behavior, I'd have serious concerns about her emotional and physical well-being. For example, Vance refuses to spend time with anyone she knew before they got married; makes it difficult for her to see her friends on her own by waiting until the last minute to inform her of his plans; and fiercely discourages her from doing so by insisting they're not good enough for her—which, incidentally, is the only time he comes close to saying she's worth a damn. He also forbids her to use their home phone for anything other than local calls, and allows her to use her cell only for emergencies. He cites financial reasons for these policies, but they're clearly designed to limit her contact with people who might encourage her to rebel, and to decimate her support system so she'll have no one to turn to for help when the going gets really tough.

In addition to making it difficult for Renee to talk to her friends, Vance makes it unpleasant by complaining when she takes incoming calls in his presence and then accusing her of keeping secrets if she goes to another room. Badgering one's partner about their behavior and accusing them of selfishness, manipulation, and deception are two of the hallmarks of emotional abuse, and Vance has them both down cold.

To her credit, Renee gets around the rules by arranging for friends to call the house when she's home alone. Although I find it disturbing that she sees nothing wrong having to go to such lengths to maintain her relationships, I'm glad to know she still has that much fight left in her.

I learned of all this over the course of twelve weeks when Renee took part in a series of workshops I was facilitating for community education. She had heard about the program and signed up hoping to improve her "poor communication skills," which Vance insisted was at the heart of all their problems. Hoping to surprise him with her progress, she told him she was taking a step class at the Y which seemed to please the man but also required her to duck out an hour early to avoid having to explain why it required her to be gone more than three hours at a shot.

Sensing from her body language and her lack of participation during group discussion that there was something more sinister behind her early departures than a desire to catch a favorite TV program or avoid getting caught waiting for a train, I endeavored to draw her out by visiting with her before class and during bathroom breaks. When eventually I heard her story—over a doughnut and decaf the first Tuesday after the workshop ended—I knew I was out of my depth and would need to get her some help before her husband kills and dismembers her, or she snaps and decides to kill him (not because I was interested in his well-being, but because I didn't want to see her go to jail for what many women would consider reasonable behavior.) Hers was a classic case of emotional abuse, I explained, and she didn't deserve to be treated that way. I then calmly, but forcefully suggested she find a shelter and a lawyer and, without a word to Vance, get a restraining order and file for divorce.

It probably comes as no surprise that this guidance was met with resistance. Although she and Vance had no kids or any significant debt besides the mortgage on their home, Renee was hell-bent on staying with the man and thus would backtrack over literally any and every negative thing she said about him in order to justify sticking around.

She was no more receptive to the idea of marriage counseling. "Vance is a very private person," she would insist each time I suggested it, "and he would sooner die than talk to anyone about our issues. Besides," she would add, "someone we know might see our car in the parking lot and realize we're having problems."

After each of these conversations, I was tempted to point to solutions to these obstacles, but decided not to bother since her excuses are like terrorists and facial tissues: Take one out and another just pops up in its place.

Given her history, I understand why Renee believes Vance is the best she can do and is reluctant to send him packing. If she had ever dated even one guy who treated her well, she may have set the bar a little higher. At present, though, Renee couldn't spot a decent man if he was standing on her foot, and she wouldn't know how to behave if she did. That could change if she were to seek help to deal with her lack of self-worth and other demons, but since Vance needs to make her feel bad in order to feel good, he's unlikely to support anything that will improve her confidence or give her ideas above her station. And, since she sees his behavior as problematic only until someone prescribes an unattractive course of action—at which point it becomes the product of her own stupidity, insanity, or faulty memory—she's unlikely to do anything about it.

With this in mind, I had long given up hope Renee would ever see the light and get the help she needs. Instead, I settled for praying Vance wouldn't graduate to violence, and e-mailing her periodically with a joke or silly photo to make sure she hadn't gone the way of Stacy or Laci Peterson. This didn't thrill me, of course, but it gave me peace of mind, and let her know I was there for her if she ever had a change of heart.

And so it was with a mixture of hope, dread, excitement and doubt that I held the phone and prepared to call her back. As much as I wanted to hear that she was leaving Vance—or had left him already—and was looking for support, I was even more afraid to find out how bad things had gotten since we last spoke. And while I knew better than to get my hopes up, it depressed me to know I couldn't dial her up without bracing myself for the worst.

The one bright spot I could see at this stage was the phone number that my cell had attributed to an unknown caller. Although it may have signaled nothing more than a new job or a change of address or service carrier, I allowed myself the faint hope that it meant something more. Among the list of potential explanations was the possibility she'd purchased a pay-as-you-go cell phone as a means of further circumventing Vance's efforts against consorting with her allies. Below that was the admittedly unlikelier but entirely preferable possibility she'd flown the coop and was now hiding out somewhere waiting for the dust to settle.

With this in mind and my fingers crossed, I pressed the send key and waited for Renee to pick up.

"Hi there," she said almost as if we spoke every day. "How are you?"

"I'm good. And yourself?"

"I'm doing great. I'm on the highway about halfway between Madison and La Crosse, and hoping you don't already have plans for the weekend."

I didn't, of course, other than to send Bunny some documents that morning and to kill time while Walker was out with Erica on Saturday night. Still, I didn't want to admit it without first finding out what was going on. I'd made that mistake more than once back in Waukesha, and wasn't about to spend two days listening to her cry only to see her go running back to Vance on Sunday.

"That depends," I said instead. "What's going on?"

Renee went on to explain that she had left Vance, and that she was looking to crash at my place over the weekend.

"You've left Vance?" I repeated. "As in, past tense? Over and done with? Done and dusted?"

"Yep."

"I was supposed to spend the weekend in Madison," she explained, referring indirectly to her parent's home and the one place she was allowed to go by herself, "so he's not expecting me to be home. Which means I can be gone for two, maybe three days before he finds out I've left."

"Won't he find out when you're parents call and ask why you haven't shown up?"

"Oh, they're not expecting me. I've already called and told them I'm not coming."

"Besides," she added with uncharacteristic confidence, "he's not home to answer the phone anyway. He left on a fishing trip with his dad and two brothers this morning, and won't be back until Monday afternoon."

Interesting. "What lake did they go to?"

"What difference does that make?"

"I'm just making sure they've gone far enough away that they won't drop back by the house for something unexpectedly," I lied.

In truth, I was checking her reaction to the question more than looking for flaws in her plan. Scott Peterson had claimed to be on a fishing trip when his wife went missing, too, after all; and just because Renee was the victim and not the abuser in her household didn't mean she hadn't put a new twist on an old ruse.

"They went somewhere in Illinois," Renee said, seemingly satisfied with my explanation. "It takes about five hours to get there, which is why they're taking four full days as opposed to just the weekend."

"Okay. Well, good. It sounds like you've got the element of surprise on your side. Do you have any money?"

"Yes. I took two hundred bucks out at the ATM this morning, and I have a cashier's check for forty-thousand-dollars in my purse."

Forty thousand dollars? "Where on earth did you get that?"

"We have an eighty-thousand-dollar home equity line of credit at the bank where we have our checking and savings accounts. We got it to cover the addition we're having built onto the back of the house later this month. So I had them cut me a check so I could pay the various contractors as their invoices come in. I figured, if I'm leaving, he sure as hell doesn't need that addition any more, and I'm definitely not walking away with nothing— especially since it was the money I made on the sale of my old house that got us the down payment for the new one, and my job and credit score that got us the original loan and the line of credit for the addition."

"Wow. Okay. So you have cash and a phone."

"And my own credit card and soon my own checking and savings accounts. I plan to open them with the cashier's check before I go apartment hunting on Monday."

"How did you decide how much to take?"

"I decided half of the line of credit was fair. That's more than I'll need to cover my bills until we reach our settlement and our divorce is final. And this way I won't be broke while we fight things out in court."

At that point, I had nothing to do but to sit in stunned silence. Renee sounded so lucid, so confident and composed—and so utterly unlike herself—I didn't know whether to congratulate her or call the police and advise them to start dragging the lakes.

"Okay, so what's next?" I asked instead. "What are your plans now that you've left?"

"Can we talk about that when I get there? I'm only about thirty minutes away and I want to save the units on my phone in case I need them later."

"No problem," I replied, once more impressed with her foresight. "I'll see you when you get here."

Having already showered, straightened the house, and remade the guest room, the only thing left to do in the few minutes before Renee arrived was to cancel my afternoon hair appointment and call Walker to warn him we were having company. Although he'd never met Renee, I'd seen enough people through crises for him to know what to expect in terms of the impact on his activities, and how to occupy himself while we were working things through.

Once that was settled, only two things were on my mind: Why had Renee finally decided to leave? And what would she do once she'd told Vance?

The first question gave me less trouble than the second. Since it was in the past, it couldn't be changed by anything I said or anything that might happen over the next couple days.

The second question, on the other hand, had my stomach in knots. Walking away from a man like Vance, although difficult, isn't the hard part; the real challenge lies in staying away from the bastard after you've made your escape. This is because abusers need their victims to fulfill their need for power and control, and while the worst of them may stalk, menace, threaten, maim, and kill their partners after they leave, those who have a reputation or an income to protect, or who lack the skill or will to cause genuine fear or harm, will instead use charm, guilt, remorse, and whatever else it takes to bring their victims back into the fold.

I had the answer to my first question less than twenty minutes after Renee appeared on my doorstep. Vance had evidently lived up to my expectations and struck her the previous weekend after they got home from an office party hosted by a colleague of his who lived down the street.

It started as they were changing clothes that evening, when she told him she didn't like the way he had flirted with two of the women he worked with, which she felt was inappropriate and disrespectful both to her and their spouses. To this Vance responded by telling Renee she was neither his mother nor his boss, and thus had no business policing his behavior.

"'Furthermore,'" Renee quoted him, "'no one has any respect for you in the first place. In fact, everyone I know—including your mother—feels sorry for me for having married you, and thinks you're lucky I don't put your sorry ass out on the street where you belong.'"

This is a common tactic among emotional batterers. They'll refuse to take responsibility for their actions or their impact on other people, and justify their behavior by twisting the facts and portraying themselves as victims. While a rational person—guilty or innocent—may deny having behaved inappropriately, or admit to doing so and apologize for it, and/or attempt to soothe the feelings of the spouse who was injured by it, the abusive personality will do none of these things. That's because the goal for an abusive person is not conciliation but control.

"He went on to say, if I don't like how he behaves in front of his coworkers, I can stay home next time."

Another common tactic: Hint at the negative consequences—in this case, isolation—that may result if the victim continues to question the abuser's behavior.

"The crazy thing is," Renee continued, "I didn't want to go with him *this* time. But when I tried to get out of it, Vance told me I had to go because if I didn't, his boss and colleagues would think there was something wrong between us, and his career would suffer because of it."

I nodded. "So you were damned if you did go, and damned if you didn't."

"Exactly. And I told him that. So then he says I'm full of shit—that he tried to get me to stay home so he wouldn't have to deal with me, and that I insisted on going along like I always do whenever he has an office function because I'm insecure and can't stand for him to have a good time without me, and because I'm a jealous, controlling bitch."

Yet more weapons in the abusers arsenal: Change the facts to suit your goals while accusing the victim of the same behavior you're displaying. That way, you not only get to play the victim, you can make the other person question their own motives and sanity. The list goes on and on.

"And the whole time he was yelling at me," Renee continued, "he kept getting closer and closer, until suddenly my back was against my dresser and I was convinced he was either going to choke me, or strangle me with his tie. So I put my hands up and pressed myself against his chest to create enough of a gap behind me to squeeze out from between him and the dresser. That's when he grabbed me by the wrist with one hand, backhanded me with the other, and sent me flying into the side of the closet.

"Thankfully I had put my arms up before I landed or there would have been marks on my face where I hit the door trim, and I wouldn't have been able to go to work without coming up with one really big whopper of a story."

"I'll say," I agreed, only then noticing the bruises on her forearms. "From the looks of things, you were damned lucky you didn't land face first or you may not have ever gotten up again."

Renee shrugged. "Not according to Vance. He said he'd hardly touched me and that I threw myself against the wall as a dramatic gesture to make him feel bad. Then he said he was only defending himself, and that he'd had no choice but to push me away to keep me from shoving him out of our bedroom and down the stairs."

I couldn't even imagine five-foot, two-inch, one-hundred pound Renee pushing her former hockey player husband backward an inch, much less across the room, through a doorway, and down the stairs. What a joke.

Laughable or not, this was a new—though not entirely unexpected—addition to Vance's playbook. Employed by many first time batterers and schoolyard bullies, the aim is to provoke a fear response in the victim that will result in physical contact, which the aggressor can then use to justify retaliation. That way, the abuser can claim he or she was acting in self-defense, and that the victim is to blame for any injury he or she sustains.

"'And don't go thinking you can run crying home to mama,'" Renee added, quoting Vance again. "'She's told me a million times you're a pain in the ass and that she doesn't understand how I've lived with you this long and haven't killed you already.'"

'I can hurt you worse than that,' is the implication here, 'and not even your own mother will do anything about it.' A frequent companion to the tactic described above, this strategy aims to convince victims that resistance is futile, and no one cares. So whereas a normal, rational person wants his or her partner to feel safe, secure, and loved, the abusive personality strives to instill fear and insecurity because doing so makes the victim easier to dominate and control.

"And this was last weekend?" I asked, surprised it had taken her six days to pack her bags.

Renee nodded.

"I decided while I was icing my arms that I had to leave, but knew it was in my best interests to take my time and come up with a plan in advance. And remembering what you said about not announcing my plans or doing anything out of the ordinary that might arouse suspicion, I acted like everything was normal. I even made sure to sulk, since that's what I would normally do after he accuses me of something or hurts my feelings. Meanwhile, I continued to work on my plan as I cleaned the house and did the gardening and the laundry on Sunday so, come Monday, I had it all worked out. I would cancel plans to visit my parents this weekend and arrange to take two full weeks off work, during which time I would get my own place and set up my own bank accounts. By then I would have already taken a portion of my share of the joint assets, so all I would need to do is find a lawyer and file for divorce."

"Wow," I mused guardedly. "You seemed to have really thought this through."

"Thanks."

"So, now, what should we do this weekend?" she asked, as if we were two friends on a road trip instead of counselor and client working out an escape plan. "I can't really look at any rentals until Monday, so we have until Sunday morning to hang out and have fun."

Although I was happy she'd decided to leave Vance—especially with his abuse having escalated to violence—her demeanor was trending a bit toward the manic, and I worried what would happen when the adrenaline that was clearly sustaining her now had been burned up and she came face to face with the consequences of her actions. She would need more than money and a place to live if she was going to see this thing through, and I needed to prepare her for that without making it sound like something she couldn't handle on her own.

Not wanting to kill her buzz just yet, I suggested a Julie Roberts movie marathon—minus *Sleeping with the Enemy*, of course—and decided to wait until morning to get serious. A good night's sleep will do her good, I reasoned, and then we'll have the whole day to fill in the gaps in her scheme.

But, as is often the case with best laid plans, I didn't have the chance to talk to Renee before the adrenaline hangover hit. Instead of waking up refreshed and ready to take on the day, she awoke with the jitters of an alcoholic who'd recently hopped on the wagon, and the expression of an addict who fears she won't make it another hour without scoring another hit.

"I have to go home," she announced after silently sipping at her coffee for the better part of an hour.

I had tried not to treat her like an inhabitant of the primate exhibit at the Brookfield Zoo, but kept finding myself looking her way and wondering what she was thinking as she stared into the light brown liquid in her mug. So I was good when she finally said something—even if it was negative. At least now I knew where to start.

"Why do you say that?" I asked rather than contradict her. It made no sense to argue, after all, since that might only induce her to dig her heels in deeper. Better to let her work through her doubts.

"Because it's the right thing to do, Roxanne. I've thought it through, and I realize I'm not cut out for this."

"Why not?"

"Well, for one thing, I don't know what to say to Vance."

"You don't have to say anything to Vance."

"He'll have to know I've left sooner or later. For God's sake, Roxanne, it's not like he won't notice I'm not there when he gets home on Monday."

"That's doesn't mean you have to explain it to him."

"Well someone has to tell him what's going on. Otherwise he might think I've gone missing or had an accident or something."

I got the impression Vance would be more concerned for the whereabouts and condition of the car than for the safety and well-being of his wife.

Still, Renee had a point. It would do her no favors with the court if her departure looked like a disappearance and caused a commotion for local law enforcement. And even if meant Vance had to sweat a little as the police looked into his means, motive, and opportunity, his suffering would hardly be worth the cost to Renee if he convinced them she had set things up to make him look bad, or out of a desperate need for attention.

"So send him a post card," I offered. "We can pop it in the mail today, and it'll be waiting for him in the mailbox when he gets back from fishing."

"It's not just that, Roxanne. I'm also thinking about how ugly things are going to get—especially when Vance finds out about the cash and the cashier's check. That's why it would be best for me to just go home, put the money back in the account, and forget this whole thing."

"And what about the unexpected forty-thousand dollar transactions he's going to find on your bank statement this month? Do you think he'll shrug them off without an explanation?"

"Of course not. But I'll just play that off like another one of my stupid mistakes. He'll have no trouble believing it since he thinks I'm a total dumbass anyway. Sure, he'll bitch for an hour or so about what a moron I am and how I've ruined his life, but I'm used to that. And it won't be anything compared to what he'll have to say to me if I don't go home and put it back."

"Well, I won't deny it, Renee. Things are going to get ugly. But as far as the money goes, it's as much yours as it is his, and you can direct your attorney to address your decision to use it as a means of temporary support when he or she drafts your divorce papers. That way, it doesn't look like you're trying to hide anything or pull something over on him."

"And when he tells our families—and mine comes screaming after me saying what a crazy, stupid bitch I am for leaving the only man who would put up with me? What then?"

"I never said it was going to be easy, Renee. But nothing worth doing ever is."

"Spare me the platitudes, Roxanne. Vance is going to crucify me, and my family is going to help him."

She wasn't wrong. Vance was not going to take this well, and neither would the monsters who primed her for life with the bastard. They depended on her playing the willing victim as much as Vance did.

"You're absolutely right," I admitted. "They will. But you're better off without them, too. Deep down, you know that."

It was then that Renee started to cry.

"I can't do this," she sobbed. "I just can't. I don't have it in me to fight both Vance and my parents. I'm just not cut out for it."

"That's not true, Renee."

"Look at everything you've done already," I reasoned. "You made a plan and waited for the perfect time to implement it. You created an excuse to explain to your parents why they wouldn't see you this weekend and arranged for time off work so you wouldn't lose your job while you set things in motion. And you managed to swipe forty thousand dollars right out from under Vance's nose and got your own credit card so he can't punish you financially or use money to blackmail you into coming home. Based on that information, I'd say you are more than capable of fighting this battle."

Renee eyed me doubtfully. There was hope there, too, but not enough to convince me I had convinced her.

Nevertheless, we continued to discuss the details of her decision—including her need for emotional support—over breakfast, and here and there between episodes from the last season of *Criminal Minds*, and during potty breaks between scenes. To boost her confidence and chances of success, I also made a few phone calls and got a couple referrals for therapists and support groups, and hoped as hard as I could that she would follow through.

Even as she said good-bye early Sunday morning, I wasn't sure she wouldn't go back home and undo everything she'd accomplished on Friday and pretend it never happened. But as there was nothing I could do one way or another, I had no choice but to let it go.

"So?" Walker asked as he emerged from his man cave later that morning. "What's the status?"

"Renee's gone. That's about all I can tell you. I don't know whether she's gone home or to a motel until she can find an apartment or what. I just know she's gone."

"I can't believe she didn't tell you what she was going to do."

"Oh, she told me what she's going to do. I'm not sure I should believe her."

"And how was your evening?" I asked since I'd been busy with Renee when he got home from his date with Erica the night before, and was already fast asleep when I climbed into bed with him several hours afterward.

Walker pondered that for a beat, and then laughed. "I'd have to say that *interesting* is the first word that comes to my mind."

Over eggs and toast, he then related to me the highlights of the evening, which featured a "Dating Game" style get-to-know-you format wherein they took turns asking questions of each other.

"Whose idea was that?" I asked, wondering if Walker had stumbled upon the perfect route to getting the information for his notes, or if Erica was the architect of the plan and he was merely an accidental beneficiary.

"Well, I'd love to be able to tell you it was mine, but unfortunately it was Erica's. And I am I glad she suggested it, since I can use it to get the information I need on future dates without looking like a deranged investigative journalist or a cop working on his interrogation technique."

"Of course, there was a huge difference between her questions and mine," Walker added with a degree of bewilderment. "For example, while mine involved open ended questions like, 'So what do you like to do on the weekends?' and 'What are your favorite books?' hers were a tad more specific."

"Such as?"

"'What is your idea of the perfect romantic getaway?'"

"Oh gross."

"Exactly."

"I can't believe anyone would ask that on the first date."

"Me either."

"But my favorite question, by far," Walker enthused, "and the one that surely would have put the nail in the coffin of our chances for a relationship were I truly looking for one, was 'What is the most romantic way you can think of for a man to ask a woman for her hand in marriage?'"

"Oh God. I think I just threw up a little."

Walker laughed.

"I'm not surprised," he admitted. "I did, too, at the time."

"What did you tell her?"

"The truth."

"Which is?"

"That I'd take the lucky lady on a camping trip and, while I was packing up the truck, I'd put a little box containing the engagement ring in the cooler so that when she went to get a beer or a soda later, she'd run across the box and jump for joy."

"Wow. I must say, Walker. That's pretty creative for an engineer. How'd you come up with that?"

"I overheard it in a bar once."

"And do you really think that's romantic?"

"Roxanne, I'm an engineer. I'm not sure I can even *define* romantic."

"Fair enough," I laughed. "So was Erica impressed?"

"Hardly."

"Although she had no problem with the idea of a camping trip," he explained, "evidently the lady does *not* fetch her own beverages."

"Well now, isn't she special?"

"That would be her take on it, I'm sure. In fact, I got the distinct impression she has already planned both her proposal and her wedding, and is simply looking to cast a man to fill the role of the groom—whom she has written not as a main or even secondary character, but as a walk-on or an extra."

"That is so sad."

"I'll say."

"Speaking of *sad*," Walker added with a laugh. "I talked to your mom while you were busy with Renee yesterday, and she said to tell you she's very disappointed by the lack of messages in her e-mail inbox this week."

"Crap. I meant to call her and explain, but then Renee arrived and time got away from me."

"That's what I said. Then I gave her a brief rundown of the challenges you faced this week, and told her I'd see to it that she got what she was looking for either tomorrow or Tuesday."

"Great, Walker. Thanks."

"No problem. So what exactly was it she was looking for?"

"Are you kidding?"

"No."

"So you seriously made a commitment on my behalf without even knowing what it was you were committing me to?"

"Why not? It's not as if you haven't done something similar to me in the recent past."

"That isn't completely true," I advised with a grin. "In your case, *you're* the one who made the commitment to *me* without knowing what it was *you* were committing to."

"Whatever," he replied with mock denial as he took my hand. "I say we just forget about all our commitments for a while, and go upstairs and try to rescue what little is left of our weekend."

Seven

As per Walker's promise, I scanned and forwarded Bunny the data the following week, along with instructions on how to use the spreadsheet I'd created to record it, and a gentle reminder not to share any conclusions she might draw from what she learned about the women Walker had met thus far—no matter how irrelevant or innocuous they might seem.

Also among the materials I forwarded were the responses to the surveys I had distributed, which I'd previously printed and placed in a pile to be read later.

The latest addition to the stack came from Natalie, who is one of the most interesting and audacious women on planet earth. Despite having been dumped by her mechanical engineer and occasional conspiracy theorist husband for a personal banker who apparently liked his blog, she has as much confidence as can possibly be contained within one body. She is also the most open-minded and adventurous person in my acquaintance. These are admirable traits when you're looking to introduce her to someone from a foreign country or a member of a non-mainstream religion; they can make it a bit unnerving when she calls to ask if she can bring another guest to dinner since she is just as likely to befriend an ex-con or a member of a radical vegan cooperative as she is a poet or a petrologist. For although I enjoy talking to new people and generally try to learn something from everyone I meet—some of our neighbors and associates are visibly less comfortable around folks who spend a lot of time off the beaten path.

As one would expect, Natalie's *joie de vivre* and affinity for the unconventional have influenced her romantic life and landed her in situations even the craftiest author couldn't invent. Evidence of this can be found not only in her survey, but also in a supplement she had attached containing highlights of her most memorable dates, and from the phone call I had to make immediately after reading the first entry.

"He brought an RV?" I asked as she picked up, knowing she would have seen my name appear on caller ID.

"It was actually more of a camper. You know—one of those pop-up jobbies that you pull behind your car or truck."

"So does he live in the damned thing? Or does he just have nowhere to park it?"

"Neither. In fact, the man has a house with a two-car garage and a camper pad. He only brought the camper along so he didn't have to pay for a hotel room."

"You are kidding."

"I wish."

"And he wasn't even remotely subtle about it," Natalie continued. "He just waltzed up, introduced himself, told me I was pretty, and announced that we wouldn't need a motel room after dinner because he had brought his *Jayco*."

I couldn't imagine Walker—or anyone, for that matter—dragging a camper along on a date in hopes of getting laid, much less admitting to it. I confess to being somewhat naïve due to having been off the market for over a decade, but it seemed to me that the singles scene had gotten really creepy in the electronic age.

"That is unreal," I breathed for lack of anything useful to contribute.

"I know, right?"

"Where do guys like that get their nerve?"

"Beats me."

"You have to wonder if that's worked for him in the past," I mused aloud, "or if he's one of these idiots who keeps trying the same old crap and never realizes what a loser he is."

"Well, in truth, it might have worked with me—if he hadn't looked so different from his picture, which clearly was taken about twenty years and twice as many pounds ago."

"Are you serious?"

"Well, yeah. I mean, the guy tries to pass himself off as my age and thinks, not only would I ignore the fact that he's old enough to be my father, but also that I'd sleep with him afterward? Please."

"So you might have slept with him if he wasn't old and out of shape? Or you might have slept with him if he hadn't lied about it?"

"Either one. Maybe both."

"It may sound impulsive," Natalie continued without prompting, "and insanely risky to sleep with a stranger in a camper in a parking lot, but it sounds kind of exciting at the same time. And is it any more risky or insane to sleep with someone under those conditions than it is to go home with someone you've just met in a bar? I mean, at least in a parking lot there's a chance someone will hear you calling for help if the guy turns out to be a psycho."

She had a point. Of sorts. Still, it seemed to me that it would be better not to have to rely on the kindness of passing strangers to save you from a psycho in a camper when you could have just avoided the psycho by not getting into the camper in the first place, but that's just me.

"That's fair," I observed genuinely. "But I wasn't judging. I was just clarifying."

"No problem. In truth, it wasn't the fact that he was older or heavier than he'd led me to believe that kept me from sleeping with him; what bothered me was how he handled himself when I brought it up—which I did as sensitively as anyone could. I mean, we all try to paint ourselves in the best light in our online profiles, but there's a big difference between saying you're a Stephen King fan when you've read just one of his books and telling someone you're in your thirties when in fact you're in your fifties. And I suppose I could have kept my mouth shut and let him move on to his next mark without saying anything, but I wanted to give him a chance to explain—if not because what he had to say may have changed my mind about him and allowed us to salvage the date, then because it would give him some insight into how women respond to things like that and help him be more successful in the future."

That's Natalie. For some people life is a contest or a competition; for her it's experience and education. That perspective is what makes her such a fun and interesting person. Unfortunately, it also leaves her vulnerable to a lot of pain and frustration. Seems to me her personal security settings should be set a little further toward exclusive, but she prefers them wide open.

"But I guess he just wanted me to pretend the emperor had clothes or something," she was saying now, "because instead of acting embarrassed or explaining himself like any reasonable person would, he pointed out how different I looked from my photo, and said that, at my age, beggars can't be choosers."

"Oh my God."

"Tell me about it."

"I didn't even finish my meal," she huffed. "I just threw a twenty-dollar bill on the table, and walked out."

"What an ass."

"One hundred and ten percent."

"Still," Natalie added with an audible shrug, "he's not the worst. That distinction goes to the guy who told me only *after* we had ordered dinner and a bottle of wine that I'd have to get the check because he'd driven further and had to pay more for gas."

Wow. "So did you?"

"Hell no. He knew how far he had to drive and how much the meal would cost when he suggested that location, and could have arranged to meet somewhere closer and less expensive. The fact that he had done neither—and that he hadn't bothered to tell me until we were sitting in this posh place surrounded by people that we weren't splitting the bill— told me that the guy was a cheap-ass son of a bitch who planned to have himself a nice dinner and stick me, the desperate single woman, with the tab all along.

"But rather than argue with him," Natalie explained almost serenely, "I decided to play along. So I smiled as we ate our appetizer, smiled as we enjoyed our meals, and smiled some more as I listened to him yammer on about his job and watched him drink most of the wine. I continued to smile as he ordered coffee and dessert, and then smiled as I excused myself to the ladies room and left him to wait for them to arrive. I was still smiling when, instead of going to the bathroom, I went to the bar, paid for my dinner, half of the appetizer, and one glass of wine, plus tip, and walked out, leaving him to pay for everything else."

"Well played. Did you ever hear from him again?"

"Sure did. I had a lovely one-word message waiting for me the next morning at the website where we'd met. I'll give you two guesses as to what it said."

"Hmm. By any chance did it rhyme with *witch*?"

"Funnily enough—it did."

"My, how decent of him to confirm what you had already gleaned about him the night before."

"My thoughts exactly."

"What amazes," Natalie added with a touch of fascination, "is how many men lack the basic social skills to build a friendship with women, never mind a romantic relationship."

It didn't amaze me at all. Annoy, irritate, frustrate? Sure. But *amaze* carries with it a degree of curiosity that for me is simply not there.

What does amaze me is how people who are successful at relationships are typically able and willing to look at their behavior and adjust it to improve things between themselves and others, while those who are historically unsuccessful at relationships never even consider that they're doing something wrong. Instead, they'll blame and cast aspersions on their former partner—or on their former partners' friends or new partners for interfering or horning in—and never put an ounce of time or effort into examining, much less changing, their own actions, habits, or attitudes.

Obviously this tendency isn't unique or common to the men populating the Internet. We need only look at Dean and Marty to know that arrogance and assholes predate the web, and to all the gentlemen who don't bring campers on dates or lie about their age to know that the net isn't solely the province of scoundrels and pigs.

Nor is it unique to men. Although at times it may seem as though men have cornered the market in the mate-from-hell department, according to my male and lesbian sources, women can be just as arrogant, controlling, and otherwise obnoxious as the next guy.

The sad truth is, like other recent inventions, the Internet as a dating tool is a double-edged sword. On the one hand, it has the potential to help shy, awkward, or busy adults connect with people whom they might otherwise never encounter. On the other hand, it gives assholes and others with poor social skills access to people who normally wouldn't want anything to do with them. So while the web has made it easier for normal people to interact with potential viable mates, it also allows losers, monsters, and weirdoes to hide the fact that they drool, have horns, or collect hair or nail clippings until who-knows-how-long after you've started chatting with them.

"It's a jungle out there," Natalie concluded as if she'd read my mind. "You're so lucky to be out of that game."

She didn't have to tell me. I didn't date strangers before I started seeing Walker, and no amount of money could convince me to start now. In fact, if Mr. Browne and I ever split up, the only thing I'll be looking for on the Internet will be an alarm system or a Schutzhund-trained German shepherd.

Of course, Natalie didn't have to be in that particular game either. She could opt to sit the bench until she met someone *in person* whom she wanted to spend time with, but apparently that approach is too old-fashioned or slow to bear fruit in the age of smartphones and speed dating. It's as if the fact that you *can* look for love on the net dictates that you *must*.

An avid believer in the *Thumper Principle—if you can't say something nice, don't say anything at all*—I decided to keep these observations to myself.

"Well, I guess I should get back to work," I offered instead. "Thanks for your help with the research."

After spending the weekend with and worrying about Renee, it was refreshing to talk to someone who consistently lives life on her own terms and takes no crap from anyone. Although she didn't actively choose to start over again at thirty-five, as always, Natalie did what she could with the cards she'd been dealt and made them work for her.

Of course, there are some who think she should have played them differently. Her mom, for one, says Natalie should have been a more available and accommodating spouse, and accuses her of taking her marriage for granted. Her view is that Natalie was so focused on her job, hobbies, and causes that she failed to give Curt the time and attention he needed, which forced him to look elsewhere for comfort, support, and companionship. Others in her large, outspoken—and apparently incredibly sexist—family share this position, asserting that Curt wouldn't have left if Natalie hadn't failed to make him feel like a man; that she should have been more attuned to his needs; and that she was crazy to let him go without a fight.

Aunt Charlotte echoed this position after I had related that conversation to Bunny one day while she was visiting, adding that women should align their interests to suit their men, and intimating that those who fail to do so basically deserve what they get. "Like satisfaction," Bunny offered dryly in reply, "and the freedom to find someone with a smaller, less fragile ego?"

Charlotte had let the remark pass—assuming she'd understood it, that is, bless her clueless little heart—and instead of taking the bait or seeking clarification, shared a couple of deliberately chilling anecdotes about her own divorced friends to further illustrate the perils of independence.

To be honest, I had expected as much from Charlotte. She is a product of her time and her upbringing, after all, and has never been particularly curious or contemplative. Younger than her brother and sisters by several years, Charlotte processed their father's death quite differently than her siblings did, and was required to do nothing to help the family cope in his absence. Coddled and cosseted by well-meaning relatives, neighbors, and foster parents, she never learned to think or care for herself, and instead came to rely on the kindness and favorable opinion of others for happiness and survival. Meanwhile, having been too young to remember her father, she conjured an impossibly virtuous image of the man that would influence her impressions and approach to the opposite sex for the rest of her life. This is hardly uncommon among women who have lost a parent in their youth; but whereas most of them see their fathers' characters as the standard by which other men are measured and often found wanting, Charlotte wanted to love and be loved by everyone, and consequently painted all men with the same flattering brush. "Charlotte views men as gods to be worshipped and praised," Bunny explained to me years ago, "and those who could not were to be excused and loved even more."

This philosophy, combined with her beauty and abundant charm, enabled Charlotte to enjoy an active social life, and to get whatever she wanted from nearly any man she encountered. Given her naïveté and tendency to overlook the bad in the opposite sex, it was only dumb luck that she didn't wind up with her generation's version of Dean, Marty, or Vance. To Bunny's interminable relief, she instead landed Uncle Gene, proud owner of a direct mail printing firm, who puts the appropriately attractive, bubbly, and domestically inclined Charlotte on a pedestal, and approaches less innocuous women like creatures from another galaxy.

With this in mind, one can almost forgive Charlotte's perspective, but the same can hardly be said of Natalie's mom, Temple, who manages to find fault with nearly everything Natalie does while offering a seemingly inexhaustible stream of excuses and praise for Natalie's brother, Russell, who's been through drug treatment twice and in jail three times. Her attitude, it seems, is not rooted in the loss of a father figure, but in a tradition of gender bias for which Natalie says her entire family is famous.

To illustrate this point, Natalie once shared a story involving her cousin Kelly, who was the first member of their family to earn a college degree. To mark the occasion, Kelly and her then-fiancé planned a big party that no relatives but her parents and her cousins attended. Later, when she inquired as to why her grandparents, aunts, and uncles had skipped the celebration, she was told the event didn't warrant a two-hour drive; but they all would be up to visit when she has a baby.

I would go insane if I had to face that kind of thing on a regular basis, but Natalie—as usual—zeroed in on the silver lining.

"That's why the girls in my generation are all so successful," she explained. "We've seen what having most favored status has done for the boys in our family—most of whom dropped out of school, have gotten into trouble with the law, and have fathered at least one child without the benefit of marriage—and decided that we want something—and someone—better. So we work hard, do well in school, go to college, make our own way, and with a few exceptions, choose partners who appreciate intelligence, education, and independence in women."

I couldn't be so blithe about it all if I were her. In fact, it maddens me to think that anyone could blame her own daughter for her son-in-law's infidelity. While Natalie's confidence and adventurous streak may have contributed to the demise of her marriage insofar as they moved her to take up causes and projects that held no attraction for Curt and that kept her too happy and satisfied with her life to wonder if her husband was banging someone on the side, they were in no way, shape, manner, form, or fashion the direct cause for their divorce. Curt is a grown man, after all, who isn't the least bit lacking in confidence and—not unlike my friend Janine— could have spoken up if he was unhappy or unsatisfied, instead of slinking off to play doctor with any one of the *seven* women Natalie ultimately learned he had screwed since their wedding. The fact that he didn't say anything until six months into his latest affair—and then only because his paramour was pushing him to move in together and Natalie most certainly would have noticed the lack of clothing on his side of the closet or a third toothbrush next to the bathroom sink—should prove to anyone that he was less a lonely man than a womanizing bastard.

Even if you buy the idea that it was due to dissatisfaction or neglect that Curt strayed, that wouldn't excuse the fact that he carried on multiple affairs—three of them lasting more than two months—behind Natalie's back. Although the fact that she was totally content with her construct of their lifestyle and trusted Curt to *communicate with* rather than *cheat on* her may have made it easier to deceive her, it hardly justifies his infidelity or makes it her fault.

How could she not have known? some might ask; *there had to have been signs.* People ask this kind of question because they like to think they couldn't be duped this way. They don't want to imagine themselves being blindsided and hurt as others have been. So they'll point to this event or that behavior, and describe how it would have tipped them off if they had been in that relationship or situation.

And they're not necessarily wrong. There may have been signs of Curt's infidelity which a less secure or more suspicious woman would not have missed or allowed him to explain away.

But it's not healthy to spend your life waiting for the other shoe to fall, and you could drive yourself crazy looking for symptoms of infidelity and duplicity in every word or action. The fact is that people in relationships have to be able to trust one another, and because the healthiest and most trustworthy among us are generally the most trusting, the liars will occasionally get the better of them.

Including yours truly. That's right. For all my training and experience, I never imagined Natalie and Curt wouldn't make it. When they were together, they seemed happy in a genuine, natural kind of way. They were openly affectionate and visibly appreciative of one another's attention. Although they spent less time together outside of the home than other couples I've known, they called one another often, flirted frequently via text message, and occasionally met for quickies when they were between meetings. It was for these and other reasons that even Kristin and Laurel, who've known Natalie twice as long as I have, were just as floored as I was to hear Curt was leaving and—until they found out about all the mistresses—predicted the two would ultimately work things out.

The same cannot be said—it's worth noting—of Alethia Dornquast. In addition to having declared herself an authority on all subjects from common to obscure, Alethia fancies herself a clairvoyant of sorts and claims to have predicted the demise of Natalie's and other marriages well before they dissolved, based purely on her unmatched interpersonal intelligence. The fact that she kept all such prophecies and prognostications to herself—ostensibly out of respect for the parties involved—until each divorce or separation became common knowledge is irrelevant, of course. Alethia would never let a lack of evidence undermine her assertions, especially when she knows her cohorts are all too polite to challenge them. But I digress…

In addition to claiming to have predicted the failure of Natalie and Curt's marriage, Alethia has—without compunction or compassion—

placed the blame squarely on Natalie's shoulders. Her theory, which she revisits whenever the conversation veers toward some broken relationship or another—no doubt in hopes of reminding us all how wise and prescient she is—is that Natalie was bored and wanted out of her marriage, so she drove Curt into the arms of other women in hopes that he would leave her and then ignored evidence of his infidelity so she didn't have to be the bad guy.

Words could not express my disgust the first time I heard this. While it's true that people don't always recognize their own feelings or act in their own best interests, you don't say shit like that to someone whose husband has just broken her heart, and you don't continue to repeat it at regular intervals for months afterward.

Predictably, Natalie is far less offended by Alethia's hypothesis than Kristin and I are on her behalf. So instead of sitting there frozen with shock and disbelief like we did the first time we heard it, she simply smiled and nodded as if giving it serious consideration.

"You could be right," she then offered earnestly as I bit my tongue and nearly died of oxygen deprivation. "I'll have to give that some thought."

Subsequent visits to that topic area have terminated at roughly the same point, which suggests that either Natalie finds the idea as preposterous as Kristin and I do but doesn't want to reject it outright and inadvertently entice Alethia to elaborate or make a stronger case, or that she really does intend to ponder it a bit but keeps forgetting to do so. In truth, with Natalie, neither scenario is any more or less likely than the other.

In any event, she has bounced back. Gone are the puffy, bloodshot eyes. Gone are the gloomy grey sweats and yoga pants she lived in for weeks on end. In their place are the vivid green eyes that literally sparkle with enthusiasm, and the jewel-tone blouses, scarves, and jackets she likes to pair with her trademark black jeans and leather boots. More importantly, instead of lying in bed awash in rage and despair, she's back on her feet and marching again to the beat of her own drum.

Which is good, since in my experience, people who can't move on or who fail to chart their own course generally come to regret it. Whether they do so out of guilt, fear, anger, insecurity, misplaced selflessness, or just sheer stupidity, those who wallow in their misery, let other people call the shots, or consistently place the needs of others ahead of their own are rarely happy or fulfilled, and almost always become sad, bitter individuals in the end.

A classic example of this is my Uncle Mel, who as mentioned earlier, has in his wake a string of failed relationships with lovely but damaged women and now—approaching sixty—is angry, broke, and alone. Ruled by profound insecurity and a need to play the hero, he is unable to forge a relationship with any damsel who is not in some kind of distress. Like my Aunt Charlotte's husband, Gene, he can only relate to women as mothers, daughters, sisters, or potential lovers. Thus, we who prefer to be treated as intelligent, independent individuals simply do not compute. In fairness to Mel, intelligent, independent women are no more likely to be attracted to him than he is to them given his creepy propensity for innuendo and gratuitous displays of gallantry. That said, if such a woman were ever willing and able to overlook his appallingly awkward social skills, he likely would find an excuse to reject her before she had a chance to run away.

At any rate, with these and other issues having deprived Mel of a mutually acceptable committed relationship, he now sits among the angry white men who blame women, lawyers, judges, and—by association— the government (which happens to include the police, thanks to one dazzlingly well-enforced restraining order) for their problems. Never mind that it was he who gave his last fiancée access to his bank accounts, only to have his assets seized by her former bank to settle a previously undisclosed debt; lent his car to a woman whose estranged ex had both a temper and a penchant for property damage; and turned up at another woman's workplace to request a more detailed explanation for breaking up with him. It is not Mel, but women, their lawyers, the judicial system, and the government as a whole who are responsible for his being solitary and nearly penniless.

Another example is Walker's friend and former colleague, Heath. Divorced after fifteen years of marriage to a woman he would describe at literally every opportunity both before and after their split as Evil Incarnate, Heath stayed with Cindy out of an unwavering and oft-repeated conviction that the courts are biased against men, and that she would not only get the kids but also take him for everything he had. Doubting the premise of his assertions—and, privately, his characterization of the conveniently unseen and unheard source of his discontent—I would now and then get dragged into a debate with Heath over the wisdom of staying in a loveless marriage. In return for my imprudence, I would be treated *not* to examples of cases that had been heard in his jurisdiction that highlight the inherent unfairness of the legal system or even to anecdotes involving friends whose divorces were inequitably discharged. Instead, he provided a litany of Cindy's transgressions dating back to four months before their wedding when she insisted on honeymooning in the Bahamas instead of Maui, which included such diverse and mystifying offenses as campaigning on behalf of political candidates he did not like; forcing him to delay going to graduate school until she had finished her BA; dictating the neighborhood in which they bought their home; refusing to allow him to name their third child after his Uncle Oscar; and, finally, laying claim to 50 percent of their joint assets, including a motor home that—he would grumble—she hadn't even wanted him to buy in the first place.

On their face, these charges sound minor to the point of petty, but combined with his regular diatribes against teachers unions, the ACLU, the IRS and Hillary "Ramrod" Clinton, they suggest to me that it is not Cindy—nor any advocacy group, government body, or political figure— that is responsible for his misery. Rather, it is his own deep sense of powerlessness and refusal to do anything but bitch about his situation that transformed the handsome and otherwise successful Heath from a warm and friendly man into an embittered old crank.

Of course, those who don't make the full journey from dissatisfied and unhappy to resentful and bitter—due to some unexpected intervening factor like, say, a midlife crisis or sudden twist of fate or fortune—may appear much more pleasant, but they'll make for no less frustrating companions. They may not annoy you with persistent grousing or arouse your sympathies with their endless tales of woe; but they will bore you senseless with talk of bucket lists and wake-up calls, and platitudes like "Today is the first day of the rest of your life." The more miserable they were, the more exuberant they'll be as they prattle on about some new hobby they've taken up or some feat of daring they've just completed as if no one else had ever done or even thought of it before. As if that weren't enough, if you decline to join them in one of these pursuits, they'll gaze upon you with pity and accuse you of being repressed, boring, or chicken shit.

What they don't seem to get, and as I've told Janine more than once— most recently when she tried to talk me into getting a tattoo after one of her dates mentioned that he finds them sexy—is that people who consistently run their own lives are generally satisfied with who and where they are and therefore won't have a litany of things they want or need to do before they die. They may have a goal or two that they're putting off for a better time—like, say, when they have the money or the kids are older—but because they've never let guilt, selflessness, or fear of disapproval get in their way, they aren't obsessed with what they haven't done, and thus have nothing to prove to themselves or anyone else.

Of course, as Natalie and countless other people have found, living life on your own terms won't guard you against infidelity, fraud, or any other calamity or misfortune that has ever befallen humankind. It will, however, make whatever challenges you happen to encounter far easier to manage, and ultimately make your life more satisfying.

No one in my circle seems to grasp this better than Kristin, who knows a thing or two about sticking to your guns, and who both embraces and embodies the notion that what doesn't kill you makes you stronger. Having amicably split from her boys' dad, Jared, years ago (amicably, that is, until two years ago when he called to inform her of his impending acquisition of a new wife and a three-year-old stepdaughter, and to make a case for cutting her child support—soon after which she was forced to haul his ass into court and let a judge to do the math, thereby drawing first blood in what has since become an all-out war) she generally does what she wants and, with few exceptions, manages to do so without pissing anyone off in the process. A fellow adherent to the *Thumper Principle*, she may not always say exactly what she's thinking when it comes to the likes of Alethia, but she is someone you can always count on to keep her word, tell the truth when asked, and to stand her ground when it comes to what she feels is right.

Remarkably, this has not always been the case. By her own account, Kristin was a late bloomer in terms of assertiveness and self determination owing to the fact that, until a reality-shattering encounter with unplanned pregnancy, she had never needed to stand up to or for anyone, and had little to no experience with adversity.

Raised in a close, middle-class family of six in Sparta, a town of just under a thousand people about thirty miles northeast of La Crosse, she had what she characterizes as an idyllic childhood filled with love, laughter, and as much excitement that a place with a bicycle museum and an annual butter festival has to offer. In fact, until she got herself knocked up at the ripe old age of twenty-one, the only real hardships she had ever faced were the death of an old family dog and a handful of unusually harsh winters. With her closest comrades similarly situated and her parents lacking the vast network of colorful (as in crazy, self-destructive, et cetera) relatives, friends, and associates with whom families like mine have been blessed, Kristin never had the opportunity to learn even vicariously about divorce, delinquency, abuse or addiction, or to appreciate their role in promoting resiliency, conferring survival skills, and curing naiveté.

This lack of experience with domestic drama and dysfunction, as she tells it, was a mixed blessing. On the one hand, it enabled her to acquire the character and confidence to pursue a variety of interests without the angst, guilt, insecurity, and bad habits she now knows can hamper people from more chaotic homes. On the other hand, the relative comfort in which she advanced from birth to young adulthood also gave her the false impression that her entire life would be a cakewalk, and left her utterly unprepared to deal with conflict, crisis, tragedy, or failure.

It could have been worse, I reasoned privately upon hearing this. *That sort of upbringing could have rendered her ignorant of those less fortunate than herself, and compromised her ability to feel or express compassion, kindness, or sensitivity.*

Fortunately, these and other positive characteristics—loyalty, honesty, generosity—were modeled well and often by her mother, who could always be counted on to provide a week's worth of hot meals to a grieving family; donate a pint whenever the bloodmobile was in town; and to organize a pancake breakfast or chili supper on behalf of someone in need of costly medical treatment. That her efforts were directed at helping victims of involuntary crises such as disaster and disease might be an issue for people who devote themselves to bigger causes and problems of a more self-induced variety, but the important thing—in my view, at least—is that, although Kristin knew little of sacrifice or suffering, she was not raised to be shallow or spoiled.

Ultimately, however, the so-called gaps in her education were filled, thanks to her affiliation with Jared, whom she met over spring break during her junior year at the University Wisconsin right here in La Crosse. Then a senior at Ohio State, Jared was slated to attend Army Officer Candidate School that June, and report to his first duty station soon afterward. With that in mind, and knowing the prospects of forging a successful long-term relationship from a whirlwind romance—even without the added complication of distance—they agreed to keep in touch, and take things slow.

All was going well in that regard until a few weeks later when Kristin missed her period and subsequently discovered why. Unwilling to terminate the pregnancy but steadfast in her goal of finishing her degree, she decided to have the baby—which was due around Christmas—and stay in school on a part-time basis, if necessary, after that. This required her to give up her apartment near campus and move back in with her parents, who while disappointed by the circumstances, were thrilled to be having a grandchild and therefore completely supportive of her decision.

That arranged, and with no intention of pressuring him to help, Kristin shared the news with Jared, who immediately—and unexpectedly—proposed. Having known him for less than sixty days, and convinced he was only "doing the right thing," she declined his proposal, and told him of her plan to move in with her folks, have the baby, and finish college. There was no need to rush, she reasoned; instead, they should continue in their individual pursuits and maximize their respective earning potential. In the meantime, they could get to know one another and, if it still seemed like a good idea, revisit the issue of marriage at some point down the road.

Everything was going according to plan until that November when Kristin went into preterm labor and landed in the hospital. Determined not to fall behind in her studies while the doctors kept labor at bay long enough for the baby's lungs to mature, she arranged with her instructors to complete the semester on a correspondence basis, and for her brother Zach, then a freshman at UW-L, to courier papers, exams, and other materials to and from the school on her behalf.

Eventually Kristin's dedication—or stubbornness, as her family fondly called it—paid off, since one week before Christmas she managed to deliver an eight-pound baby boy and pass all four of her courses without losing her spot on the dean's list.

Jared didn't make it to Wisconsin in time for the big event, but he did turn up the day before New Year's Eve bearing gifts that included a half-karat princess-cut diamond engagement ring. Rendered senseless by the mood of the season and the post-partum hormones, she succumbed to Jared's charm and the not-so-subtle encouragement of the well-meaning friends and family who had unanimously declared him a keeper, and imprudently—to use her term—agreed to marry him. In the back of her mind, she says, she knew even then it was a mistake, as she resisted setting a date until well into the new year, and then only did so to get people to stop asking.

"The only smart thing I did during that entire episode," she says with a sigh, "was insist on delaying the wedding until after I graduated. If I hadn't had the sense to do that, I probably wouldn't have ever gotten my degree, and I would have never again been able to look myself in the mirror."

The baby, whom she named Nicholas, was perfectly healthy, and surprisingly mellow and easygoing. As a result—and thanks to her mom's rather conveniently timed "retirement" from volunteer work and her gardening club, Kristin was able to complete her remaining credits in one term, and to finish her degree in business administration right on schedule.

With her graduation all but assured, and Jared having proven both acceptable to the army and sincere in his desire to have and support a family, Kristin set about to plan their wedding, and by the end of the summer had joined him at his command in Memphis. Not long after she arrived there, they had a second son, Patrick, and things seemed to be going—outwardly, at least—swimmingly.

That perception changed, however, when Kristin's mom came down with lymphoma, prompting her to pack up the boys and return to Sparta. Amid talk of radiation, chemotherapy, and bone marrow transplants, Kristin happily played the dutiful daughter—taking care of the house, the shopping, and her younger brothers, all the while caring for her own now school-age boys—so her dad could be at her mother's side for every appointment, test, and procedure.

Although the circumstances were grave, they proved secretly convenient for Kristin, who had been miserable as a military wife, and desperate to find a means of escape. Unable to cultivate a career of her own due to the demands of two small children and the nature of army life, she had grown to regret the series of choices that had brought her to this point, and to resent Jared and his success. Thus, while she was alarmed by her mother's illness and what it might mean for her family, she was privately grateful for the excuse to return to Wisconsin. Even if it meant she still had two kids and no recent experience on which to build a career, she welcomed the chance to leave Jared before her resentment evolved into hostility and their home became a combat zone.

Confessing all this to him several weeks later when he was in Sparta on leave, she was surprised to find him puzzled, hurt, and desperate to make changes that would entice Kristin to come home and work things out. Convinced she had already ruined his life and not wanting to make matters worse, she rejected his offer to leave the military, but agreed to give him time to find a billet on a base closer to Sparta so they could reunite and give their marriage a second chance. In the meantime, she would stay with her parents and find a part-time job to give both her resume and her self-esteem a needed boost, but take no actions that would have permanent consequences for the future.

Due in equal parts to a dearth of available billets in Jared's field in the upper Midwest and Kristin's devotion to her various interests and commitments—not to mention what she describes as an abject lack of anything in common apart from an overwhelming physical attraction— the two grew steadily apart and eventually divorced. For the sake of the boys, they agreed to keep their demands fair and their interactions civilized, and to manage as many issues as possible without involving the courts. With these goals in mind, and the assistance of a mediator, they devised a custody and visitation arrangement that suited them both and negotiated a child support figure that, when combined with Kristin's wages from her part-time job as the substitute coordinator for the local school district, would allow her to afford her own place once her mom's condition improved and she no longer felt the need to live under the same roof.

By the time that day came, Kristin had already traded the substitute coordinator job for a full-time position in the personnel office and was eyeing a management slot that was likely to be vacated soon. Later, when budget cuts prevented the county from filling certain positions and doctors had confirmed that her mom's cancer was firmly in remission, she gathered the nerve to cast a wider net and landed a job in the HR department of the *Post-Courier*, where she was when we met. She has since left that role to work for the county, thanks to their superior medical and dental benefits, and her intense distaste for Ken Lawrence, whose lack of ethics prompted her to look elsewhere not long before he was unexpectedly dismissed. These and other timely choices enabled her to avoid asking for increases in child support, which eased her guilt over having left Jared, and gave her back the personal pride and autonomy she had lost upon getting married and becoming—in military terms—his dependent.

Thus it was out of neither greed nor spite that Kristin objected to his request to decrease his monthly payments. If that were the case, he would have found himself in court a lot sooner and a whole lot more often. The real issue was that, having never asked him to increase his support since they first went to court, she knew Jared was getting off pretty easily. A reasonable woman who hadn't complained on any of the handful of occasions his payments arrived late, she would have considered a temporary reduction, or even one necessitated by unforeseen and unavoidable circumstances; but having never petitioned for an increase in support even as Jared worked his way up to the rank of major—and knowing that the cost of raising her boys was more likely to go up rather than shrink as they got involved in sports and started driving—she was definitely not prepared to accept a *decrease*, much less one prompted by Jared's admirable yet essentially irrelevant decision to support someone else's child.

Not surprisingly, the judge saw it her way and not only refused to reduce Kristin's child support, but also raised it significantly. He also backdated the increase to the month of his promotion to captain four years prior, but instead of ordering it paid as a lump sum, allowed him to pay it along with his regular installments over the next two years.

With Kristin's own career having begun to bloom, she had neither asked for nor anticipated the back pay, but this was of no consequence to Jared. Displeased by the ruling and the impact it would have on his new family, he vowed to appeal the judge's order at his earliest opportunity. He argued that because Kristin was living with her folks when he was promoted to captain, her expenses did not warrant an increase in child support. He also threatened to sue for full custody on the grounds that he could now provide a two-parent home, which would require Kristin to pay him instead of the other way around.

Although he could not see it, Kristin knew that Jared's problem wasn't with her, but with the fact that he wasn't used to losing. Like her up to the point of their fateful meeting that spring, he had never suffered or wanted for anything. Meanwhile, having always gotten what he wanted in life by virtue of his personality, intelligence, and wholesome good looks, he had no experience with loss or failure until Kristin left him, and then lived in a sort of state of suspended reality—working hard, and saying and doing all the right things in the hope that life would one day be again what it had been. When he finally snapped out of it—thanks in no small part to the woman who would eventually become his fiancée—he was angry at all the time he'd wasted, and at Kristin for having already moved on. Thus, he viewed a decrease in child support as his right—a sort of compensation, if you will, for his time and effort—and her opposition to it as both evidence of selfishness and an obstacle in his own pursuit of happiness.

That he ultimately wound up paying even more did not help matters. Even though it was a point of law and not a demand made on Kristin's part that triggered it, Jared blamed her for the outcome since it was she who had petitioned the court for a new hearing. Disregarding the fact that she wouldn't have sought relief from the court if he had just followed the original order and not shorted her support payments three months in a row, he now treats her like a gold-digger and fights her for literally every dime. Add to that the fact his efforts to get the case moved to Ohio have been thwarted by his home state's refusal to grant him a hearing, and one can imagine how pleasant things can be when there are medical bills, vacations, and holidays to negotiate.

Despite his hostility and pettiness, Kristin has vowed to remain patient and to give Jared time to work through his issues. Without absolving him totally of his sins—he did, after all, violate a court order and their pact to remain fair and civil—she bears the bulk of the blame for their problems since it was she who allowed herself to be talked into getting married before she was ready; she who allowed herself to be talked out of divorce when she knew her feelings weren't going to change; she who let Jared cling to false hope by not encouraging him to move on; and she who failed to seek more support earlier, as if letting Jared keep more of his own money would somehow make up for having deprived him of the life and family he had envisioned.

Of course, Kristin wasn't the first person to be punished for her good intentions and she won't be the last. That said, she claims to have learned from her mistakes and seems determined not to repeat them. Having basically fallen into motherhood and been all but railroaded into marriage in her youth, she now plots her own course rather than being force-marched toward a given path, or drifting along like a scent on a breeze. Like anyone with a conscience, she's also eager to make amends for the problems caused by her failure to honestly communicate her needs.

"Don't get me wrong," she had said after recounting her story to me over a protracted lunch break not long after we met. "I love my boys and don't regret having either of them. I just know that if I'd been more intentional and responsible in my actions, and if I'd been more honest with myself and others about what I wanted, I could have saved my kids, my ex, myself, and my parents a whole lot of pain and frustration."

Unlike many who've learned the hard way to assert themselves and to call their own shots, Kristin does so without a chip on her shoulder or even a hint of cynicism in her tone. Rather, she is probably the most positive, openhearted person I know of after Natalie, Pollyanna, and Mother Teresa—the latter of who was venerated and, technically, compensated, for her goodness and therefore doesn't count.

Perhaps her sunny disposition is the result of having been raised in a loving family in the middle (or rather, the upper middle) of America's heartland. Or maybe it's the product of nature and therefore would have materialized regardless of when or how she came into her own, or where or by whom she was raised. Either way, by regaining control over her life, trying to make amends for her missteps, and maintaining a positive attitude, Kristin has improved her chances for a satisfying future and, by her example, is giving her boys the tools to do the same.

Happily, Kristin's boundless optimism and receptiveness haven't compromised her ability to appreciate irony. This works in my favor given my knack for finding the absurd in everything and almost pathological need to explore and share it. Especially when it comes to some of the e-mails we get from Alethia—which, variously, lecture us on some topic that someone happened to mention in a previous message; entreat us to donate to some obscure cause she's supporting for the singular and entirely obvious purpose of looking hip and socially conscious; or invite us to take note of some success achieved by Mr. Dornquast that she'll insist on recounting using *we* and *us*, as if she, personally had set pen to paper and designed the schematic for upgrading the electrical grid or slapped on a hardhat to pour the foundation for some fancy new parking structure—I can always depend on Kristin to join me in a game of e-mail pong consisting of delightfully catty private messages relating to the quality and quantity of obnoxious self-promotion to which we had been jointly and unwillingly subjected. As a grown woman, I'm almost ashamed to admit to wasting hours and untold kilobytes of code riffing on Alethia's e-mail excrement or dissecting some load of crap she offered up the evening before—but not quite.

Kristin, on the other hand, does have a conscience, which apparently starts to plague her after this kind of exchange. This is evident from the way she'll end a volley with something like, "God love her, but does she seriously think she knows Natalie's hair better than Natalie does?" or, "I'm sure she means well, but would it not have occurred to her that one of us might also know *something* about the origin of Mardi Gras?" Clearly I have a thing or two to learn about contrition since I find nothing at all wrong with taking the piss out of someone who is so deeply and unrepentantly convinced of her own superiority—especially if it's done behind her back and the purpose is primarily cathartic.

Not that Alethia would know we were talking about her if we did *not* do it behind her back. In fact, as a self-described expert on everything, if asked for advice on managing an insufferable narcissist, she probably would be more than happy to elucidate. But again I digress…

Just as Kristin's positivity and sincerity haven't diminished her sense of humor, neither have they impaired her ability to perceive danger or deceit. In this way she differs from Natalie, our reigning Queen of the Silver Lining, who can't spot the bad in anyone until it's smacking her in the face, and who refuses to jump to conclusions about people even when they're standing over her exsanguinating body with a knife.

With all this in mind, I took a moment to locate Kristin's survey and see what she'd been up to as a single woman in the new millennium. Unlike most of the other submissions, it was fairly empty. Although she was a member of two online matching sites, she had yet to exchange messages with anyone and therefore had nothing to report. Moreover, apart from the dozen or so men she spoke to at a speed dating event she'd been cajoled into attending by Natalie—who else—last fall, she otherwise had not had a conversation with anyone of the opposite sex who wasn't a relative or colleague in more than three years.

Speaking of colleagues, I mused, recalling her workplace crush. *I'd better call her one of these days and see how that's going in case I need to nip a little something in the bud.*

Meanwhile, in the comments section at the end of the survey, she shared her new philosophy toward the opposite sex: *Men are like jewelry. They're nice to have but not essential. So if you're not going to get exactly what you want, you may as well just not bother.*

Eight

I nteresting thought, Karla Collier observed after I'd shared this quote—anonymously, of course—over coffee the following week. As a single member of my circle, she had received and responded to my survey, and was making inquiries as to the findings now that she'd handed back the printout of the copy I'd submitted earlier for my next Sunday feature.

"It's not as bad as it looks," she assured after catching me reacting to all the red ink gracing the margins. "Most of it is commentary, not criticism."

"*Most?*" I wondered aloud. I found that hard to believe given how much she had crossed out.

"Well, okay, maybe not most, but certainly not as much as you think."

"Just read it later," she instructed, "and take from it what you will."

I nodded, knowing that whatever I took from it, she would print only what she wanted, and I was perfectly fine with that. As Mack would put it, *if I'm ever in charge of a small metropolitan newspaper, I'll get to print what I want. Until then, what she says goes.*

"It's quite similar to my own philosophy," she continued, referring to Kristin's remark—I immediately gathered—not to my submission or Mack's wisdom. "Only mine likens them to couches."

Our conversations are often like that—dynamic, circuitous, and oblique. Sometimes we can carry on five discussions at once, taking turns switching from one topic to another as we respond to one another's questions or comments. In fact, only when one of us is in a hurry to do we ever get straight to the point, and even then we have trouble sticking to one subject. Walker jokes that it's because we both have multiple personalities, but with one of her cousins having a history of mental illness, that's something I'm planning to keep to myself.

"I used to be a lot less selective," she began as I slipped the packet of paper into the file folder inside my purse. "My first one was too low, but I made it work by putting blocks under it. The second one sagged, but I made it work by putting a board under the cushions. The next one was ugly, so I threw a slipcover over it. Another one smelled like dog, so I bombed it with air freshener. It was ridiculous. I mean, I wouldn't even consider buying jeans that didn't fit, but I was willing to move heaven and earth to make a cheap couch work in my dinky little apartment."

"Well, that was like, how many years ago? When you were young and just starting out? Who hasn't been there?"

"Oh, I'm sure everyone's been there. But most people grow out of it when they start making money. Not me. So there I was, long after I could afford to buy new, plunking down my hard-earned credit card to buy some designer piece of crap with killer lines that was about as comfortable as an ice block and miles too long for its designated space in the living room, and then arranging and rearranging the furniture until everything fit—only to spend the next four years with bruises on my shin from banging it on the end table whenever I needed to get to the closet.

"Then one day, after lusting for two hours after this chic onyx number because it was leather and made by Cappellini, I finally asked myself, why? Why do you keep putting yourself through this? If it's extreme discomfort and frustration you're looking for, you can have that with the junk you've already got. For once, why don't you save your money and hold out for exactly what you want instead of spending another four to six years waiting for something to wear out because it cost too much to throw away?"

From there she went on to explain how she had a similar epiphany in January about men after dating yet another shipwreck in dreamboat's clothing whom she'd met in October and continued to see through the holidays just so she wouldn't have to be single on New Year's Eve.

"Now tell me," she sighed as she finished her confession. "How sad is that?"

Pretty sad, I had to admit. Just not aloud.

"So I've decided it's just not worth it," Karla added after a pause. "It makes absolutely no sense to keep trying to fit the wrong guy into my life, or to wait for him to grow up, wake up, step up, or whatever. From now on, the only men I'm going to date are those who are already the complete package because I would rather hold out for exactly what I want and wind up spending evenings, weekends, and the rest of my life with friends, than waste another second on someone who either can't commit, needs to be fixed, doesn't get me, or doesn't share my values."

I couldn't fault her logic, of course. It's my stock-in-trade. Yet, knowing some people cloak their fear in selectivity, I was moved to inquire further.

"I agree," I said to that end, "so long as you don't throw the baby out with the bathwater."

"What does that mean?"

"Just that I'd hate for you to set your standards so high because subconsciously you don't think anyone can measure up, and have you end up watching television sitting on the floor—to borrow your analogy—just because you're afraid that's what's going to happen anyway."

Karla laughed. "I'll try to keep that in mind."

"Anyway," she continued, "back to your research on Internet dating. How's that going?"

"Pretty well. I've collected all the data—with the exception of a couple responses from folks I totally expected to blow it off. So now I just need to review it, analyze it, and see what, if any, conclusions there are to draw from it."

"Great. So how long will that take?"

"I'm not sure. But as I promised—nothing I print will be attributable or traceable to you or any other source."

"I'm not at all concerned about that."

"Nor will this project interfere with my other commitments," I offered, supposing my Sunday features, if not anonymity, were the issue, "if that's what you're worried about."

"Also not an issue. You're the one person I can depend on to get her copy in on time."

That wasn't exactly a huge compliment, I knew, since all but a handful of the contributors reported to an assistant editor. Only those of us who wrote exclusively for the lifestyle section submitted our work directly to Karla, and that would change as soon as she demonstrated to the publisher that the addition of that section to the Sunday issue was a good idea and he gave her the go-ahead to hire another assistant editor. Until then, Karla planned to nurture its content and design like a first-time mother of a newborn babe.

"Okay. So then what's with all the questions about the survey results?"

Karla shrugged. "Just making conversation."

"Making conversation? Or changing the subject?"

"No. Seriously," Karla insisted in response to my doubtful look. "I'm perfectly happy to sit here and talk about my impossibly high standards and their potential to render me couch-less, if you prefer. I just thought you might want to talk about something more interesting."

"Fair enough," I laughed. "So is there any aspect of this that you're most curious about?"

"Actually, there is."

"And what would that be?"

Karla looked around at the tables behind us. The place had started to clear out somewhat now that it was well past ten. Business would likely start to pick up again as we got close to the lunch hour, but for now the tables around us were empty except for a few cups, crumbs, and napkins left behind by the less courteous of our fellow patrons, and two elderly ladies who were far more interested in the various elements of the shop's warm, urban motif than anything Karla and I had to say.

"Okay, here goes," she warned. "Do you recall when you first sent out the surveys and asked everyone who got one to forward a copy to all the single people we know as well?"

"Of course."

"Well, I sent a copy to Nathan Goddard."

"As in, the new assistant city attorney, Nathan Goddard?"

"Yes."

"Okay. And?"

"And...I'm wondering if he responded."

"And?"

"And...if he happened to indicate whether he's seeing anyone."

"Karla—I am surprised at you."

"I'm not asking you to tell me who. I just want to know if. Well, that," she added somewhat bashfully, "and what, if any, matching services he subscribes to."

"Are you serious?"

Karla nodded. "I know someone who'd like to get to know him," she explained. "So I thought, if she knew what sites he uses, she could subscribe to them too, and perhaps they might find their way into each other's orbit."

"Let me get this straight: You want me to violate my own confidentiality agreement so that one of your friends can stalk a man with a background in law and a close relationship with the local police force?"

"I would hardly call it stalking, Roxanne. Plus, I can assure you she'll be totally discreet and that any contact between them would be strictly as his initiation."

"Besides," she continued, "it's not like I don't know him already. We're both members of the Chamber of Commerce and we worked together on the committee for the United Way last year."

"Okay. Okay. You're buds. I get it. So why don't you set the two of them up?"

"I can't."

"Why not?"

Oh my God.

"Because it's you," I exclaimed as it came to me—and way too slowly, at that.

"What?"

"It is. It's you."

"Karla, your pupils are enormous," I added, offering her my compact before she could deny it. "In fact, if they were any bigger, you wouldn't have irises."

Flipping open the compact, she looked in the mirror and laughed. "You're right."

"On both counts. Yes, I know."

Not that dilated pupils are always a sign of sexual interest. Sometimes it's the lighting, or drugs. But the café was fairly bright this morning, thanks to the sunny weather and its southward orientation, and Karla wasn't nearly mellow enough to have recently been smoking marijuana.

I shook my head as she continued to blush.

"I can't believe you tried to run that old 'I have this friend' routine," I admonished, "and on a therapist, no less."

"Yeah, well, I can't believe you almost fell for it."

"Touché."

We exchanged wry smiles as we both took a sip from our mugs.

"So what do you say?"

"I'm sorry," I sighed, cursing somewhat my unyielding professional ethics. "The best I can do is to send you a list of sites where he may or may not be registered. You'll have to figure out which of them are real and which are fakes. That's assuming, of course, that he's registered with any.

I haven't even looked at his survey yet, so for all I know he prefers to find women the old-fashioned way."

"Fair enough."

"In the meantime," I continued, "I think you should consider taking a more direct approach with respect to Mr. Goddard. I mean, if you already know each other, you shouldn't have to do an end run to get on his radar. Instead, you should just invite him to dinner or a ball game, and let nature take its course."

"No way."

"Why not?"

"Because that's not how I operate."

"And how exactly *do* you operate?"

"A lot more subtly than you think I should, evidently."

"You can say that again. I mean, really, Karla. What do you expect to happen after you find out what sites he visits? Do you think he's going to find you there, realize you're in the market for a mate, and—presto— you're living happily ever after?"

Karla laughed. "Yes. That's exactly what I had in mind. How did you know?"

"And what happens if he sees you there, recalls that you've never shown even the least bit of interest in him any of the times the two of you have spoken in person, decides he's not your type, and never makes contact?"

"That's an excellent point," she conceded, "but I'm still not going to ask him out."

"Okay. Well, in that case, I need a sheet of paper."

"What for?" she asked as I reached back into my purse and produced a notebook.

"I'm going to use it to write a note asking Nathan if he likes Karla with a check box for yes and another for no. Then I'm going to take it over to the city offices, give it to him to fill out, and bring it back to you with his answer."

"Very funny."

"Well, if you're trying to avoid the mature, adult approach, you may as well go all out."

"Ha ha."

"Seriously, Karla. Why are you so against doing something that tens of thousands of people do every single day?"

"Because I don't want to make the first move."

"Why not?"

"Because I want him to pursue me."

"I see."

In addition to being twisty, tangential exchanges, my conversations with Karla routinely morph into social transactions that venture into the personal realm. No doubt it's because we have similar attitudes and interests, are about the same age, and share a sardonic and sometimes silly sense of humor that we find it hard to stay on course. This used to make me nervous since she's my boss and therefore outranks me, but having since learned how well she separates the personal from the professional realm, I now know I can speak candidly to her without having to worry about repercussions.

This has not always been the case with my peers, never mind my superiors, which is why for a time I had stopped offering my two cents to friends and colleagues who would confide in me, and would instead take on a listener-observer role. This may sound illogical and a bit heartless, given that people expect more from a confidante than a sympathetic nod and a generic supportive comment every now and then. But after enduring a shunning by a stressed-out neighbor to whom I had suggested drugs as a reason for her son's distant behavior and falling grades, I decided to save my wisdom for clients and total strangers. Eventually, though, I learned to distinguish those who could handle the truth from those who could not, and—more importantly— recognize when someone wanted nothing more than to blow off steam, and became less tightlipped with friends and acquaintances, including editors.

As one might expect from someone in her position, Karla is supremely confident and put together. It probably helps that she's six feet tall, has gorgeous strawberry-blond hair, and style enough for the entire tri-state region, but one gets the impression that she'd be no less assured of herself if she were a short stack who shopped at Costmart or Targét. Then again, it's because she is a long drink of water that she dresses the way she does since she can get away with things that the average woman can't, and can't shop anywhere that doesn't stock talls. Not willowy enough to be a model but well proportioned, she is no more satisfied with her body than anyone else in my acquaintance; she just prefers to spend her money on clothes that will enhance her figure than waste any time or energy complaining about it.

It was with all that in mind that I was so surprised by her remark, and anxious to alter her perspective.

"Are you being serious?" I asked to that end. "About wanting to being pursued, I mean?"

"Actually, I am."

"Does that mean you think a woman shouldn't be the one to make the first move?"

"Well, no. I'm not against other women asking men out. I just prefer, when it comes to my relationships, not to be the one to make the first move."

"Why? I mean, is it just a matter of your being risk-averse, or is there another element at work here?"

"Well, yes and no. I mean, yes, it is about the element of risk. But to be perfectly honest, I think, by taking the risk and asking me out, a guy is proving he has confidence in himself and telling me, in essence, he thinks I'm worth the risk of getting shot down."

"Interesting."

"What?"

"Well, I'm with you on the confidence thing. It does take confidence to ask someone out. The problem is, among the guys who have the confidence to ask someone out are a fair number of arrogant jerks."

"Meanwhile," I added with chagrin, "a lot of decent guys with a lot going for them will find it difficult to approach you because they don't consider themselves God's perfect gift to womankind and therefore aren't sure that someone as attractive, smart, successful, and confident as you would want to go out with them."

"So you're saying I'm intimidating."

"No. What I'm saying is that getting a date with a beautiful, successful redhead with a great personality and her own money is an incredibly ambitious goal, and that by expecting men to run the gauntlet, as it were, you are almost ensuring that the men who approach you stand among the most self-assured on the planet and as such have a better than average chance of being arrogant pricks or total assholes. At the same time, you run the risk of never getting to know all the decent guys in your midst who have everything going for them but because they are smart and sensitive enough to realize they're not the embodiment of perfection and allow for the possibility that you may not be interested in them., will never take up the challenge."

"I see your point, Roxanne. But bear in mind, there are men out there— good and bad—who prefer to make the first move."

"Maybe. But in my experience, a woman immediately becomes more interesting to a man the moment he realizes she's interested in him."

"Really?"

"Really."

"So if you're not going to officially ask Mr. Goddard on a date," I cautioned, "you should at least consider putting yourself in front of him and conveying your interest some way, since from what little I know of the man, he may not be on the market very long."

"I see."

"It doesn't work the same way in reverse, by the way," I noted as she processed this snippet of guidance. "Sometimes, it does—especially if the man is, by cultural standards, considered highly desirable. But, for whatever reason—it's evolutionary, I imagine—men don't require that the attention come from a highly desirable woman in order to have a positive response. She just can't be, by established cultural standards, extremely undesirable."

Karla smiled indulgently at this entirely unsolicited flurry of useless information. "Good to know."

Not wanting to emulate Alethia by continuing to lecture and monopolizing the conversation, I decided against presenting the second element to my case. Instead I privately bemoaned the fact that, after all this time and the countless sacrifices that have been made in the fight for gender equality, women were still insisting on having men make the first move and take all the risks. It seems to me, as a now thirty-seven-year-old woman, if we're going to expect a level playing field when it comes to job opportunities and demand equal pay for equal work, maybe it's time to inject a little fair play into the dating game as well. I mean, it's bad enough that many women over thirty won't date a man who makes less money than they do—even as increasing numbers of men are choosing to stay at home after the kids are born and let their wives bring home the bacon. Is it too much to expect women to let go of the sexism on their part as well?

"Not to sound like I'm inventing excuses," I heard Karla say as I pondered my private indignation, "but I did have another reason for seeking an online introduction."

"Which is?"

"Well—and this depends entirely on what sites we're talking about, since some just post member profiles, while others suggest matches based on some technology or other—but I was hoping he was on one of these latter sites so I can put my information in and let the system tell me if they think it'll work."

"Seriously?"

"Seriously."

"That way I'll know in advance if we're compatible," Karla added without invitation, "and whether or not to even bother."

Oh my God.

Had it come to this? I mean, I admit I'm a little behind the times— what with my aversion to things like Twitter and my tendency to use my cell phone just to make calls—but do people think software can judge better than humans whether someone is right for them or not? I get that people want to embrace technology as a means of increasing efficiency. I even understand why some are attracted to things like nanny cams and GPS; but surely no one truly believes a computer can do a better job than people can of can of screening potential mates or recognizing the makings of love.

"So you'd rather let a website decide if you're compatible, instead of getting to know the man and doing it yourself?"

"Not necessarily. But if it's available and potentially more efficient, why not?"

"That's true, and you're not getting any younger."

"Hey!"

"Oh, you know I'm only joking. As far as I'm concerned, age isn't an issue. What is an issue," I added grimly, "is whether these Internet matching sites can do the things they claim to do, because if not, it's getting about time for someone to debunk that myth."

"Myth?"

"That compatibility can be accurately assessed based on logarithms and a questionnaire."

Having not yet shared with her the second aspect of my project, I went on to tell Karla about what else I'd been up to as a result of my research, and of Walker's adventures meeting women with whom he'd been matched in cyberspace.

"Sounds intriguing," she declared, having slipped back into editor mode. "Do you think there's enough there from which to build a weekend feature?"

"I'm not sure. A bigger issue is whether there is anything really to tell. The data is still being collected, and even after it's all in, the results may not be conclusive.

"Worse still," I continued, "even if my results indicate that *thematchcafe. com,* and by association, others of its ilk, can accurately predict compatibility, there is a bigger issue that needs to be addressed, which is that it will still say nothing at all about chemistry, which is a biological matter and therefore cannot be gauged by software—at least not until serious progress is made toward understanding genetics and DNA."

Out of respect for time and a desire not to—again—lecture or monopolize the conversation, I decided against saying so, but my argument was based on some articles I'd read a few years ago on the science of attraction and MHC.

MHC, which stands for major histocompatibility complex, is a set of genes that certain researchers believe influence attraction and therefore reproduction, by conveying information about one's health, fertility status, and genotype. This information, they believe, is carried by pheromones that are released by the body and are detected subconsciously by others around us. In short, this is how—some believe—humans identify who has the stuff they should be mating with, and who does not.

It would be this MHC that makes kissing and other types of close, nonsexual contact so crucial to the dating process, since exchanging MHC requires proximity. Hand holding and hugging work too, but you can't get a whiff of someone's MHC unless you're breathing what comes directly out of the pores.

The larger function of the MHC, some believe, is to create combinations that will produce offspring with the traits most favorable to survival, and to avoid creating combinations that will not. Thus, it encourages people to mate with people with different genes and discourages them from mating with people with similar genes, which explains why mothers can't stand the smell of their teenage son's rooms, and why teenage boys can't get along with their teenage sisters. This makes sense since breeding with one's immediate or close family members is generally considered the least reliable means of producing offspring with traits that are favorable to the continuation of the species.

Of course, MHC can be overridden by alcohol and other mind-altering substances such as estrogen, serotonin, and chocolate. This explains why women are more confident and bubbly on days ten through sixteen of their cycles, and why men find them less attractive on days twenty-one through twenty-eight. It also explains why the girls all get prettier at closing time, as the Mickey Gilley song goes, and why so many women wind up in bed with men whom, without that third vodka appletini, they would have rejected out of hand. Popular culture has it that these actions occur as a result of lowered inhibitions, but if that were the case, the appeal of the people we're waking up with the next day could be plotted on a perfect bell curve. The fact that they are not suggests that our MHC knows better than we do when it comes to mating, and is beyond grateful for the advent and popularity of contraception.

Available research also suggests that MHC can also be overridden by birth control pills and other hormone-based medication. This explains why couples who start trying to conceive can find themselves on the road to divorce. Especially if the woman was already on the pill when they met, her MHC may communicate things it could not impart while she was under the influence of estrogen and progesterone. People tend to blame stress for the rate of divorce among couples struggling with persistent infertility, but it's at least as likely that their MHC has realized they're genetically incompatible and is trying to nudge them in different directions.

MHC may also explain the seven-year itch, and why many otherwise faithful men wind up cheating on their wives while they're pregnant or nursing. While people typically point to other explanations for these phenomena—e.g. pregnant women look fat (or more accurately, have a different waist-to-hip ratio than they did before they conceived), which causes men to find them less attractive; the seven-year itch occurs because the spark is gone, not because of any age-related drop in the production of estrogen, testosterone, or human growth hormone—no doubt the real culprit is, like germs before the invention of the microscope, undetectable by the naked eye. That's not to say anyone with a sociological perspective is completely off the mark; I just think there is more to the picture than what scientists can currently prove, and way more beyond our comprehension than most people would like to believe.

I let these and related thoughts run in the background as Karla and I finished our discussion of what may come of my investigation.

"I still have to review the notes from Walker's first three dates," I told her, "and those from his date this coming weekend. Meanwhile, I plan to continue checking *thematchcafe.com* periodically to see if anything has changed. I would hate to go through all the trouble, only to find out Walker and I had been matched while I was doing something else."

Not that I expected anything to be different. With my matches having topped out in the high forties, and the rate of increase among Walker's matches even having slowed to two or three a week, I was convinced that any new profiles that appeared in either of our list of matches would result from the addition of new members and not because either one of us had suddenly become a hotter commodity.

"I'll be going over Walker's notes after his fourth date," I added, "and conferring with my research assistant on any preliminary findings."

Karla's eyes widened. "You have a research assistant?"

"Don't be too impressed—or start thinking you're paying me too much. By research assistant, I mean my mom, who offered up her time and considerable Excel skills for free."

"Wow. That's pretty generous, even for a mother."

"Don't be too impressed by that, either. I love the woman to death, but she wasn't motivated by any innate generosity, altruism, or humanity, but by an intense and often disquieting curiosity, and the knowledge that being part of this project would give her more excuses to talk to me."

"Not that I mind," I added quickly. "Mom is great, and we get along beautifully. I just don't want to leave you with the impression that our relationship is somehow different from any other mother-daughter pair, or that because we can work together she doesn't make me nuts."

"So noted. Okay," Karla continued by way of wrapping up our meeting. "Well, I guess that about covers it for me. Is there anything else you wanted to discuss?"

"I don't think so."

"Great."

With a nod, I gathered up my things and waited for Karla to do the same. The process took a little longer for her, since in addition to a purse and workbag to pack up, she also had gloves, a scarf, and her trademark belted jacket—one of the seven I had seen since our first meeting—to arrange on her person, plus a pair of black oversized sunglasses to perch atop her head in case any blinding rays of sunshine should come her way as she drove to the office or wherever her calendar required her to be next.

"Oh—one more thing," she said suddenly as she made the final adjustments to her ensemble like an expert chef casually putting the finishing touches on a fabulous meal. "Did you get the e-mail from Jennifer about the volleyball tournament?"

"I did."

"And? Are you interested?"

She was referring to the annual indoor volleyball tournament hosted by the chamber of commerce. Area businesses, nonprofit organizations, and other civic groups compete in the tournament, which raises money for the chamber's education fund, which in turn awards two scholarships each year to deserving business majors attending one of the local colleges.

The *Post-Courier* had participated in the event every year since Karla had taken over, but had yet to make the finals. Consequently, she was eager to attract some new blood and to fire up the veterans whom she feared would give up if the team didn't make a better show of it this year.

Knowing this—and mindful of the buzz it would generate for the *P-C* if we were to surprise everyone by making the quarterfinals—I was definitely interested. Unfortunately, I'm not cut out for that kind of pressure and, as much as I hated to disappoint Karla, I knew I had to decline.

In truth, I had been avidly sports-averse since middle school. It wasn't the physical activity or the challenge that deterred me, but my highly competitive and empathetic nature, which made it impossible for me to enjoy the experience no matter the outcome. I would get so angry at my teammates if one of them screwed up—and even more so at myself when I did—that I could never shake things off and move on. Moreover, I'd feel depressed if we lost, and even worse for the other team if we won, and thus couldn't even enjoy my victories.

The same turned out to be true for non-team sports. Even with no one to blame, accost, or console, I couldn't control myself when it came to either winning or losing. Just playing tennis with my family—as they liked to do on those rare weekends that Mack wasn't deployed and no one had a prior commitment—was too much for me. As likely as not I'd wind up shagging balls by the ninth or tenth volley, having been ordered to do so by Bunny or Mack for hurling my racquet, or having stormed off the court in an effort to avoid launching my racquet in the first place.

My feelings about competition spilled over to non-sporting activities as well after I took part in my first debate and discovered I was no better at controlling my emotions while standing at a podium without a racquet or other potential missile in my hand. Not wanting to embarrass myself with ridiculous verbal and physical displays of emotion, I decided to avoid situations that might stir my pot, as it were, and to stick with behind-the-scenes activities such as painting sets and writing for the school newspaper and yearbook.

Thus it was with a great deal of certainty but very little detail that I declared myself too busy to join Team *P-C*. Although Karla was visibly disappointed, I knew I was doing her an enormous favor and one for which—if she had any idea of my true nature—she would definitely have thanked me later.

Nine

Walker's fourth date, with Dawn, a divorced party planner who was originally from Iowa, took place in Madison. According to the post-date briefing he provided in our hotel room later that evening, Dawn was also a trivia enthusiast with a dream of appearing one day on *Cash Cab*, *Jeopardy!* or *Who Wants to Be a Millionaire?* This explained her choice of meeting places, he divulged with a laugh, having found upon his arrival there that the place hosted nightly trivia competitions, and that night's game was for couples.

Apparently this woman had done her research.

"Ah, so she was checking out your viability as a mate," I teased as I put away the laptop and other work paraphernalia I'd brought along to keep myself occupied while he was out, "trying to make sure you're smart enough for her, huh?"

"Maybe."

"If so," he added proudly, "I must have passed, since she invited me over for coffee as we were leaving the bar."

"Coffee, huh?" I mused, recognizing the offer as an invitation to make out and/or engage in casual sex. "And you turned her down?"

"Of course I did. I mean, who drinks coffee at ten o'clock at night?"

Poor Walker. The man may be brilliant when it comes to science and technology, but like many of his colleagues, he can be as bright a black hole when it comes to reading women.

"Obviously *she* does," I pointed out with a laugh, "or she wouldn't have asked."

"I guess."

"So was she disappointed?"

"To put it mildly."

"I offered to walk her over to the Starbucks down the street so she could pick up something for the road," he continued with genuine bewilderment, "but that didn't seem to make her any happier."

Now I felt as sorry for Dawn as I did for Walker. The poor girl took a risk and went down in flames thinking he didn't like her when in fact he was just missing a clue.

Well, that and *married*.

"That's because she didn't want *coffee*," I explained, hoping to spare him similar confusion in the future. "She wanted *you*."

"Me?"

"You."

"You're joking."

"No I'm not."

"Think about it," I suggested. "Did we have coffee the first time I invited you back to my apartment?"

"Yes."

"No, honey. We didn't."

"Yes, we did. I distinctly remember us making coffee the first time I set foot in your apartment."

"And I distinctly remember us *not* drinking it."

I watched him process that thought, and waited for him to respond.

"So you're saying the point was never to have coffee?" he asked finally.

"Well, we *would have* had coffee if I'd lost my nerve and not jumped your bones before it was ready. But once I realized you honestly thought the point was to have coffee, I decided to take charge of the situation rather than let the moment pass."

"Wow. And to think this whole time I thought the idea to jump my bones came to you *after* we got to your apartment."

"Then why did you come? Given your aversion to drinking coffee late at night, that is."

"I just assumed we were going to continue talking. Or, more accurately, that *you* were."

"Besides," he added before I could defend my loquaciousness by pointing out his lack thereof, "back then I didn't have to be up at oh-Christ-hundred in the morning."

"Fair enough."

From the way he stared at the air above my head in the mirror, I could see his wheels were still spinning as we prepared to turn in for the evening.

"So what's on your mind?" I wondered aloud. "Are you going back over the events of that night to see how they would have looked if you'd had more information?"

"No," he admitted with a laugh. "I'm thinking back to all the coffee I've turned down over the years and wondering what I may have missed."

When Walker's notes on his visit with Dawn were ready, I scanned and e-mailed them to Bunny, then allowed myself a quick peek at the demographic and other details of each of his dates to see if there were any obvious similarities between the four of them that might explain what prompted the system to deem them more compatible with Walker than I. *No real harm could come from doing so*, reasoned the miniature Bunny on my left shoulder to the consternation of her more scrupulous but, alas, less persuasive counterpart on my right, *since the forms he was using to gather data were already written and, therefore, could not be influenced by anything I might find at this point as long as I didn't revise them.* The only danger, in fact, lay in the possibility that reading the notes could spawn a theory or a conclusion that, in turn, could influence the data gathered in the future. As long as I didn't change the instructions I gave Walker or the tools he used to carry them out, I conceded, it probably wouldn't hurt to learn a little something about the women he had met so far.

The first things I looked at were age and occupation. Though all four women were younger than both of us by a couple years, all were over thirty and employed. All worked in a fairly conventional field—the most exotic of which was Tara the flight attendant—and all but she did work that required them to synthesize information and make decisions or recommendations, or build a case for some kind of action on the part of a group or organization.

This didn't seem terribly significant, since I too pool information and either report on my findings or advocate for some kind of action. Okay, so maybe issuing advice and writing about relationships isn't exactly the same thing as providing career and other guidance to high school students, or planning weddings and other events. Still, the differences between me and the four of them were no more striking than the differences between any two of them. Not that I expected it to be that obvious. After all, if the devil was in the demographics, then there would be no need for the fancy questionnaires or the personality profiles that *thematchcafe.com* seemed so proud to present. And I wasn't about to get into issues like height or hair or eye color since if that was the kind of thing their matches were based on, I would have to drop the matter altogether and declare war on the site as a complete and utter fraud.

Moving on to personality, I decided to take another look at our own profiles. Having already declared them accurate, I read them now not with an eye for content errors, but with the goal of identifying elements that would render us incompatible, and with a view to discerning their underlying logic.

The first element in the profile was entitled Amiability, wherein Walker and I predictably both scored average. In addition to being accurate, it boded well in terms of compatibility, I reasoned, especially since I was more inclined to be friendly and concerned about the welfare of others—including strangers—and Walker tended to be interested only in people he knew, and to ignore others unless they approached him first. This created a good balance that was evident in our social circle to which I tend to draw people, and Walker manages not to drive them away.

The results were similar in the area of Receptivity. Apparently the system felt we were both open to new ideas and experiences, and not at all threatened or paralyzed by the introduction of new people or information. This rendered us both flexible enough to change our mind in the face of new data, and able to compromise in the interest of the big picture.

Although people say that opposites attract, I could see no basis for that when it comes to a quality like receptiveness. Call it a personal bias—since people tend to value more in others the qualities they perceive in themselves—but I could find nothing to support the premise that two people would be better suited to each other if one of them was open-minded and the other was not. Although more rigid, reserved, or timid people might be repelled by others of their ilk, and open-minded individuals more tolerant thereof, I could identify no basis to believe that two open-minded people did not belong together, nor any evolutionary advantage for keeping them apart.

The findings in the area of Stability and Security were no less predictable. As my profile indicated, I tend to be hyper-analytical and to second-guess others, but am fairly comfortable with my gifts, flaws, relationships, and circumstances. Although I tend to *feel* a lot—for both myself and others—I am not prone to sentiment or passionate displays of emotions, with the exception of the occasional justifiable rant or sarcastic expression of frustration. With Walker's score in this area being even higher than mine, I again could see no obstacle to compatibility. While it was possible that men like Walker—who is mellow almost to the point of comatose and has not a shred of insecurity—are more tolerant of women of a more volatile or anxious nature, it didn't necessarily follow that they cannot have healthy relationships with women whose scores in this area were closer to their own.

This pattern continued through to the area of Responsibility and Reliability. According to our profiles, Walker and I are both mature, conscientious people who can be counted on to use good judgment and follow through on our commitments. Although Walker tends to have a routine and prefers to schedule his tasks, while I am more of a list person who takes a more organic approach to my day and tackles goals and duties when the need or mood strikes, we both manage to juggle our respective balls without dropping any of the glass ones.

Upon reviewing this information, I was once again struck by how the two of us could be any more compatible. Does one of us have to be a drooling mess for us to be suited to the other, I griped to myself, or would it be better if we were both total slackers who forgot to pay their bills or failed to keep appointments?

Sensing I was taking things a touch too personally, I set our profiles to one side and took a look at the ones I had assembled for Tara, Jamey, Erica, and Dawn from Walker's notes and responses to my proxy questionnaires.

The information here was inconclusive. Of the four women, all were moderate to high in terms of Amiability, and likewise for Receptivity, Stability and Security, and Responsibility and Reliability. In terms of personality, Walker had declared them all extroverts with moderate to high levels of creativity, and a tendency to favor reason over emotion. Even their hobbies and interests—100 percent of which obviously could not have been covered over the course of a single lunch or dinner date—were not all that different from mine or one another's, judging by the responses they gave to Walker's questions and commentary about his own. Jamey, Walker, and I, for example, are readers, while Erica, Tara, and Dawn are not; and Erica, Walker, and Jamey are all outdoorsy, while Tara, Dawn, and I are not. In areas where there are more than two options—e.g. religious or political affiliation, or favorite time of day—there was even more variation between us, which suggested that nothing but degrees distinguished me from these women and them from one another, and rendered us different as not apples and oranges, but rather Galas, Braeburns, Pink Ladies, and Honey Crisps.

Figuring I must be getting hungry, I stopped to put a pork loin in the oven and prep some cauliflower for steaming, then grabbed a can of almonds and went back to my analysis.

Walker arrived home as the timers were going off and after kissing me hello and tossing the mail on the table, inquired as to my progress. Having the time but not the energy to provide a detailed account of my activities and finding, I opted instead to give him a synopsis that would let him know where things stood and still give him a true sense of the depth of my frustration.

"So you spent the whole afternoon reviewing the profiles," he accurately and sympathetically summarized after enduring my diatribe, "and have come up with nothing?"

"Pretty much. In fact, the only discernable difference between me and your four lady friends is that they're all younger than I—which tells me little about them but makes me wonder what you entered on your list of Absolutes and Absolutely Nots.

"And while we're on the subject of age," I added as Walker smiled at my mild consternation, "have you noticed that all of your matches are under forty, while all of mine are over?"

I'd come across this latter little detail while doing my daily search for Walker's name among my matches. Having discounted age as a factor in the system's failure to match us—since our birthdays are less than a year apart—I hadn't more than glanced at this information until, upon finding only forty- and fifty-year-olds in my pool of potential suitors, I located the list from which we'd chosen Walker's dates and realized that all of the women on it were under forty, not just the four he'd already met.

"Actually I hadn't," he admitted with a laugh. "But now that you mention it, maybe you should be the one spilling about Absolutes and Absolutely Nots."

"Ha. Ha."

There wasn't anything else to do but laugh since I was no more convinced age was a factor now than I had been that morning. I had just been trying to inject a bit of humor into a situation that was making me nuts.

"Maybe it's time to add another element to your research," Walker offered later as we divided up the leftovers into lunch-size portions and put them in the fridge.

"Okay. What exactly do you have in mind?"

"Well, you're not getting anywhere with analyzing my matches so far; maybe it's time to look at yours."

"I don't think so."

"Why not?"

"Because the only men who aren't already taken are the ones nobody wants."

"How do you know that?"

"Because I have single friends—and they date."

"Perhaps. But just because the men they've met haven't all been princes doesn't mean the ones you meet won't be. In truth, you have no idea who is even on your list, or what kind of people they might be."

"Actually, I do. In fact, given how much I have in common with four women you've dated so far, it's a safe bet the men on my list will be like you in every way but one."

"And what would that be?"

"They're losers. I'm not saying they're all unemployed drug addicts with shocking criminal records," I explained. "Rather, I fully expect them to have jobs, cars, and a decent to excellent education. What they won't have—and thus what makes them losers—is confidence, personality, social skills, good personal hygiene, or all of the above."

"You don't know that."

"Walker, they're over forty and single. If they had all of those things—plus a job, and their own car—they'd be in a relationship and not trolling for women online. I promise."

"They could be divorced."

"In which case, there would be a reason. Next pitch."

"You could meet a widower."

"Not likely. Widowers who are good at relationships usually end up remarrying within a few years."

"Now you're just shining me on."

"No, I'm not. Look it up."

"Fine. So maybe you'll catch one before he meets his next wife."

"Doubtful. Guys like that don't have to go looking for women. The women come to them."

Walker laughed. "You have an answer for everything, don't you?"

"Pretty much."

"Then I give up."

"That was the point."

Walker shook his head as he joined me on the stairs. "Don't forget about my hunting trip," he advised out of the blue. "Carson and I hit the sticks three weeks from today."

His message made me smirk, not just because he's more likely than I am to need a reminder of his plans, but also because he and Carson were planning to try their luck at pheasant hunting this fall, which I found amusing in light of Walker's intense dislike of canines.

"What's so funny?" he asked, noting my amusement.

"I was just picturing you pheasant hunting again, and wondering how long you'll hang in there before shooting one of the dogs."

"Dealing with the dogs may be difficult," he admitted sincerely, "but hunting pheasant is something I haven't tried before, and I think I'd like the challenge of shooting something in the air besides clay pigeons."

"Well, I can't imagine why you'd want to shoot them in the air in the first place. Like Eddie Izzard says, it's much easier to hit them after they land."

"That's incredibly amusing, Roxanne. Truly."

"Why, thank you."

"You know what I find amusing?" I asked as I waited for my turn at the sink. "That middle-class Americans do for fun what pioneers and the poor have historically done for survival.

"Oh really?"

"Really. In fact, I bet Charles Ingalls, Daniel Boone, and Grizzly Adams would laugh their asses off at all the bankers, engineers, and other white-collar warriors blowing on duck calls and covering themselves in doe urine when there are vast quantities of fresh and frozen domesticated animal parts available for sale at the store or already waiting for them at home."

"I disagree. Throughout history various societies—from the Native Americans, to lumberjack camps, to the ancient Greeks—have held contests of speed, strength, accuracy, and agility for the sake of sport. And while few of those skills are essential for survival in modern times, I see no reason to think people of earlier times would find it incongruous that we continue to challenge ourselves in this way today."

"Apart from the fact that you don't have to, you mean?"

Walker sighed.

"You'd better be careful," he warned, shaking his finger playfully at my reflection in the mirror. "Or I'm going to visit my parents this weekend and you won't have anyone to meet Heather in Tomah on Saturday."

I cringed.

"Fine," I groaned, hanging my head in mock shame. "I'll behave."

Ten

The trip to Tomah was a relaxing one and Walker and I passed it listening to comedy spots on the radio. Like television, the medium had changed a lot over the last several years, and one of Walker's few indulgences was his subscription to a satellite service that enabled him to take long trips without being limited to what could be found on the local airwaves. In addition to having expanded our listening options, the satellite service eliminated the frustrations of signal bleed and loss as we moved from one broadcast area to another, and helped make the trip go by much faster. Thanks to a lack of traffic—and a little help from Walker's need for speed—we arrived in Tomah well ahead of schedule, and nearly an hour before he had to meet Heather.

Knowing in advance I was going to be in the area, I had called and arranged my own date with Bunny, who was happy to make the two-hour drive since Mack was off at his cabin doing whatever manly men do in the woods when the deer and turkeys are active but sadly off limits. With time to kill before Bunny's SUV came zipping down East McCoy Boulevard—assuming, of course, it hadn't taken an unavoidable detour on its way past the Ho Chunk exit—I had Walker drop me off at a thrift shop up the road from where she and I planned to eat. It was a safe distance away from where he and Heather were planning to spend the next couple hours, yet close enough to our eatery for Bunny to swing by and pick me up on her way into town.

"Thanks for being flexible," I said to her as I got into her vehicle and gave her half a hug.

"My pleasure," she replied. "I'm just glad I called to let you know I was in town instead of heading straight for the restaurant and waiting for you to turn up."

And pretending you'd been there for hours, I mused. Bunny hates the fact that she is always running late, and never fails to seize the chance to give you the impression that she's punctual.

"Don't worry," I assured her. "If I hadn't heard from you by a certain point, I would have called you myself. In fact, you beat me by five, maybe ten seconds."

Bunny laughed.

"You're lucky I was free tonight," she observed. "Mack and I originally had plans to spend the weekend with Dodie and Perry."

Aunt Dorienne, as I knew her, was Bunny's eldest younger sister. She and Uncle Perry make the drive down to Oshkosh from Green Bay about once every other month or so, depending on the weather. They used to visit every month but have cut back in recent years because Highway 41 is always under construction and Uncle Perry hates our governor. It's not clear what these last two pieces of information have to do with each other—much less what the latter has to do with the frequency of Perry and Dodie's visits—but since nearly everything that comes out of Perry's mouth lately seems to end with "that bastard Scott Walker," it likely has everything to do with politics, which means I'm never going to ask.

"So what happened? Did he decide to head south to protest the budget repair bill instead?"

Bunny laughed again. "No. Their sump pump failed so they decided to stay home and fix it."

"That's awful."

"I know."

"But apparently keeping water out of the basement is more important to some people than playing cards," she added with mock delusion, "so try not to hold it against him."

"So how's Aunt Dodie holding up these days?" I asked. "Now that Perry's retired, I mean."

Newlyweds and even people with several anniversaries under their belts may find it hard to imagine, but there can be such a thing as too much togetherness in a marriage, and according to my sources, Dodie and Perry had it in spades.

Bunny shook her head.

"Between you and me, I don't know how she stands it," she added. "After spending less than four waking hours a day with her for more than three decades, the man is suddenly so clingy and overprotective—and jealous of any time she spends away from home."

This is not uncommon behavior among male retirees who, after working long hours for forty years or more, find themselves with no real responsibilities and lots of unstructured time. Still, it did seem odd for Uncle Perry, who always seemed to have more than his share of hobbies before he no longer had a job to go to every day.

"Is that why she didn't just come down on her own this weekend?" I wondered aloud. "Or did something else come up?"

Bunny shook her head again. "Unless by 'up' you mean Perry's dander. He was giving her so much grief," she explained, "about the cost of gas, the dangers of driving through all those miles of construction, and how bored he would be without her for two days that she finally decided to cancel the trip and stay with him in Green Bay."

"That's too bad."

"It is, but that's the way it goes."

"Not for you."

"No, but then I'm not married to Perry. And Dodie won't put up with that kind of crap very long," Bunny predicted. "She'll give Perry some time to adjust to their routine, but eventually she is going to put her foot down."

Dodie is younger than Bunny by about two years, and the only one of her siblings she admires. Being second oldest, she essentially became Bunny's lieutenant after their dad died, their mom went to work, and Bunny took over the run of the home. In addition to helping with chores, it was Dodie's job to keep Mel and Charlotte in line so they didn't exhaust the goodwill of the relatives who took them in now and again, or wear out their welcome in the foster homes they periodically occupied. Bound by their shared experiences and responsibilities and their similar yet oddly compatible personalities, Bunny and Dodie talk on the phone at least once a day, and look upon each other's kids as if they were her own.

"Rory said the same thing," I replied. "But she's also afraid Perry will become even more insecure and demanding if Dodie puts him in his place, and that things will get not better, but worse."

Rory is Aunt Dodie's daughter, my primary source of information on events in Green Bay, and the sharpest and most creative member of our family. Her folks are unique among my aunts and uncles in that they're the only ones who visited us during our time outside of Wisconsin.

An only child, Rory spent the odd summer with us back when Mack was still on active duty because Aunt Dodie wanted her to see the world and "not be trapped in a Wisconsin mindset for the rest of her natural life." Her creativity comes, no doubt, from the fact that as a singleton she often had to entertain herself, and from having the sort of parents who never asked her to tone it down. The fact that she has an outsize and unusual name, Aurore Dorienne Gatziger, may also have something to do with it, but I suspect she would have turned out to be just as much fun if her name were Mary Jones or Susie Smith.

When we were kids, Rory liked to announce her arrival in the third person using what she said would one day be her stage name, Aurore Dorienne du Bonnet—du Bonnet being both our moms' maiden name and of French origin, and thus a natural choice for a budding luminary—and say that someday we would see the whole thing up in lights. Uncle Perry used to say that was fine with him so long as the lights weren't over the wrong kind of theatre. Rory and I didn't know what that meant back then, but it never failed to make Mack and Bunny smile. Bunny once suggested that Rory was a drag queen trapped in a girl's body, due to her affinity for wigs and costume jewelry and the way she would belt out Barbra Streisand songs for our parents when they were playing canasta. I didn't get that at all at the time, but upon seeing Wesley Snipes and Patrick Swayze in *To Wong Foo, Thanks for Everything, Julie Newmar* as an adult, I had myself a pretty good private laugh.

Today Rory D. Gatziger, Esquire, as she now calls herself, is an associate with a product liability defense firm near Minneapolis, which is why we see so little of each other these days. We manage to get together about once a year—usually when a big case of hers draws to a close and she realizes how long it's been since our last parley—but mostly we keep in touch via e-mail.

Our most recent exchange was two weeks ago, when she returned the survey I'd sent her, along with a brief update on her parents, and a slightly more detailed report on the status of her love life. Consequently, I was not surprised when, upon moving on to the topic of her niece, Bunny mentioned she had a new girlfriend and was doing pro bono work on behalf of a GLTB advocacy group.

"So now on top of dealing with Paranoid Perry," Bunny lamented, "Dodie's worrying about all the publicity Rory's getting, and waiting for some kook with a gun to come along and take her out.

"I told her," she continued more positively, "if there's anyone who can handle all that attention, it's Rory, and that as far as kooks with guns are concerned, she's in less danger of one of them 'taking her out' in Minneapolis than she would be in Wisconsin."

I couldn't have said it better myself.

It would be an understatement to say that Rory's parents aren't entirely comfortable with her sexual orientation. In keeping with their desire to let her be herself—which underpinned their approach to her unique gifts and eccentricities—they strive to be supportive and nonjudgmental, and mostly they succeed. Although I find it unfortunate that people still have to work at being tolerant and supportive of non-heterosexuals, I know that Dodie and Perry are good people who are dealing with something they didn't anticipate in the best way they can.

Uncle Perry has an easier time of it, since Rory's lifestyle hasn't altered the nature of their relationship very much. Other than depriving him of the thrill of running horny boys off the porch with a shotgun, conversations between the two of them are about the same as they were before she came out; Perry just doesn't want to hear about her love life.

Aunt Dodie, on the other hand, has a bit more trouble with things. Analytical and solicitous, she wonders if it was something she did that caused Rory to be attracted to girls and if there was something she could have done to prevent it, and worries how being gay will adversely impact Rory's chances of long-term happiness. As such, Dodie's concerns aren't all that different from those that other mothers have in relation to their children; they just happen to come from a place that presupposes that gay equals unnatural and flawed. No doubt her perspective will change as time goes by and she realizes that life can be just as rich and fulfilling for lesbians as it can be for women who prefer men.

"So where too?" Bunny asked, apparently realizing just then that were still at the thrift store.

Having assumed we were still planning to go to the restaurant we discussed on the phone, I figured the only we hadn't left yet was that she'd been too busy chatting to put the car in gear.

"I thought we were headed to O'Hara's," I reminded her.

Not that a reminder was necessarily called for in this situation. Bunny can be fairly fickle when it comes to what she wants to eat, so she was more likely to have lost interest in dining at O'Hara's than she was to have forgotten we had planned to go there.

"We were. I just thought it might be fun to go somewhere else."

"That's what you said about O'Hara's." More or less. In truth, she had said the place looked *interesting*, and that she'd wanted to go there ever since she and Mack drove by it the first time they came to La Crosse after Walker and I moved there.

"I know. And I still want to try it sometime—just not tonight."

"Okay."

"Then where *should* we go tonight?" I asked, assuming she was looking to quench a craving for KFC, Perkins, or one of the other more pedestrian options available to locals and travelers looking to refuel, refresh, or reprovision at the nexus of highway 21 and I-94. "The nominees include: one family restaurant famous for its pancakes and eggs; one sandwich shop offering five-dollar foot longs; one Chinese buffet; and Colonel Sanders."

"What about the Mr. Ed's?"

"*Mr. Ed's?*" I repeated as if she'd lost her mind. Then again, since spying on Walker and his date is something Bunny would do in her normal state, I could have omitted the editorial. As R.J. says, the time to question Bunny's sanity isn't when she does the unexpected, but when she *doesn't*.

"No way," I ruled before she could make her case. "Out of the question."

"Why?"

"Because that's where Walker and Heather are meeting, that's why."

"So what? It's a big place."

"Not big enough for the four of us."

"Come on, Roxanne. Aren't you just a little curious about the women Walker's meeting?"

"Obviously. If I wasn't, he wouldn't be meeting them in the first place."

"Exactly. So here's your chance to be the fly on the wall without attracting attention like you would if you were to go in there alone."

"I wouldn't go in there alone or otherwise, Mother. And I can't believe you're suggesting it."

Actually, I could. I just didn't want to.

"What do you think we're going to accomplish by going in there anyway?" I asked. "If we even have a choice of tables at this stage of the game, we're certainly not going to be able to sit near enough to hear their conversation unless we want them to hear ours, too; and there isn't much we'll be able to tell from watching them, even if I was willing to let you sit there and stare at them while they eat."

Bunny shook her head. "Roxanne, sometimes you have no imagination."

"*Au contraire, Maman.* I happen to have an abundance of imagination—which is precisely the reason we are not going to Mr. Ed's."

"What is that supposed to mean?"

"You know exactly what it means," I charged, casting my mind back to one of several occasions when Bunny's curiosity got one or both of us in hot water. "And I do not need you causing a stir or making Walker uncomfortable."

"I am not about to cause a stir, Roxanne, and I'm not going to make *anyone* uncomfortable."

"Funny—you're making me uncomfortable just talking about it."

"Oh come on," Bunny sniffed. "Now you're just looking for excuses."

"I am not. I honestly don't think it's a good idea for us to go over there. Even if you were on your best behavior and didn't attract Heather's notice, our presence alone might distract Walker and inhibit his ability to remember his instructions, gather information, and recall it later when sits down to do his notes."

"So your objection to going over there boils down to the impact our presence might have on your research?"

"Of course it does."

"So what if we do it in such a way that there's no way it can have any impact on Walker's performance?"

"And how do you propose to pull that off?"

"Do you have some sort of disguise stashed in the trunk?" I added, recalling the Carmen Sandiego trench and other items she kept on hand for costume parties and such. "Or were you thinking of bribing a waiter to plant a bug on the light fixture above their table?"

"Ha ha. I'm just proposing that we could go to the restaurant and arrange ourselves in such a way that Walker wouldn't even know we were there."

"We've been over this, Mother. If we sit far enough away from them to escape Walker's notice, we'll also be too far away to learn anything."

"Well I don't know what you have in mind, but I really just want to get a look at the woman, and to maybe see Walker in action. You know, to observe their body language and such."

"That's all?"

"That's all."

"Swear?"

"Swear."

"And you won't do anything to draw attention to yourself? No approaching people at the other tables to tell them how lovely their shoes are, or to ask how they like their fish?"

"No."

"And no running over to greet someone you recognize from high school or Camp Fire Girls or kindergarten?"

"No."

"Even if he or she looks at you with a spark of recognition, and rushing to the door as they leave is the only thing standing between renewing an acquaintance with a long lost friend and leaving them with the impression that you've grown conceited over the years and now think speaking to them is beneath you?"

I could see she was having trouble with that one. Fortunately Bunny won't outright lie and she doesn't believe in crossing her fingers for anything but luck so I knew I had her. Check and mate.

"Good God, Roxanne," she huffed finally, proving once again that her Worst-Case Scenario Syndrome has its perks. "Why do you have to make things so complicated?"

I shook my head.

"Pot—meet kettle," I said, offering her my hand in greeting. "And I don't believe that's an answer."

"Fine."

"Fine *what*?"

"Fine—I won't do anything to attract attention or distract Walker— even if it means I wind up old and lonely because your research was more important to you than letting me reconnect with someone from the past whom I really, really miss."

"Good. Then Mr. Ed's it is."

Like all decent supper clubs, Mr. Ed's houses its restrooms near its front doors, thereby allowing Bunny to use the facilities before being seated, and affording me the chance to shoot Walker a text to let him know we were on site so it wouldn't be too much of a shock if he noticed us. In the message I assured him we were not there to spy on him, and that we would be discreet. I had no idea if he had his phone on or if he would be so bold as to look at it if a message came in as he and Heather were talking. Nevertheless, I had done my best to apprise him of our presence and, having secured Bunny's promise to behave, had made a good faith effort at keeping things from spinning out of control.

To my delight, Bunny kept her word and, despite being seated only two rows back and one row over from Walker and Heather's table, managed to both enjoy her dinner *and* carry on a conversation without calling attention to herself in any way. Even more impressive, she was able to make two passes right behind Walker's chair, thereby getting a closer look at his companion's face—which she graciously declared above average—without making eye contact with her.

"Doesn't seem very pleasant, though," she mused as she squeezed over her vodka tonic one of the lime wedges that had served as the excuse for her promenade to and from the bar. "Either that or things just aren't going well."

"What do you mean?"

"It's hard to say, since the conditions under which I'm allowed to operate didn't permit me to linger long enough to hear more than a few words. All I know for sure is that the woman seemed a bit tense—as if she just heard something incredibly offensive or has a six-legged arthropod wedged in her backside."

While Bunny obsessed over Heather—and how much more she could learn about her *if only* she'd been allowed to sit closer or make a few more passes by their table—I kept one eye on Walker to make sure he wasn't in over his head or preoccupied with our presence. It occurred to me then, as I noticed how attentive and calm he seemed (even as Heather seemed to have—as Bunny had suggested—a bug up her butt) that he really was quite a catch. There can't be many guys, after all, who could handle me—much less Bunny, Erica and Heather—with such skill and confidence, or who would be willing to attempt it without the promise of serious monetary gain.

"Thanks for the entertainment, Sweet Pea," Bunny as we rode back to the parking lot from which she had retrieved me earlier that evening. "I can't wait to hear Walker's version of events."

"Me either."

Our visit had come to an abrupt end when he and Heather suddenly left their chairs and all but marched single file to the lobby. Their timing was excellent from my perspective since it settled the question of whether

Bunny and I would have a third cocktail or switch to decaf (a matter of great import since she had a two hour drive ahead of her) which we had been weighing just nanoseconds before Heather grabbed her purse up from the floor and demanded her check from a passing server. No doubt the timing was less fortuitous for Walker, who favors dignified departures over those that attract an audience—at least 50 percent of whom probably assumed the lady had cause to treat him like a cad.

Finding no sign of him or Heather outside after taking care of our own bill, Bunny and I concluded that they had skipped the good-byes and headed straight from the front door to their respective vehicles. Unsure as to where Heather had parked and whether she might still be in the parking lot, I climbed back into Bunny's SUV and sent Walker a message that we had left the restaurant as well, and would meet him back at the thrift store.

"I'll give you a call Monday," I added, knowing she was hoping to get the scoop tomorrow, if not sooner—and preferably from the horse' mouth. "Mid to late morning, if I can swing it."

"You would really make me wait *that* long?"

"Would you rather I made you wait *longer*?"

Bunny scowled.

"You know, sometimes I could just pound your dad for teaching you kids that," she said, referring to the technique, perfected by Mack, wherein you stop Bunny from stretching an inch out to a mile by raising the price of a commodity rather than lowering it in response to her counter offer, thereby rendering further negotiation unattractive.

"I'm sorry," I laughed. "My intent is not to torture you. I'm just trying to manage your expectations since I may not have the opportunity to get back to you any sooner."

"Fine."

"So how many more of these trips do you think you'll be taking?" Bunny asked, having apparently survived her disappointment. "Assuming Walker is willing to continue after tonight, that is."

"If I'm lucky, less than three."

"That's kind of specific—not to mention ambitious. So why three?"

"Because turkey season starts in four weeks, and if this drags on past opener, Walker will *not* be happy."

"I beg your pardon," Bunny laughed. "Did you just say *Walker* won't be happy?"

"Okay, *I* won't be happy," I admitted, knowing as well as she did that Walker wouldn't give up turkey hunting for anything less than global apocalypse or his own funeral. "But he won't be any happier than I when he gets back if I haven't solved this puzzle before he leaves."

"Ah."

"Well, thanks for dinner," I said as Walker pulled into the space to my right. "Next time it'll be my treat."

"You'll have plenty of chances to treat when I'm old," Bunny countered, "which won't be any time soon if I have anything to say about it."

"So?" I wondered aloud after buckling myself in and setting my handbag on the floor behind Walker's seat in preparation for the drive home. Having gotten the hugs, kisses, greetings, and salutations out of the way before waving good-bye to Bunny, I was eager to get down to business. "Dare I ask?"

"That depends. Are you referring to the question of how the evening went? Or to how the terms of our agreement may change as a result thereof?"

So he is *willing to continue. That's promising.*

"Let's start with the former," I suggested. "That way you can build a case for renegotiating your contract as we go along."

"Good idea."

"Well, as a means of getting to know someone," Walker began, "it went fairly well. As a means of determining if someone is crazy, it went even better."

"Oh my."

Walker nodded gravely.

"She seemed totally normal at first. A bit chatty due, I assumed, to the truth serum she'd had in the bar before we moved to the dining room—but otherwise lucid, intelligent, and pleasant."

"Interesting. So when did things start to go south?"

"About twenty minutes after you texted me."

So he did get the message that Bunny and I were there.

"I ignored it when it first arrived because I didn't want to seem rude," Walker added, "but then took the opportunity to read it while she was complaining to our server about how long it had taken him to refill her water after the appetizers arrived."

"Hmm."

"I know."

"In her defense," he offered with a sigh, "she'd already asked him once. I just didn't think it was that big of a deal since she had a brand new Long Island iced tea in front of her."

"Number two?"

"Three."

"Yikes."

"I should have known then that things were headed downhill," Walker laughed, "but ever the optimist, I attributed both her drinking and irritability to nerves and decided to push on. Or at least, I would have, if she had *let* me."

"What does that mean?"

"Let's just say she took issue with the fact that she'd had to voice her dissatisfaction with the waiter by herself. Apparently where she comes from, 'real gentlemen' handle things like that for their female companions."

"Did she actually say that?"

"Oh yeah."

"What did you say?"

"'Noted.'"

"That was pretty ballsy," I laughed, "considering how volatile she had already revealed herself to be."

"Perhaps. But where I come from, 'real women' fight their own battles, and 'gentlemen' are not required to apologize when they've done nothing wrong."

"Nevertheless, I too expected things to escalate at point," Walker admitted. "But then our food arrived, and I guess she decided she was more hungry than angry, because she started eating as if the last few minutes had never happened."

"That's odd."

"You're telling me."

"But I don't understand, Walker. If she calmed down after the food arrived, why did she suddenly storm out of the place later?"

"Because she's crazy."

"No, seriously."

"I *am* speaking seriously, Roxanne. That woman is not right, and neither is that matching service if it thinks she and I are remotely compatible."

"What I meant," I said, laughing appreciatively but treading lightly, "is 'What happened to cause her to suddenly storm out of the place later?'"

"Oh, we'll get to that. But first we've got to get through dinner."

"We were about halfway through our meals and making small talk," he explained, "when Heather noticed two women staring at us from a table behind me. Assuming it was you and Bunny, I tried to brush the matter off by suggesting they were probably admiring her hairstyle. Unwilling to accept that possibility, she then started asking questions like 'What is their problem?' and 'Who do they think they are?'"

"Oh my God."

"I tried to reset the mood by steering the conversation elsewhere, but she just would not let it go. The next thing I know, she's talking about going over and giving them a piece of her mind about staring and bad manners."

"Oh. My. God."

"Walker, I don't know who she was talking about," I interjected before he could continue, "but I swear to you, it was not us. Sure, we each gave her a subtle once-over when we first arrived and Bunny did walk by your table once to get a closer look, but we were *not* staring at her."

"I know that."

"You do?"

Walker nodded. "I didn't know it at the time, of course. All I knew then was that my wife and mother-in-law were about to be confronted by someone who may or may not be dealing with a full deck."

"How did you know she wasn't dealing with a full deck?"

"Have you ever been stared at?"

I shrugged. "Lots of times."

"And have you ever confronted the people doing the staring?"

"Not since grade school when I'd walk over and tell them to 'shake your head, your eyes are stuck.' Nowadays I generally ignore them or give them crusty looks until they get the message."

"Exactly. And did you or Bunny notice anyone giving you dirty looks or even looking your way as if they were offended by something you were doing?"

"No."

"So either she's crazy for thinking you were staring at her, or she's crazy for planning to confront you—or someone else—for staring at her. Take your pick."

"You mean you gave us the benefit of the doubt? Even though you knew Bunny was there?"

"Not at first. In fact, I was just about to excuse myself to the washroom and send a text asking you guys to clear out when Heather suddenly announced 'They're leaving.' Still thinking it was you and Bunny she was talking about, I figured you'd noticed how uncomfortable you were making her and decided to take off. It was only as I followed her out and saw you and Bunny still sitting there that I realized it wasn't you two who had her knickers in a twist."

"Wow. So someone else happened to be staring at you while Bunny and I were spying on you?"

"Or, Heather is a paranoid fugitive from the local asylum. Again—take your pick."

"Wow," was all I could say.

"Anyway, things got back to normal, so to speak, and stayed that way until about thirty minute later when I failed to jump in and echo her opinions on this budget battle—which is when she decided it was time for us to part company."

Ah.

We don't talk about it much at home since neither of us is all that politically oriented, but Walker tends to be slightly to the right of center on financial issues, and thus isn't as worked up over the contents of the budget repair bill as some of our neighbors and family members would have him be. Although he thinks it's pretty crappy that the governor has tried to ram a bunch of bills through the legislature without sitting down and talking to the teachers unions and other public workers whose wages and benefits are on the line, he thinks it was equally cheesy for the Democrats to have left the state to prevent the matter from coming to a vote when the members of the Republican majority had been elected fair and square.

"So in addition to being paranoid," I observed, "Heather is a little opinionated."

"To put it mildly—yes."

I found this interesting, and wondered if his previous dates had exhibited a similar tendency.

"I don't know why you're surprised," he replied when I shared this thought with him, "since you're hardly lacking in opinions yourself. I mean, we may not spend enough time in the political realm for it to manifest itself that way, but you have plenty to say on other topics."

I thought this was a bit harsh given how much I tend to leave unsaid, but then, what I do have to say sometimes comes across pretty forcefully, so I decided to let it go.

See how willing I am to let others have their way even when I don't necessarily agree?

Walker smiled as if he'd heard every word of this inner dialog.

"Just because you don't always speak your thoughts out loud," he said with a wink, "doesn't mean you don't like to have the last word."

Busted, I trained my gaze forward and pursed my lips to suppress a guilty smile.

"I guess we should talk about your new terms now," I suggested, "so I know whether or not I can still afford you."

Walker laughed. "I was only teasing about that. I really don't mind helping you with this project. I just like to give you hell."

Don't I know it.

"On that note," he added suddenly. "I should ask: Are *you* still happy with our arrangement?"

"Of course. Why wouldn't I be?"

"I'm just thinking about the notes and wondering how helpful they have been."

"They're getting better."

"*Better*?"

"You must admit," I chided as he assumed a look of mild offense. "That first batch was pretty light on details. You almost couldn't call them notes."

"And what exactly did you expect from someone with a lousy memory and precisely zero psychic powers?"

I laughed.

Although I didn't totally endorse his use of the term "psychic powers," I too had questioned the wisdom of trusting an engineer to interpret and describe human behavior and character traits. With the volume and quality of his submissions having improved, however, I had concluded that the initial dearth of detail was a matter of inexperience rather than a lack of talent or will.

"Maybe I'm not the right person for this?" he offered despite my assurances. "Since my strengths are systems and processes rather than people and personality, maybe you should talk to one of your colleagues at the paper."

That sounded a bit like what Aunt Dodie would call dishpan colic, a condition that afflicts children and conveniently sends them running for the bathroom when it's time to do the dishes. I could hardly blame the man if that was the case since dealing with Heather would've made even the most dedicated helper think twice about getting his hands wet; but since Walker was the *only* helper I had on staff, I could not afford to lose him to any infirmity—real or imagined.

"Oh no," I said, aiming for a playful rather than bossy tone. "You're not going to weasel out of this now. I've got too much invested here—and I've already spent the night with those German business associates of yours."

Walker crossed his arms. "Have you now?"

I laughed as I realized how it had come out. "You know what I mean."

"Seriously, Roxanne," he said gently. "Maybe you should get someone else."

"I can't get someone else. I mean, setting aside the fact that I don't know anyone else I would ever want to date, much less sleep with, I honestly don't want to start over with the surveys and profiles and all that crap. Besides, even if there were someone out there I would consider dating, there's no guarantee we'd be compatible and—based on *thematchcafe. com's* failure to put the two of us together—there's no guarantee the system would get it right if we were."

"Maybe you don't have to go all the way back to square one."

"What do you mean?"

"Maybe you could continue to use my profile, but find someone else to go on the dates."

"You mean like a stand-in?"

Walker nodded. "I would have probably said pinch hitter—but, yeah, that's basically what I'm driving at."

"It could work," he continued. "After all, it's not as if I've posted any pictures on my profile page, so no one but the women I've dated knows what I look like. And while I do send a photo when I make first contact, that can be overcome by taking a picture of the stand-in once you find someone for the job."

It was an interesting proposition, and I was impressed he had come up with it—even if his motives weren't entirely unselfish.

"I'll look into it," I said, hoping it wouldn't come to that. Finding someone more socially perceptive than Walker—and who could still pass for an engineer—would be tricky at best; and letting Walker off the hook while I conducted such a search might lead to unacceptable delays.

Walker sighed. "So I guess the beatings will continue until morale improves?"

"Or at least until sufficient information is obtained."

Eleven

alker's next beating, as he would have put it, involved another trip to Tomah, where he was to meet a thirty-five-year-old English teacher named Joy. Having already committed to a night out with Kristin and the gang, I asked Walker to make the excursion solo, and after some verbal and physical cajoling, he agreed.

Thus it was with a dollop of guilt—on top of my usual ration of Alethia-induced nerves—that I entered the bar and made my way to our favorite table.

"So how's the survey project going?" Natalie asked after all the requisite inquiries into the well-being of our respective families had been made. "Did you get everything you were looking for to give that dude his answer?"

"I did, actually. Or at least as much I can reasonably expect from such an informal research method. I'm not going to be able to give him exactly what he's looking for due to the sheer number of sites that are out there, and how different they are from one another. So instead of recommending any particular service, I'm going to approach my response like a literature review, and just sort of summarize what the data says about each one. That should give him, and readers as well, a sense of how the services work so they can choose which ones they want to access."

"Are you planning to give us a preview?" Kristin asked. "Or are you going to keep your findings a secret until they come off the press?"

"I have a little bit more work to do yet," I stalled as I considered the question.

Having not yet finished my review of the *themated cafe.com* and—more importantly—having no idea how long it would be until I did, I knew Kristin and Natalie were unlikely to see the fruits of their labors anytime soon if I made them wait for the item to appear in the paper. With this in mind, I offered to share a draft of my report if the interested parties could see fit to meet me for coffee or lunch the following week.

"Could we make it dinner or drinks again?" Alethia asked. "My new office is too far from any decent eateries for me to come during my coffee or lunch break."

The request took me even more by surprise than Kristin's had. Although I hadn't intended to exclude her by proposing a daytime meeting, neither had I expected her to want to come.

"Never mind," she suddenly added before I could reply. "Just send it to us via e-mail."

Us?

Inside I was shaking my head in disgust. It was just like Alethia to hijack a plan, and to try to keep her court from assembling without her. Oh, it was perfectly fine for her to back out of an event with the four of us if something else more interesting or prestigious came up, or if Laurel wasn't going to be there to play her muse; but to allow a plan that she couldn't be part of to be made in her presence, well, that would *never* do.

"Actually, I can't," I said politely, recalling the syndication agreement that barred me from releasing my product to anyone who wasn't a subscriber until thirty days after an item had run.

"I guess we'll have to shoot for dinner or drinks as you suggested," I added helpfully, "or wait a few more weeks until it's available in print or online."

"A few more weeks?" Natalie repeated. "I thought you already had all the data?"

"I do. But like I said, I still have a little work to do."

Kristin eyed me sideways. "So much that it's going to take weeks for the full item to run?"

I sighed as I realized the jig was up. Having painted myself into a corner, I had no choice but to spill the beans about my investigation into *themated cafe.com*, and the methods I was using to determine whether or not its claims were valid.

"Wow," Kristin marveled when I'd finished my tale. "I can't believe you got Walker to do all that."

"Why not?" Alethia sniffed. "Greg would do just about anything for me."

Laurel shook her head. "There's no way Marty would do any of that for me."

"Curt already has," Natalie announced with a shrug. "He just did it behind my back and without recording any data."

There was a pause as we all absorbed the remark, followed by a gust of laugher as Natalie cracked a smile. It was great to see her making light of Curt's indiscretions, and we all raised a glass to that as much as to the quality and timing of her joke.

"What I want to know," Alethia asked as the giggling subsided, "is why you would ask your man to do this in the first place. I mean, honestly, doesn't the idea of him spending time with other women make you just a little bit nervous?"

"Why would it?"

"Why would it?" she repeated, looking around the table for support. "Aren't you at all afraid he might leave you for one of them?"

"No. Is there some reason you think I should be?"

Alethia smiled as the other three almost physically backed away. "Look, Roxanne, I admire your confidence, but you and I both know what they say about the greener pastures."

"I suppose. But I don't see how having Walker spend time with strange women creates a problem that doesn't otherwise exist. I mean, he's no more likely to leave me for one of them than he is to do so for a colleague, a coworker, or one of my wonderful friends."

"But colleagues, coworkers, and your friends all know he's off limits," she argued, "And they're not going to lead him into temptation, as it were."

I certainly hope not.

"This is silly," Laurel interjected. "You only have to see the two of them together once to know that Walker only has eyes for Roxanne."

"That's true," Kristin agreed. "You're barking up the wrong tree here, Alethia."

Alethia shrugged. "Maybe. But what about these poor women," she began again. "Doesn't it bother you—as a woman yourself—that they're expecting to meet a single guy who wants to settle down when in fact they're meeting a married man who's only there to collect data for his wife?"

"Not really."

"Well, it seems a bit heartless to me."

"I don't understand why it would," I countered. "It's not as if he's promised them anything and then reneged. They know going into it that things may not click. Besides, how many men do single women go out with that they later decide not to see again? So is it really any worse that he knows in advance he won't be seeing them again than it would be for someone to decide not to see the other person again after meeting them?"

Alethia, shrugged again. "Maybe not," she allowed. "I just couldn't do what you and Walker are doing, I guess. That's all."

I found it bizarre that Alethia was even remotely interested in this project, much less worried about my research subjects. But to say so would have been beside the point, and would have led me to say things about her behavior that would have made our companions uncomfortable.

"Well, we're all different people," I offered, referring to the entire table with an illustrative nod. "There are probably lots of things some of us would do that others of us wouldn't."

Like put other people on the spot and attack their character.

"But it may ease your mind to know," I continued with a sly smile, "that we do have a plan in place to prevent anyone from becoming too smitten with Mr. Browne. If he senses, for example, that his date is picturing him walking down the aisle in a white tux and tails or imagining what their children would look like, he's been instructed to take out his reading glasses, spill his drink on the table, and dump hers in the process of wiping his up. In the event this strategy backfires, because, say, the woman finds clumsy men appealing or is a codependent who wants someone she needs to fix, he is to immediately start exhibiting unattractive behaviors, starting with the mildly irritating—like cracking of the knuckles—to the totally revolting, such as picking his teeth or cleaning his ears with a car key."

Although Alethia did not appreciate my attempt at levity, the rest of the gang did, and so the conversation took a sharp turn for the absurd as Natalie, Laurel, and Kristin speculated as to the means by which their spouses might repel an admirer. Eventually Alethia had to choose between holding her tongue, which would preserve the myth of Mr. Perfect but keep her in the shadows, and reclaiming the spotlight by sharing information that would dispel the Gregory Mystique.

When the lunacy had passed—with Greg's reputation as our generation's answer to Einstein and Dionysius still intact—the conversation again turned to the column, thanks to Laurel, who had a comment about my reply to a woman who had written about an issue she was having with her teenage daughter.

I was more than ready to stop talking about work—especially given its propensity to incite Alethia to vileness—so I kept my response to Laurel short and sweet, and then quickly asked her about her new car.

"I saw that letter," Alethia remarked, trampling all over Laurel's reply in the process. "And I hate to keep picking on you, Roxanne, but do you think it's responsible for you to answer parenting questions having never been a parent yourself?"

I must have turned several shades of red with embarrassment, and then several more from anger. She was like one of those annoying little dogs with a yappy bark who refused to let go of a bone. I would have been perfectly within my rights to let her have it with both barrels, but I wasn't about to lose my cool.

"Actually, I don't think my having or not having kids has anything to do with it," I said instead, taking care not to reveal my inner tumult. "After all, one needn't have experience with, say, a condescending coworker or pretentious in-laws to competently advise others on how to deal with people like them; likewise, one doesn't need to be a parent in order to advise them on how to resolve issues with teenagers or small children. Perhaps personal experience might come in handy with issues such as teething and ear aches, but when it comes to things like getting kids to do their homework, avoid the wrong crowd, or treat others with respect, you're basically talking about discipline, problem solving, and conflict management, so all you need is an understanding of human behavior and communication, and a solid grasp on emotional and cognitive development—all of which I have, thanks to six years of college, four years of fieldwork, and a counseling certificate from the great state of Wisconsin.

"So, yes," I concluded blithely. "I do think it's responsible for me to give parenting advice despite having never been a parent myself. And you can rest assured that, when I do encounter something that's out of my depth, I don't overstep. Depending on the nature of the question, I'll address the writer privately and refer him—or her—to someone more qualified, or I'll do like I did with the question about online dating: Poll the experts and do the research."

Oh why, why, WHY do we put up with her? Kristin asked via e-mail the next day, as much in the hope of gauging how I was doing, I assumed, as expressing her own frustration. Although I had managed to keep my cool, it was no doubt obvious to Kristin that I had struggled to do so. Thus, I knew she would be looking to my response for clues as to how I was holding up, and whether I needed to vent my frustrations out loud.

With this in mind, I shot her a quick reply that included a suggestion that we pool our considerable good karma—banked over the course of the years that we've been putting up with Ms. Dornquast—to effect her relocation to a place from which she is likely never to return.

It wouldn't have to be an unfavorable event, I reasoned. In fact, the rules of karma dictate that it be a favorable one if we don't want something terrible to befall us. So let us hope that either she or Greg receives a great job offer or other opportunity that requires them to move to a place they love or have always wanted to go. This part will be a major struggle for me, as I generally prefer to condemn evil people to hell or a life of unrelenting frustration. However, as that would likely backfire and deliver them instead to paradise while simultaneously subjecting us to copious amounts of emotional anguish or physical harm, I will entreat providence to handle them with the utmost kindness and care.

From there, I asked about her plans for the week, and inquired as to her interactions with the colleague who, unbeknownst to Kristin, had confessed to being a member of *ashleymadison.com*.

Forget him, she replied. He is a total ass. I found out yesterday that he was two-timing one of our social workers while he was seeing another woman from my department.

Reading her message, I breathed a sigh of relief that I didn't have to break it to her myself.

I've decided I'm holding out for Matt Damon, her note continued. I had a dream about him the other night. I won't go into detail, but I am convinced he is worth waiting for.

Interesting, I replied. Last night I had a dream about George Clooney. I was at his house in Italy, which was filled with beautiful young women who were wandering around crying, sobbing, and pouting. Disgusted, I told them all to leave and forget about George. Then I ordered him to sit his ass down and chastised him for his inability to commit and his refusal to date women his own age. Then I cleaned the house, did the dishes, and went home.

Yes. I know it's sad. Other women dream about having sex with celebrities. I dream about fixing them.

All jokes aside, I continued in the next paragraph down. *What the hell is Alethia's deal? I mean, normally when someone act like that, it's because they're compensating for some kind of distress, disappointment, or deficiency. So I have to wonder, what the hell is going on with her or between her and Greg that makes her so obnoxious? Given her height, my first guess would be Short Woman Syndrome, but since she's always bragging about how tiny she is, I doubt that's her problem. So what gives?*

I don't know what scientists call the next smaller unit of time after the nanosecond, but it seemed like barely three of them had passed from the moment I sent the e-mail to Kristin to the point at which her number appeared as an incoming call on my cell phone.

"Hey," I said cheerfully. "I literally just replied to your e-mail."

"I know. That's why I'm calling."

"I just couldn't hold it in any longer," Kristin explained, "so if Laurel ever finds out I told you, you have to promise to tell her that you guessed."

"Guessed what?"

"Okay, do you remember that time Alethia offered to let me and the boys *vacation* at her and Greg's place while they went to Bermuda?"

"And you declined? Of course I do. Why?"

"Well, since they couldn't find anyone to housesit for them and Laurel had no plans, she offered to run by their place every few days to check things out, water the plants, skim the leaves from the pool, et cetera. Well, on one of her visits she got caught in a downpour and her clothes got soaked, so she decided to toss them in the dryer."

"And?"

"*And,* when she opened the dryer, she found a load of clean socks, tee shirts, and so forth. Thinking it would be nice for Alethia and Greg if they didn't have to put laundry away when they got home, she decided to carry the load upstairs and do it for them."

"And?"

"*And,* when she opened the drawers to what she thought was Greg's dresser, she found several sets of bras and panties with matching silk robes."

"And?" I breathed. Although I could see where she was going with this, I didn't want to jump to any conclusions until I'd heard all the evidence.

"*And yet,*" Kristin obliged, "when Laurel went to the other dresser thinking she'd made a mistake, she found several more pieces of ladies' lingerie."

"Okay—so Alethia is a clothes horse. What else is new?"

"How about the fact that the sets Laurel found in the first dresser were all size XXL, while those in the second were all extra *small*."

"Get out. You're making that up."

"I swear to you, I am not."

"Then there must be some other explanation."

"Like what? Like Alethia used wear extra large women's underwear, which she now keeps in case she gets fat again or to motivate herself to keep the weight off?"

"Seems plausible," I allowed unconvincingly. "We don't know what she looked like before they moved here, after all, and it would explain why she's always pointing out how petite she is."

"Yeah. Well how about this: After noting the differences in the sizes of the lingerie in the two dressers and wondering what it meant, Laurel decided to have a look in the closet. Care to guess what she found?"

"Go ahead," Kristin challenged me with a laugh. "Guess."

"Several pairs of women's pumps in size ten and a half?" I offered with a cringe.

"Close. Size eleven—extra wide."

"Oh my God."

"I know. Explains a lot, doesn't it?"

"Well, it may explain Alethia's need to brag about Greg's accomplishments, since she can hardly talk about his taste in lingerie. Then again, assuming she's uncomfortable with it—as opposed to accepting of or turned on by it—Greg's cross dressing could be a source of friction, which would definitely explain why she's wound so tight and why their daughter's such a mess."

"That's what Laurel said."

"Now listen," Kristin admonished. "No matter what happens, you cannot say anything about this to anyone. Because Laurel would die if Alethia found out she'd been in her drawers."

"And Alethia would die if she knew what Laurel found there."

"Exactly."

"And while that may not be incentive for *us* to keep our mouths shut," Kristin advised, "my promise to Laurel is. So can I count on you?"

"Of course. I don't need for Alethia to know I know. It's enough for me to know I know."

"I hoped it would be. That's why I called."

"Thanks."

"You're welcome. Now, I'm sorry to cut this short, but I've got to get back to work."

Even after swapping e-mails and gossiping with Kristin, I was still more than a little annoyed by my exchange with Alethia the night before. Somehow, even knowing her handsome, brilliant, and highly respected husband had a fondness for lingerie did nothing to rouse my sympathy for her or quash my urge to see her get her comeuppance. In fact, so great was my irritation with her behavior—past and present—that I couldn't concentrate, and basically wasted the entire morning and much of the afternoon revisiting the conversation.

I knew it was stupid to let her words get to me—and to let them keep me from getting anything done; but whenever I tried to think about something else, I found my mind wandering back to what she'd said and how I had responded. It was as if I were trapped in a maze wherein every thought I had reminded me of one of Alethia's remarks, which in turn reminded me of her comments the previous night.

Normally, when people have trouble moving on from an experience like mine, I'll suggest they break down what was said and identify specifically what part of the exchange is bothering them. Oftentimes the snag results from an unconscious suspicion or belief that what was said is true. The offended party, therefore, is upset at having heard something she or he doesn't want to face. Other times the problem is that what was said was untrue, and the offended party is afraid other people will still believe it and resents that she or he is powerless to do anything about it. Still other times the problem is one of perceived injustice wherein the offended party is upset at the offending party simply because his or her own code of behavior prevents her from saying or doing whatever it was that the offender did—or from responding in a way she feels is deserved—and thinks the offender should be admonished and/or punished for her actions.

While it is true I would never have said the things Alethia said to me—or many of the things she has said in my presence, for that matter—this was not the source of my discontent. Nor was the problem that I'm afraid I'm not qualified to do my job, or that I thought Alethia's suggestion that I'm not qualified might somehow resonate with the others.

What it boiled down to, I realized—after a few hours of HGTV programming observed without sound—was not what Alethia had said, then or ever, but that she kept getting away with saying things like this because I was afraid of how the other gals would react if I ever told her off. Plainly put, it disgusted me that a woman my age was unwilling to risk social isolation to stand up against a narcissistic bully.

And while I knew it wasn't what she said that had upset me, I couldn't help but wonder why she had said it. One could speculate, I suppose, that she attacked my qualifications after Laurel mentioned the letter from the parent because her own kid has given her a lot of grief and she resents the idea that someone without kids would dare to think she could handle it better. Then again, for all I knew, her only reason for speaking up at all was to point out that I don't have children in the hope that it was a sore spot for me.

Oh my God, I thought as it hit me.

I don't have children.

I don't have CHILDREN.

I DO NOT HAVE CHILDREN.

With my heart pumping wildly, I raced back to my office for my notes. Recalling the fifth packet that Walker had left on the table before heading to work, I ran to the kitchen and grabbed that too. Then I scrambled back to my office and settled into my chair.

It never even occurred to me, I announced aloud as I flipped through the packets. *But it's the only thing that makes sense.*

So far from my mind was the matter of offspring that I hadn't even made a space for it in the forms. Walker had noticed this on his first date and had been forced to record what he gathered on the subject in the comments section of his survey, or in the blank spaces along the margins. Thus, I couldn't be sure if what I would find in the packets would be complete and accurate since for all I know, a blank space may have meant that Walker had forgotten to write it down or that the subject simply hadn't come up.

Locating the printouts of the basic profiles of his matches, I soon realized they would be no help. In the interest of member security, the profiles contained first names but not last; ages but not birthdays; and cities, but not street addresses. Meanwhile, in order to keep pedophiles from targeting single parents, the system didn't indicate on members' profiles whether or not they even had children. Rather, it relied on the software to quietly sort out who was compatible with whom and left it to the members to decide how much information to divulge to the people with whom they made contact. With this in mind, it became clear I would have to rely on Walker and his dates to have talked about children, and on him to have recorded what he'd gathered if this particular expedition was going to yield any useful details.

As I worked my way through Walker's notes, my excitement over the possibility of finally finding the key to this mystery started to fade. Two of the ladies he'd met apparently mentioned they had children, but the other three either did not have kids or didn't say. Or they did say and Walker hadn't recorded it because there wasn't space for it in the notes. Or he'd simply forgotten.

Damn. Damn. Damn. Damn. Damn.

I was about to close the door on this subject and let Walker resume his work—with a new and improved research tool, of course—when I recalled that the profile questionnaire contained not one but several questions about children, which in retrospect were clearly designed to yield a more nuanced analysis of members' compatibility than could be generated simply by asking whether or not they have children. It made sense, therefore, to take another look at that part of the questionnaire before ruling the issue of parenthood a red herring. With this in mind, I logged on to the site and poked around until I found what I was looking for.

Do you have children? It read. *If so, how many?* It then asked for the gender of each child and the year they were born before posing a few questions about the future. These included:

Are you interested in or open to having any/more children?

Are you interested in or open to a long-term relationship with someone who has children from a previous relationship?

Are you interested in or open to a long-term relationship with someone who has children from a previous relationship who live with him or her?

Are you interested in or open to a long-term relationship with someone who has children who would not live with him or her but who would visit regularly or occasionally and spend evenings and/or weekends at your home?

So the issue wasn't simply whether members have children or not. Of equal if not greater importance was whether they were willing to make a life with someone who already had them; whether they were willing to raise someone else's kids or merely put up with them from time to time; and whether they were hoping to have more kids of their own at some point.

And I—despite having answered all these questions when I completed my profile; despite their being so precisely phrased that one might entertain the idea of consulting an attorney before answering them—had deemed them all immaterial and essentially forgotten they existed.

Talk about research bias.

No one with children would have made such a mistake, I admonished myself. *Nor would someone who wanted them, or who was interested in meeting someone else who wanted them.*

No. Only someone with zero interest in children—their own or someone else's—could have made such an error.

That's not to say I dislike children. I won't go so far as to say I *love* them, but they're okay as people go, provided they're well groomed, well behaved, and in good health. As with adults, I prefer them sentient, articulate, and self-toileting, but I can tolerate infants and toddlers now and then as long as their parents are standing by to whisk them away at the first sign of hunger, thirst, or other form of distress. In short, I can abide children in small doses, but I've never felt the need, urge, or desire to have my own.

Teens and preteens are a slightly different story. Unlike most people I've encountered, I prefer the company of older kids over that of young children, and enjoy engaging them in conversations about music and movies, and social and cultural issues. It's amazing how much they know and understand but keep tucked away, and how much they care and what they could accomplish if adults took them more seriously. Even the rebellious and remote among them have a lot to offer and would be more cooperative and involved if they could trust that they would not be dismissed or ridiculed for being too young and inexperienced. Unfortunately humans don't come into the world walking or talking in complete sentences, so barring the adoption or foster care route, you can't parent teens or preteens without spending a few years with infants, toddlers, preschoolers, or kindergarten through third graders, which is too high a price to pay in my book.

It isn't so much the diapers, the dirt, or the daily chaos I object to—although they're all major deterrents—I just don't want someone else's physical, social, and emotional well-being to turn on my knowledge, skills, or abilities. That may sound odd coming from an advice columnist, but there is a huge difference between caring for helpless creatures who are counting on you not to screw them up, and corresponding or conferring with adults who are already screwed up and looking to you only for advice and support.

When I was younger and would tell people I wasn't planning to have kids, more often than not they would look at me as if I was a monster or shouldn't be walking the streets. Those who didn't doubt my sanity would instead question my morality—as if voluntary childlessness were a crime or a social disease. Even Bunny, who says if it were up to her, people would have to get a license to bear children, didn't take me seriously. "Most people who say they don't want kids eventually change their minds," she would insist, "and likely as not you will too."

In response, I would warn her not to hold her breath. I knew damn well I wasn't cut out to deal with the stuff my brother and I, and Mel and Charlotte put her through, and I wasn't going to force it or fake it. Given the consequences of failure, it just wasn't worth the risk.

"I sure as hell wouldn't want me for a parent," I would offer if pressed. "So why on earth would you wish me on your own grandchildren?"

That usually ended the conversation, although sometimes it prompted a lecture instead, so I tended to invoke that logic sparingly.

I can recall only one time in my life when I regretted my lack of maternal instincts. It was following a miscarriage I had about five months after my wedding. Having been on the pill since I was sixteen—not because I got around, mind you, but to manage a case of endometriosis—I typically had light periods and sometimes no period at all. Thus, I didn't realize I was pregnant until the night I was brought to my knees by pain in my lower abdomen. Suspecting appendicitis, Walker rushed me to the hospital only to find that I did not have a hot appendix, but a tubal pregnancy that was threatening to burst and convey me and my errant zygote to another realm.

The credit for this breathtaking adventure goes to a little-known condition called SIN—or *salpingitis isthmica nodosa,* which is a fancy name for inflammatory fallopian tube disease and a not uncommon byproduct of endometriosis. I may have never known about it if it hadn't been for the antibiotics I'd taken a few weeks earlier, which had dampened the effect of the pill and allowed an egg to sneak out, get fertilized, and take up residence where it didn't belong.

In order to prevent a recurrence of a potentially fatal kind, a surgeon removed my faulty reproductive components and sent me home to convalesce. Per the protocols of her profession, she left my ovaries intact, which would allow me to continue charming the loved ones with my fascinating mood swings and violent carbohydrate cravings—or vice versa—at least until I ran out of estrogen. And so, after losing a pregnancy that I had neither planned nor wanted, I only had to deal with the guilt of not being unhappy with the outcome.

It wasn't on any particular person's behalf that I felt guilty. Having kids wasn't something in which Walker had ever expressed an interest. Although he had never explicitly ruled it out before my surgery, whenever friends or relatives would ask if or when we planned to start a family, he had always brushed it off with a "Maybe someday" in a way that implied that *someday* would likely never come. This suited me just fine, so I didn't sweat it.

Even after that ordeal, all Walker had to say on the subject was "I'm so glad you're okay." He never referred to the pregnancy as a baby, or expressed sadness over it coming to an end; nor did he treat the event as a tragedy or seem devastated or even disappointed that I could no longer reproduce. Consequently, I concluded he was perfectly content to remain childless and that the issue—or lack thereof—was effectively but not unhappily closed.

It probably helped that there was already some doubt as to my ability to have kids before we got married. Along with severe pain and excessive bleeding, infertility is a common feature of endometriosis. While the pill can be effective in treating its symptoms, they often come back after contraceptives are discontinued. Thus, there was no guarantee I could have had children even if I had wanted them.

That history, combined with my haste to complete my profile and discover whether Walker and I would be matched, had made it easy for me to breeze through the questionnaire without a thought as to the significance of any specific area of inquiry. On second look, however, I was suddenly convinced that the key to this mystery could be found in the section on parenthood, and anxious to see if I was correct.

And so it was with more than a trace of excitement that I pondered the various combinations of responses it would take for the system to match Walker to the five unwitting participants in my study. Unfortunately, after running a few logic models, it became apparent that, given my limited data, I was going about this all wrong.

Setting aside my papers, I faced my computer and logged back in to my *thematchcafe.com* account and started playing with my own responses.

And then, as if by magic, Walker was on my list.

I couldn't believe it was that simple. After all the miles we had logged driving all over the state for Walker's dates—after all the time and energy I'd put into analyzing the data, I finally had what I was looking for. And it practically had been right under my nose the whole time.

Overcome by the thrill of victory, I gave myself a mental high five and salivated at the prospect of telling Walker that his note-taking days were over.

And then the other shoe fell: Walker wanted children.

I didn't know how many he wanted, or whether he wanted boys or girls, but the man clearly wanted children and I couldn't have them. More importantly, I didn't want them.

This posed a big problem. For even if I had no objection to a couple having a child that only one of them wanted, our only option was to adopt. And even if I thought I had what it takes to keep a stranger's child alive for eighteen years, Walker and I didn't have the financial means to make that happen.

And so, realizing we were pretty much screwed in terms of our future together, I switched my answer back to what they'd been that morning, put away all the printouts and note packets, and sat down to reflect.

I'd been naive to think he would tell me. A guy can't walk up to his wife after she's been rendered sterile and inform her he wants children. And he can't leave her to pursue a relationship with someone whose reproductive system and nurturing instincts are in working order. Even if he knew from the beginning that the woman didn't want kids and might never be able to have them, his only option—unless he wants the rest of the world to think he's a complete ass—is to shut up and suck it up.

But now the cat was indisputably out of the bag, and the only thing left to resolve was what to do about it.

Obviously I had to let him go. You can't have a relationship with someone knowing he wants something you don't and then pretend the problem doesn't exist. More importantly, you can't have a relationship with someone you know is sacrificing something for you, and not have it color every other aspect of that relationship.

But Walker would never admit there was a problem. He wouldn't want me to feel bad, so he would deny everything even if I asked him about it outright. Even if I showed him the evidence, he would say he'd misread the questionnaire or simply marked the wrong box. Either way, he wouldn't leave me over this. Walker wasn't that kind of man.

And so I decided to do the only smart thing I could under the circumstances: I would have to leave him.

Upon realizing that Walker and I were not meant to be—*congratulations, thematchcafe.com; I hope you're happy*—I started making plans for our separation. The first step in this process would be securing a steady income. The *Post-Courier* was fair in how it compensated its contributors and my syndication deal was pretty good; but I certainly wasn't getting rich off of either arrangement and what I was getting wouldn't pay the bills. I would also need to find a place to live, but until I had a job, I wouldn't know what I could afford or where to look. The final step would be to tell Walker that I was leaving and without letting on as to why. I wasn't about to tell him the truth and have him then try to talk me into staying out of some noble sense that it was the gentlemanly thing to do.

It did not escape my notice that I was acting against my own interests. If I wanted to be with Walker—and I did—all I had to do was keep my mouth shut and go on with life as if nothing had changed.

Nor did it escape me that I was ignoring all the advice I had dispensed over the years and violating my own belief in speaking one's mind and confronting problems head on. For the first time in my life, in fact, I was starting to understand why people stuff their emotions and leave things to fester. If I—a woman who was encouraged to rock the boat and had always had the love and support of her family—was reluctant to talk to a man so decent that he would subvert a desire to have kids in order to spare his infertile wife pain or embarrassment, how on earth could I expect those who've been criticized, punished, and otherwise mistreated virtually all their lives to confront assholes who have always ignored them and have never taken them seriously? And was my plan to abandon Walker any more honorable or assertive than Janine's decision to move into the guest room or start sleeping with Dr. Ron?

The difference, of course, was that I wasn't acting from a position of anger or frustration, and my goal wasn't to punish or provoke. I was just trying to give the man I loved what he wanted so I could have a clear conscience. At least, that's what I told myself.

"What are you doing?" said man inquired as I pondered these thoughts in my office later that evening.

Having not heard him come into the house, much less the room, my heart nearly stopped. I waved at him so I could dedicate my mouth and lungs to catching my breath.

"Just updating my resume," I replied, hoping he interpreted my look of panic as part of my startle response.

"Oh?"

"There's an opening for a lifestyle editor at the paper," I lied as I minimized the window to prevent him from seeing my actual job target. "So I've decided to throw my hat into the ring."

"But I thought you were going to start working on your book as soon as this matching service project was over? Isn't that why you haven't been running workshops and seminars? Because a full-time job would get in the way?"

"I'll get around to that stuff, don't worry. In the meantime, the editorial work will be great experience and preparation for putting the finishing touches on the book."

Not wanting to arouse his suspicions by my refusal to reopen the windows on my computer screen, I got up to lure him into the kitchen so we could discuss something other than my lie while making dinner.

"So what did you think of my notes?" he asked proudly, having noted they were no longer on the table. "I see you found them."

"They were great, Walker. A big improvement on the other batches, and very detailed."

"Wonderful. I guess it helps to do them when your mind is still fresh," he pretended to marvel as he watched me season the steaks I had sentenced that morning to the broiler.

"Yeah," I mused. "Who would've ever thunk it?"

Walker laughed. "I'll try to get the next ones done the same night too," he promised. "That way maybe you'll get more out of them and figure out what's going on with that software."

"That won't be necessary. In fact, you don't even have to go on another date, unless you've already set something up and it's too late in the game for you to cancel."

"Are you firing me?" he asked with a charming combination of concern and hope.

"No. I'm not firing you. I'm just not sure it makes any sense to continue, given how little I've come up with. So I've decided to suspend the research for now and rethink my project design."

"So no more dates?"

I nodded. "And no more notes."

"Aw man," he said with mock dismay. "And just when I was getting good at it."

Walker wasn't the only one I was going to be lying to in the coming weeks, as I realized upon seeing a picture of Thumper on my phone the following weekend while he was out stalking turkeys with his brother.

"Rise and shine, baby mine," she said when I picked up. "Time to greet the day."

"Mother, it's nine a.m. and I greeted the day about two hours ago, thank you very much."

"I see. Well, it sounds to me like you did it from the wrong side of the bed. Maybe you ought to go back and try again."

"I'll think about it."

"Meanwhile," I continued, placing my breakfast plate in the sink. "How are you today?"

"Excellent—apart from wondering where my notes are. Didn't you say Walker had another meeting in Tomah last Friday?"

Right. I had been so excited by what I thought they could tell me that I'd forgotten to scan and send them to her. After that, well, there didn't seem much point.

"About the notes, Mom," I began, hoping to sound convincing. "I'm suspending my research, so, they won't be coming after all."

"What do you mean by suspending your research?"

Now what? I thought. It's not like I could just announce that the system was right and Walker and I aren't compatible without her asking a whole slew of questions. This was Bunny, after all.

So after giving her a song and dance about potential flaws in my logic models and assorted other whooey I knew she'd understand but not question, I told her to e-mail her work product thus far, and dump her copies.

"Wow. You're serious."

"I am."

"Okay then. And just what do you plan to do with yourself now that you're going to have so much free time?"

"I'm probably going to get a job."

"A job? You already have a job. Actually, you have two."

"I mean a *real* job. One that has regular hours and rewards you with a regular paycheck."

"But I thought you wanted to finally get started on the book you've always talked about—the one on friendship and compatibility."

"I do. And I will. Just not yet."

I could tell from the silence that Bunny's wheels were spinning.

"Are you and Walker having financial problems?" she offered. "You can tell me, if you are. I won't tell your father, and Walker doesn't have to know you told me."

As if.

Bunny may believe in confidentiality when it comes to the women and children she has worked with over the years, but when it comes to family she makes exceptions and exploits every technicality in the interests of what she perceives as the greater good. Which is why, if I were to tell her we were having financial problems, not only would Mack know, but so would everyone on Bunny's side of the family—from whom we could expect to receive checks, gift cards, and a year's supply of canned goods.

"No, Mom. Walker and I are not having financial problems. I just think it's time I grew up and did my part around here. And stopped sponging off the rich, as Uncle Mel would say."

"That doesn't sound like you. Not the Mel part," she added with a laugh. "I mean the growing up and doing your part."

"*Mother!*"

"I don't mean it that way, either," she insisted. "I mean, you've always been okay with the fact that you didn't want a traditional career, so it sounds kind of strange to hear you equating your current lifestyle with immaturity and sloth."

Wow. Only Bunny could make that leap so quickly.

"Level with me, Roxanne. Because I can tell something's wrong."

"Fine," I agreed just to stop the inquisition. "Walker and I are separating."

"You're *what*?"

"It's a mutual thing, so don't go getting your Bunny undies in a bundle."

"I don't understand. What happened?"

"Nothing happened. We just decided it's the best thing to do."

"Does this have anything to do with the research project?"

"No," I lied. Because it didn't—at least not as she would have conceived it. The situation clearly existed before the research project. I just didn't know it yet.

"I knew this was a bad idea," Bunny was saying now. "This is just like that movie *Indecent Proposal* where Woody Harrelson talks Demi Moore into sleeping with Robert Redford, and then drives himself bat-ass crazy with jealousy as soon as the deed is done."

I sighed.

"This has nothing to do with the research, Mom," I repeated, hoping this time my tone didn't trip her lie detector. "And this is nothing like *Indecent*

Proposal. I'm not jealous of Walker for dating those women, or that those women were interested in him. Nor am I torturing myself with thoughts of what he ate when he was out to dinner with them, or worrying that he prefers their company to mine."

"If you say so. Now was this separation Walker's idea, or yours?"

"It was a mutual decision." *Or at least it will be when I finally tell him.*

"Okay, but which of you brought it up?"

"Mother."

"What? I'm not allowed to ask questions? These are the kind of things mothers ask when they get a shock like this, Roxanne. You can't expect me to act like you've just told me it's snowing."

I knew my reticence was making matters worse. I should have thought this through better.

"It was me."

It was my only option under the circumstances. There was no way I could pin this on Walker. It would totally change how Bunny and Mack saw him, and that would be completely unfair.

"You?"

"Yes."

"But why?"

"I don't want to go into it over the phone," I said, grateful for the distance between our locations and the chance to say something true for a change. "Let's just say I think it's the right thing to do. As my mother, I think you should support that."

"Fine. I'll support it. For now. Meanwhile," she added abruptly, "you should know that I do not intend to share this with your father. Instead I'm going to sit on this little bit of news and hope it was all a bad dream or that you'll have changed your mind the next time we speak."

"Fine. Okay. Whatever you want."

"Alright then. When can I see you?"

By *see you* I knew she meant see my face—which meant I would have to do whatever I was going to do before she found time to come to La Crosse and try to change my mind.

"I'll check my calendar," I offered, "and call you back tomorrow."

"You'd better. Or I'm going to plan a surprise visit, and you won't know when I'll show up."

Twelve

Behaving normally when things aren't right is a lot harder with someone you care about as much as I did Walker. I was used to holding my tongue with Alethia and other people whom I disliked or whose opinions of me didn't matter. Keeping my distance and holding my tongue with Walker, whom I loved and whose good opinion of me I prized, on the other hand, was a bitch.

The thing I missed most of all was our banter. We had always teased each other since way back in college. Some people thought we were bickering, but the majority could tell we were having fun, and several would laugh out loud when one of us made a particularly clever lob at the other. These days, there wasn't much banter flying about the house because I was trying so hard not to talk about certain things, and I couldn't think of anything else to say.

I also missed spending time with him. I'd been keeping my distance because I found it easier to avoid talking if we weren't in the same room. This part wouldn't have been so difficult for me if things were still as nuts as they used to be for him at work. Now that Walker had finally found his groove at the brewery, he was spending more time at home, which meant I was spending more time trying to avoid him. As a result, I found myself staying in bed later than usual in the morning. It was easier than being up and around as he got ready for work or holding back my tears while helping him pack his lunch and seeing him out the door each day.

Eventually I stopped getting out of bed at all except to check my e-mail and pursue job leads.

The one bright spot in all this was the fact that I had my features and columns written several weeks out and therefore didn't have to do much more than proofread them before sending them to Karla or the syndication company. I was grateful for this not only because it freed me up to mourn my impending loss, but also because any advice I would have dispensed at the time likely would have been pure crap.

Although I was spending much of my day in bed, I did my best to act like everything was normal when Walker was home, and made excuses when it obviously wasn't. As time passed, however, my sadness became harder to hide and Walker became more curious.

"Are you okay, Roxanne?" he asked one night as we were getting into bed.

I'd just had my first job interview with a counseling center in Madison, and was wishing I could tell him how it went. I could have pretended it was for something right in La Crosse, but that would have required more lying, and I couldn't stomach the thought of that even for the chance to appear more animated.

"I'm fine," I assured him with a light peck on his cheek. "Just a little tired."

I was still *a little tired* one week later when my phone rang about three hours after Walker left for work. Having not slept much since making my discovery about his interest in children, I was about to switch it to voice mail and roll back over when I noticed the gray and white tones of a cartoon rabbit on the screen, and remembered I'd forgotten to call Bunny.

"Hello, darling," she said sweetly. "Did you sleep well?"

"Not really," I admitted. There seemed no harm in it after all.

"I wouldn't have thought so, what with so much weighing on your conscience."

My heart started to race as I tried to imagine what she was driving at, since there seemed no way she could know the truth.

"I know. And I'm sorry. I was supposed to call you days ago."

"Yes, you were. And the only reason I'm not standing at the foot of your bed yelling at you in person is that the weather's bad."

"Why would you be yelling at me in the first place?"

"You mean, apart from breaking your promise to call me, and telling me and Walker both a pack of lies?"

"Walker?"

"Yes, Walker. That is sweet, hardworking, decent Walker, who oddly enough knows *nothing* at all about your impending separation."

"*Knows* nothing? As in, still doesn't?"

"Yes, dear."

"I took care not to accidentally fill him in," Bunny assured me, "when he called me on his way to work this morning to ask if I knew what's wrong with you. He said he'd tried to talk to you himself—about how sad and distant you'd become—but you kept brushing him off. Not knowing what else to do, he decided to ask me for advice."

Wow. I never saw that one coming.

"So what gives?" Bunny continued. "And this time, I want the truth.

So I gave it to her. Each and every last bitter morsel.

"Holy Christ," she breathed when I had finished.

"Exactly. Now do you understand why I'm leaving?"

"Actually, no. I don't."

"And what would you have me do instead?"

"I'd have you talk to him, for starters."

"No way."

"Why not?"

"Because I won't have him staying with me out of some misplaced sense of duty. That's no basis for a healthy relationship, Mother, and you know it."

"You don't know that's why he's staying with you. As hard as it may be for you to believe, it could be that he loves you."

"You think so? Then why on earth would he want to meet women who have children? Or women who want to have children?"

"I don't know. You'll have to ask him."

"Not going to happen.

"Seriously, Mother," I insisted in response to a disapproving sigh. "Do you think Walker would admit to wanting kids when he knows damned well I can't have them and never wanted them?"

"Maybe not. But you should definitely give him the opportunity."

"I don't think so. Because no matter what he says or does, this will always be in the background. Like a virus, infecting everything we do for the rest of our lives."

"I think you're over-thinking this, Roxanne. You know, sometimes things are exactly what they seem."

"And sometimes, they aren't, Mother. And I don't believe in fairy tales."

"Alright—I've had enough."

"What does that mean?"

"You know, I hate to say it, baby," Bunny continued, "but you're a coward."

"*A coward?*"

"Yes. Never once have you ever put up anything close to a fight. Not in school. Not on the job. Not even when it came to your friends. That's why you've always steered clear of any class that may have posed even the slightest threat to your precious straight A average, and why to this day you avoid competitive activities like the plague. It's also why you indulge people like Janine and that nutcase Lisa. You tell yourself it's because they've been through enough and that you don't want to make things worse by saying what you really think or by kicking them to the curb, but the fact is that you're afraid. You're afraid they'll get upset and you'll have to deal with their anger or hurt feelings, or that they'll argue with you or make you out to be the bad guy. And now you're doing the same damned thing with Walker. Oh, it may seem like an entirely different thing because you're planning to walk away. But since you're doing so without giving him the courtesy of an honest discussion or the opportunity to explain himself, the situation is exactly the same."

"No, it isn't," I argued, unsure if that was even the more honorable position. "Walker deserves to have what he wants. I'm only letting him have it."

"That's what you tell yourself. But deep down, Roxanne, you know you're just afraid."

"Afraid? Afraid of what?"

"Afraid he won't tell you the truth. Afraid he's not the man you think he is and that he can't really handle what he's known for years—that you and he will never have babies. And afraid he's not being honest with himself and that things may change between you two.

"Which is the part that pisses me off the most," Bunny continued. "As I used to tell you and R.J. when you were kids and didn't want to do your homework or take your chores seriously: I did not break my neck to get out of the trailer park so the two of you could land your privileged little butts back in it. The same applies here: I haven't spent my entire life teaching you manners, and to stand up for yourself, and to care and get along with people just so you can end up lonely and unhappy. Now get your sorry ass out of bed, put on your big-girl panties, and go talk to Walker."

It wasn't exactly like magic, since it took nearly three hours to take effect. But Bunny's butt kicking eventually did its job.

It started with tears that came as I acknowledged my fear that Walker might lie to me, and that I would have to leave him after finding out he couldn't be trusted. They continued to flow as I thought about life without him, which I honestly believed would be better than living with a lie.

But then I got out of bed, took a shower, got dressed, and waited for Walker to come home.

"How are you?" he asked as I met him at the door for the first time in almost a month.

I could tell he was glad I was there instead of holed up in my office or zoning out in front of the TV.

"I'm okay," I replied. "How was your day?"

"Fine."

And now I could see I was making him nervous, as if he was afraid somebody had died or was about to.

"Are you leaving me?" he blurted out when I tried to hug him. "If that's what's going on, just tell me."

I didn't know how to answer. So much depended on the outcome of this conversation—and possibly others—that I honestly did not know yet what I was going to do. On top of that, I had planned to sort of ease into the discussion and, thus, hadn't expected to deal with that question quite so soon.

"Roxanne?"

"Why don't we go into the living room?" I suggested. "We'll be more comfortable there, and then we can talk face to face."

Walker nodded and gestured for me to lead the way.

"So you *are* leaving," he said as we settled in on the sofa.

I was no closer to answering that question then than I'd been when we were standing in the foyer. I couldn't say *no* after all, since I had in fact been planning to leave. Yet I couldn't say *yes* since I no longer was—at least not until we had talked things through. *Not necessarily* may have been the most accurate response I could have given under the circumstances, but at the moment specificity didn't seem as important as calming Walker's nerves.

"It's a simple question, Roxanne. Either you're leaving or you're not."

"If it makes it any easier for you," he added with a hint of a quaver in his voice, "I know about the jobs and the apartments in Madison. In fact, the only things I don't know are when you're leaving, and why."

I didn't have to think too hard to figure out how he knew about the jobs. I'd told him myself I was looking for work; all he had to do was check the computer to see to whom I'd addressed my resumes and cover letters. A more suspicious man would have hacked my e-mail while he was at it, but I doubted Walker would have gone that far. Even if that were his style, it wouldn't have told him anything more than he knew from looking in My Documents.

As for the apartments, a check of our phone records would have led him to the numbers I'd called and, subsequently, to the ads to which I had responded. Were he determined enough, he could also have checked my computer history to see what sites I had visited in my perusal of Madison area rentals. As with hacking my e-mail account, I wouldn't have expected him to take either of these actions, but given how oblivious I was to his interest in having children, there was little I could learn about Walker that would surprise me anymore.

What did surprise me was how frightened he looked at that moment. Whether he had been hiding his fear up to this point or I had been too wrapped up in my own self-pity to notice it before wasn't clear. Either way, it was obvious to me now as he sat there, struggling to look me in the eye, just how much he was hurting, and that nothing else I could say could make things any worse than they already were.

So, I took him by the hand and told him I had been planning to leave, and that I was sorry it had taken me so long to come clean about it.

"Is there someone else?" he asked after a moment.

"No."

"Are you *looking* for someone else? Someone you think can make you happier?"

He was getting warmer, but then the idea wasn't to play twenty questions. I needed to own up to the reasons behind my actions rather than make him play guessing games.

"No, Walker. I'm definitely not looking for someone who can make me happier. In fact, I doubt there's anyone alive who could make me happier than you have."

"Then why would you leave?"

"I've just been thinking that you and I aren't really suited to one another after all, and maybe *you* would be better off with someone else."

"Why would you think that? I mean, is there something I've done—or something I haven't done—to make you think I'm unhappy with you?"

"No. Well, yes. But not in the way you probably mean."

"Well, then tell me what it is, Roxanne. For Pete's sake, I've been going out of my mind wondering what's wrong."

"I see that now. And I'm sorry. I never meant to worry you, or hurt you, or make things any harder than they had to be. I just didn't want to say anything until I had everything in place so we could make a clean break and get it over with."

"And why would we need to do that?"

"I ran across some information last month that suggests the matching program employed by *thematchcafe.com* isn't faulty, and that we're not as compatible as I wanted to believe."

"You're not serious."

"I'm afraid I am."

"Roxanne, you can't let some bullshit piece of software change your mind about something we've both known for nearly fifteen years."

"Normally I wouldn't. But I've since done some digging and discovered that when I adjust my answers to certain questions, the system finds us compatible and immediately adds you to my set of matches."

"Well, that's good, isn't it? I mean, if it solves the mystery as to why we weren't matched in the first place."

"If that's all it did, Walker, it would be great. Unfortunately, the responses I entered the second time around aren't true, which means we really *aren't* compatible."

Walker eyed me nervously. "What questions are we talking about, exactly?"

"The ones about having children. And wanting children. And being willing and able to raise someone else's children."

I watched and waited as it all sank in, then frowned with confusion as a smile crept over Walker's face.

"Is that what all this has been about?" he asked with the excitement of a man who'd just shot a trophy buck or found out he'd won a million dollars. "Holy Christ, I thought it was something serious."

"It *is* serious."

"Okay—bad choice of words. I should have said insurmountable."

"It *is* insurmountable," I insisted while privately wondering which questions, if not these, had given him pause earlier, or if the disconnect was in our respective definitions of insurmountable. "Walker, if one party wants to live in the desert and the other wants to live by the sea, there are only two choices: Either they separate, or one of them has to lose."

"*Or* they live in the desert for part of the year, and by the sea for the rest."

"Or they compromise," I allowed, immediately regretting my example. "But you can't do that with children Walker. You can't adopt a baby, play with it for six months, and then stick it in a box and send it to someone else for six more. And there is no such thing as half a kid, so I don't think we can resolve this the way we do when we disagree over pizza."

Walker laughed although I wasn't joking.

"Roxanne, I admit to having said I wanted kids on the questionnaire," he said gently. "But I only did so because you told me to answer truthfully—not because I regret not having them."

"What does that mean? Those two thoughts can't exist at the same time. I mean, either you want kids or you don't."

"It means that I would want kids if I had to start all over again, just like I was pretending to be on that questionnaire. But that doesn't mean I regret having married you, or that I resent you for not being unable to have children."

"It's not just that I can't have children, Walker. I don't want them either."

"I know that. I don't really either, at this point. I'm almost forty, for Pete's sake," he added as I eyed him doubtfully, "and I can't live on less than seven hours of sleep anymore. Maybe I should have considered that when I completed the questionnaire. I guess I just thought, having done things one way this time, it might be fun to do them differently next time—if there had to be a next time. I guess I just never imagined that part of the questionnaire would prove so crucial to the matching process."

That made two of us.

"Look," he said, sensing my deepening chagrin, if not its true source. "I've known all along that you weren't too keen on having kids, and that's never been an issue for me. I'll admit that deep down I've wondered if your aversion to having them was a defense mechanism of sorts—you know, a way of dealing with the fact that you might not be able to have them. But never have I resented you for not wanting them or for not being able to have them. I'm just glad I have you."

"But Walker, if you want kids, you should have them. Which means you should be with someone who can have them, or who at least is willing to adopt or hire a surrogate."

"But I don't want anyone else. And I don't want kids badly enough to live without you. I love you, Roxanne. How is it that you don't know that?"

"I do *know* that, Walker. We wouldn't be having this conversation if I didn't. But loving me can't possibly be enough."

"Why not?"

"Because it never is. I've seen it a hundred times," I reminded him, "with my column and in my seminars. People tell themselves they can live without something the other person wants or doesn't want, or can't or won't provide; and for a while they're okay. But over time, they come to resent that they never got to see France or that they always had to have baked potatoes with their steaks instead of au gratins, and things change."

"And you think things between us are going to change because you don't want kids?"

"Yes. Things always change between people when one of them is unfulfilled."

"Unfulfilled? Roxanne, just because we don't have kids does not mean I'm unfulfilled. You and I have a great thing going, and I am perfectly happy with our life the way it is."

"But the survey…"

"Screw the survey, Roxanne. It was a hypothetical. I answered it as if we were no longer together because you asked me to—which is also why I joined that stupid dating service in the first place, and why I went out with all those women and took all those damned notes. Do you really think I would have gone along with all that, if I weren't committed to you?"

If it were any other man, I could have said yes and given him a list of several reasons why. But this was Walker, after all. He was more likely to say he was with another woman to cover up a secret hunting trip than to use a hunting tale to hide an affair.

"Look," he continued, taking me by the hand, "you and I both know we're not like other people. Didn't you once tell me that the average couple fights nearly once every single day?"

He was referring to a report published in England in 2011 that said couples fight an average of 312 times a year. It also identified the time couples most often fight as 8 p.m. on Thursdays.

"Yes. I did."

"And did we not agree that we don't even come close to that?"

"Yes."

"And that we were more likely to be having sex at eight o'clock when everyone else is fighting?"

I smiled. "Yes."

"Well, then doesn't it stand to reason that we might be different from the average couple in a few other ways?"

"I suppose."

"Well, then I propose you and I agree we're going to stay together and be happy, because I would rather be with you and never have kids, than have kids and not be with you at all.

"Now come on," he instructed, looking at his watch while nodding toward the stairs. "It's almost eight o'clock."

Epilogue

So once again I had managed to make things harder than they had to be.

In my defense it had been a long time since I'd put that much cement into my work, and even longer since I'd done so with respect to my marriage. While that didn't take all the sting out of the embarrassment I felt over my three-week sulk and self-imposed exile, it comforted me somewhat to know that, with age, such occurrences were becoming fewer and farther between. That was about the most positive spin I could put on things for a while, but I knew that one day I would look back at my emotional self-immolation and laugh. And even if I couldn't, Bunny would.

Meanwhile, still needing to be resolved after making up with Walker was the matter of what to tell R.A. in answer to his question about online dating. Fortunately, having uncluttered my head on the personal front helped me to see the forest for the trees, as it were, in the professional realm and cleared the way for me to draft a response I undoubtedly could have written from day one if I hadn't been ensnared by the World Wide Web.

Dear R.A.

Much as I would like to do so, I am unable to either endorse or recommend any of the matching services available online. Even without the potential legal liability to which I would be exposing myself, the newspapers that carry my column, and the syndication company that distributes it were I to encourage readers to subscribe to a specific service of any kind, I am wholly unconvinced that one or more of them are any better or worse at creating matches that will lead to love, marriage, or wedded bliss.

While I don't doubt there are those that excel at identifying who among their members would be compatible in terms of values, personality, and temperament and who therefore have the greatest potential to become fast friends, boon companions, and passionate lovers, these elements represent only part of the picture when it comes to building and maintaining satisfying interpersonal relationships. For as important as values, personality, and temperament are to compatibility and happily-ever-after-ability among marriage-minded individuals, they do not function alone but instead work in concert with other factors that cannot be weighed, measured, or otherwise evaluated without the benefit of physical presence and social intercourse. Thus, online matching services are no more likely to lead to love or marriage than blind dating, speed dating, random grocery store encounters, or even televised weekly drawings.

I say this because, much as some people want to believe we humans are governed by reason, we are in fact animals—animals that are *capable* of reason perhaps, but animals just the same—and, as such, we are not above the influence of our genes, instincts, or drives when it comes to romance. Thus, it is not always or entirely with our hearts and minds that we choose whom to love and mate with, and so it matters not *how* we meet people as much as that we *do,* in fact, meet people. In person. At least eventually.

With that in mind, I advise you to meet as many women as you can via as many sources as you can and see what sticks.

In the meantime, remember the importance of communication. Specifically, communicate your needs and be willing to forego what you know you don't want without fear that what you do want isn't out there and this is the best it's gonna get. Too many people settle too soon and live to regret it. That's not to say you should set your standards too high or hold out for perfection; just decide what matters to you the most and what doesn't, and follow that prescription.

Think of the qualities and characteristics you want or expect as a shopping list with four sections. In one area, list the qualities and characteristics your partner *must* have, absolutely without exception, and plan to discount from consideration anyone who doesn't have them, no matter how beautiful, talented, or loving she may be. In the second area, list the tendencies and traits you would *like* your partner to have, but that aren't necessarily deal breakers. In the third section, list those you *prefer a partner not to have*, but that you could live with depending on how she stacks up in terms of the other criteria. In the fourth area, list every single characteristic, quality, attitude, tendency and habit you absolutely *cannot accept* in a partner, and be prepared to end any relationship—as gently or forcefully as the situation warrants—with any woman who has, holds, displays, or demonstrates even *one* of them.

For this exercise to have any meaning, you're going to have to be brutally honest—with yourself. If you're a die-hard Republican whose blood boils every time you talk to a Democrat, don't say you're willing to date someone with opposing political views because you think that makes you a nicer guy. That's just setting things up to fail. Better to find someone who matches your political stripes if you're ardently liberal or conservative than to try to reach across the aisle, as it were. If politics aren't important to you but something else is, be honest about it and your own capacity to deal with someone whose preferences or proclivities don't match your own. If you're an avid golfer, for example, you're better off pursuing women who share that affliction. (Forgive the editorial, but I can't think of anything more boring or more frustrating than chasing a tiny white ball over miles of technologically advanced turf toward eighteen little holes; that's just me.) Failing that, you should focus on women who enjoy watching golf, who have equally time-consuming and expensive hobbies, and/or who have obsessions of their own and can therefore understand your devotion to lowering your handicap and perfecting your swing. In sum, when it comes to the things you are passionate about, it's better to limit your scope to women whose feelings and opinions align with yours than to feign flexibility early on and spend the rest of your life in marital gridlock.

Also, if you're truly looking for Ms. Right, don't hop in bed with someone just because she has the potential to wear the title. Doing so just tells smart women you're not serious and gives the rest false hope. I'm not saying you have to wait until you're married—or even engaged—to have sex, as I believe there is value in making sure you're compatible sexually before making a lifelong commitment. Just make sure you're on the path to commitment before taking the plunge.

Finally, once you've found someone whom you think is the one, don't stop communicating. And if you suck at it, take a class. Or two. Better yet, take them anyway and do so together. For as I've said in numerous columns in the past—and will likely do in others hence—if couples put as much time and effort into learning to communicate and negotiate as they put into planning their weddings and buying their first home, there would be a lot more happily-ever-afters.

Well, that about covers it.

Thank you for writing, and good luck.

Roxanne

About the Author

Billie Jean Diersen is a veteran military wife with a background in juvenile justice and youth development. She holds a Master of Science in Public Administration from Troy University, a Bachelor of Arts in Communication from Hamline University, and a Black Belt in Human Nature from the School of Hard Knocks. When she's not writing, Billie enjoys harassing her two adult children and hanging out with her husband and five high-maintenance felines.

www.ingramcontent.com/pod-product-compliance
Lightning Source LLC
Chambersburg PA
CBHW070853120626
46556CB00002B/975